Sunny Days at the Beach

Sunny Days at the Beach

Morton S. Gray

Where heroes are like chocolate – irresistible!

Published 2021 by Choc Lit Limited
Penrose House, Crawley Drive, Camberley, Surrey GU15 2AB, UK
www.choc-lit.com

A CIP catalogue record for this book is available
from the British Library

ISBN 978-1-78189-456-9

Printed and bound in Great Britain by Clays Ltd, Elcograf S.p.A.

To Victoria Cornwall,
fellow author and friend.
Thank you for your invaluable support.

Acknowledgements

The idea for this novel was born when I read an article featuring a small craft gin distillery in the magazine *Landscape*. I was fascinated by the processes, the shiny equipment and particularly the botanical flavourings used. My husband was unknowingly treated to my essential research trip for his birthday, when we went on a tour of the Silent Pool distillery in Surrey! A gin maker seemed an ideal hero to set against my feisty Borteen craft centre owner, Mandy.

Mandy Vanes who owns and runs Owl Corner Crafts in my fictional seaside town of Borteen and teenage artist, Nick Crossten have both featured in my other Borteen novels and I felt it was time for them to take centre stage in this one.

Thank you to Katy Burns and Chris Longmuir for advice on foster care and abandoned teenagers. Some of this has been adapted, especially time scales, to fit the story, but the background was very helpful. Any mistakes are mine alone.

One of my favourite television programmes is *Long Lost Family* and when you've read this novel you will understand the connection.

Thanks for support and encouragement go to Victoria Cornwall, to whom this novel is dedicated. We live miles away from each other, but ever since we have both been published by Choc Lit, we message almost every day. A bonus is that we get on just as well on the few occasions when we have managed to meet together.

My support network also includes The Apricot Plots authors – Carol Thomas, Caroline James, Mariam Kobras, Angela Barton, Julie Houston, Angela Petch, Jane Cable and Vicki Beeby, plus my local coffee authors – Janice Preston, Lynn Forth, Georgia Hill, Elizabeth Hanbury, Nell Dixon and Alison May.

My main supporters are my family, particularly my husband, who can now tell when I am dealing with sticky plot points or edits and has to judge whether to drag me out for fresh air and a walk, or to leave me be and cook tea!

Thank you to my editor for helping me beat the novel into shape, the Choc Lit team and the members of the Tasting Panel, without whom this book would not have been considered for publication: Lucie Wheatcroft, Kirsty White, Mel Fairbairn, Jenny Mitchell, Melanie Russell, Bee Master, Lorna Baker, Fran Stevens, Deborah Warren, Isobel Mcilwraith, Yvonne Greene, Alma Hough, Gill Leivers, Cordy Swinton and Ruth Nägele.

Chapter One

Mandy shivered in the cold morning air and groaned at her reflection in the mirror. Dark rings beneath her eyes were topped with the remains of last night's smudged mascara. Her face looked tired and strained and a splitting hangover headache drummed inside her skull without mercy. It was going to take a lot of make-up to look half decent today. A lot of warpaint to face the world at all.

'You're getting too old for this, girl.' She spoke aloud before sighing miserably.

In the shower, she scrubbed her skin with self-disgust, trying to get lost in the aroma of her favourite shower gel with its rich rose scent. At least she'd slept at home last night and not in yet another stranger's bed. *Be thankful for small mercies, Mandy.*

Savagely blow-drying her hair, she fought the tears that threatened to overflow as she brushed, remonstrating with herself with each vicious stroke.

Beginning to feel a little more human when she'd straightened her shoulder-length, dyed blonde locks, she studied her reflection in the mirror again.

It felt as if a stranger looked back. A stranger playing a role Mandy had outgrown.

Was this even Mandy Vanes any longer? Was this really who she wanted to be?

Scooping up the skimpy clothes she'd thrown on the bedroom floor in the early hours of the morning, she shuddered when she realized they held the scent of a man's sickly aftershave; she couldn't even remember the face of the guy she'd obviously been so close to in the pub. She marvelled that she hadn't caught a chill going out in that outfit in winter. Self-loathing surfaced again and she ran down the stairs to throw the clothes straight into the washing machine. She slammed the machine door, immediately regretting it, as the noise jarred her delicate head.

'Why, oh why do you do this?' she yelled aloud, her fists clenched tightly. The reason why surfaced from her memories as it did every time she asked that question. She shuddered. Better not go there.

Stamping into the kitchen, she took two slices of bread out of the packet in the bread bin to make toast, then thought better of it and put them away again, her stomach churning like the washing machine. Eating was probably not a good idea right now. She took painkillers and gulped some water instead.

She sat down on one of the kitchen bar stools. Her eyes felt so heavy, as if someone had attached weights to her eyelashes in the night. It was a good job she could walk to work; she surely wasn't fit to drive.

Mandy decided that the worst thing about the morning after the night before was the self-recriminations. Her skin was still smarting from her punishing scrub in the shower and her head throbbed, not just from the effects of too much alcohol, but from the tirade of shouting at herself she was continuing inside.

Stupid girl! Trouble is you're no longer a girl! You're thirty-five, Mandy. Washed up, stupid singleton. Who's going to want you? Your reputation's awful. You've no self-respect. You drink too much. You sleep with anyone who shows an interest in you.

Slag!

Slapper!

Stupid, stupid.

Idiot, idiot.

She clenched her fists so tightly that her nails dug into her palms and drew blood. Then, before she could think to stop herself, she was pinching her arms hard. This was why she no longer kept razor blades in the house. In this mood, she would self-harm in a heartbeat. She didn't want to go to that dark place of her late teens ever again.

Deep breaths, Mandy.

Don't look at the old silvery scars.

I think I'm searching for something that doesn't exist and I don't deserve it anyway. Nice guys want a girl who makes them feel special, not someone who puts it around like I do. So, I attract the sleazes. Even the men I think are decent turn into sleazes.

Something needs to change.

And soon.

Mandy shrugged on her jacket. She couldn't be bothered to go back upstairs for her scarf and winter coat. She pulled on gloves, grabbed her keys and bag, checked her phone and shut the door gently in deference to her sore head. She took deep breaths of cool sea air as she walked down the hill towards the seafront. When she reached the promenade, she looked around to make sure no one was in hearing distance and yelled to the sky, 'I need a change, please. I need to change!'

She stomped off towards Owl Corner Crafts, the craft centre she owned and ran near to Borteen beach. Negative thoughts about herself continued to swirl around her painful head. She vaguely noticed that the sea looked grey and cold, the beach and the high street deserted. It was the middle of February, early yet for the majority of tourists. They would begin to arrive in droves at Easter.

Before she could begin yet another tirade of self-abuse, she stopped in her tracks. Someone was sitting hunched over on the steps of the craft centre.

For one horrified moment, she thought it could be the unknown man she'd spent the previous evening with, but this wasn't a man, it was a youth, and now she was closer, she recognized his profile – Nick Crossten.

Mandy had been displaying artwork for Nick ever since

he'd won an art competition at Borteen High School and she'd been persuaded by the competition organiser to sell his canvases. His pictures sold well too. The lad was extremely talented.

Nick glanced up as Mandy approached. His face looked ashen, just as hers had been in her morning reflection and his eyes were hollow and dark ringed too. He was shivering in the cold air.

'Nick? What's up?' She tried to sound bright, even though her heart lurched as she could tell something was terribly wrong.

'Mum's gone.'

'Gone? What do you mean gone?' All thoughts of herself, her reflection in the mirror and even her sore head fled.

'Met a man and left with him.' The unhappy youth shrugged and looked away, as if he didn't want her to see his expression.

'But she can't just leave you. Can she?'

He looked back at Mandy, his eyes full of tears. 'Well, she has.' He shrugged again.

'Are you absolutely certain? She's not just gone on holiday?'

'She's gone, Mand. Gone forever. Said horrid things to me before she went.' His thin shoulders began to shake, no longer able to hold back the sobs.

Mandy didn't quite know how to react. You thought twice about putting your arm around someone else's child these days. 'But who's going to look after you? Did she at least leave you some money? A phone number for emergencies?'

'Nope.' He gulped the bleak word out through his emotion. 'Said I didn't deserve anything, that I could support myself with my "poncy" art. Left her keys on the table, took her suitcases and slammed the door.' He looked up at Mandy, blatant fear in his eyes. 'What do I do now?'

Mandy sank down to sit on the step next to Nick and an ache started up in her chest in response to his woeful expression. 'First of all, Nick, your art is wonderful. Never let anyone say otherwise. And you, young man, deserve the best the world can give to you.'

Nick had always appeared scruffy and slightly neglected, but this was the first time she'd seen him looking beaten down by life. He'd always had a ready smile before.

'What about your dad?' Her tone sounded falsely bright even to her own ears.

'Never known a dad. Mum always says I haven't got one.'

Mandy resisted the obvious retort that he must have been fathered by someone and wondered how Nick's mother could have been so cruel to her son to say such a thing. She felt a spark of determination growing inside of her. 'We'll work this out together. You can come and stay with me for now, until we decide what to do.'

'Really?'

She nodded.

'Thanks, Mand.' His face brightened for a couple of seconds, before darkening again. 'I'll end up in a children's home, won't I?' His expression was heart-wrenchingly fearful.

'Not if I can help it.' Mandy couldn't shake the thought that she'd asked for a change in her life and while she'd actually meant a new image – maybe this was it? A sign? Not quite what she'd imagined, but then the universe worked in mysterious ways.

She glanced at her watch. 'Aren't you supposed to be at school today?'

'Nah, teacher training day.'

'That's fortunate. You can do some jobs for me if you like, earn a bit of pocket money.' She noted that he wasn't wearing gloves and his hands were turning red with cold.

His smile returned at once. 'Great.'

She took off her glove, picked a twenty pound note out of her purse and handed it to him. 'First job, go and get me a takeaway latte from the beach café, with a drink and breakfast for yourself too.' She guessed he wouldn't have eaten anything in his distressed state.

'Yes, miss.' A hint of his cheeky self was back as he mock saluted. He ran off along the promenade towards the beachside café without a backwards glance.

She watched him go, reflecting that she didn't know anything about Nick's mum at all. Mandy had been born in the seaside town of Borteen and lived here all her life, but, of course, she didn't know everyone.

Who could turn their back on a fifteen-year-old like this? She'd need to ask Nick more questions later, but she'd have to tread carefully in deference to his raw emotions.

She knew she really ought to get up and open the craft centre for the day, but there were unlikely to be many customers this early in the year and it was helping the remaining dull ache in her head just sitting on the steps and breathing in the fresh, if cold, sea air. She could hear the lap of the waves from here and, despite the cawing of a couple of seagulls, it soothed her senses so much that she almost fell asleep.

When she looked along the road again, Nick was coming back, clutching a takeaway cup, a bottle and a paper bag. There was something strange about the way he was walking – fast, looking behind at regular intervals. Mandy stood up and went up two steps so she could see more clearly and realized he was being followed by a man. Her hackles rose. Who was he?

Nick spotted that she was watching him and sped up to reach her.

Mandy put her key in the lock to give them an escape route if they should need it, as Nick raced up the steps and almost threw the coffee cup at her. His face was flushed, his eyes wide.

'You okay, Nick?'

'Am now. That guy's following me.' He pointed

unnecessarily with his bottle at the man hurrying along the road towards them.

Mandy stood up to open the door to Owl Corner Crafts and pushed Nick through it. 'Inside.'

The stranger stopped at the bottom of the steps. He was out of breath, his chest rising and falling rapidly from the fast walk. Tall, broad shouldered and clean-shaven with copper-coloured hair that flopped long over his forehead, his eyes glinted like malachite in the early light. 'Good morning.'

She dispensed with any pleasantries. 'Why are you following Nick?'

'As I've been trying to explain to him, his mother wrote to me. She claims that … that I'm his father.'

Mandy couldn't speak at all for a moment, as if the air had been sucked out of her lungs. She scanned the stranger's face again but wasn't sure what his expression meant. He didn't look comfortable as he stood shifting from foot to foot in front of her.

'His father …? He hasn't got a father.' She realized as soon as the words were out of her mouth that it was a pretty stupid thing to say. 'And, how did you recognize him anyway? Have you been stalking him?'

It was the man's turn to look shocked.

'I went to the address on the top of the letter from Sally Crossten and he came out of the front door. I followed him, because I need to get to the bottom of all this. I lost sight of him for a while, until I saw him walking along the seafront. When he came out of the café, I asked if he was Nicholas Crossten and he bolted.'

'I'm not surprised he ran off.' She crossed her arms, barring the way up the steps in case the man made a move to follow Nick inside.

'Look, I'm not a weirdo or anything. I'm just a normal bloke who received an unexpected letter about a son he didn't even know he had. My name's Graham Frankley by the way.

Could we all go somewhere to discuss this? Maybe back to that café?' He waved his arm in the general direction of the beachside café. 'I'll buy the drinks,' he added, giving a half smile, obviously hoping the offer would make his suggestion seem more appealing.

The stranger ran a gloved hand through his unusually coloured hair and Mandy was annoyed to feel a quiver of attraction. *Not now, Mandy. For goodness' sake, girl. Time and place.*

'I've got the letter from Sally with me.' He pulled a battered envelope out of his fleece pocket and waved it in the air, as if it would lend him legitimacy and provide bait for a meeting. 'You are both welcome to read it.'

Mandy turned to Nick, who was peeping around the edge of the door behind her. 'Your call, Nick. What do you want to do?'

'I got freaked out, Mand, but I want to see that letter, see if Mum wrote it. But – will you come to the café too?' His eyes held an appeal which made it difficult to refuse.

She turned back to Graham Frankley. He took a step backwards as if he thought she might hit him and she consciously tried to soften her expression. 'You go ahead to the café. We'll join you in a moment, after I've spoken to Nick. Probably best to sit outside even though it's cool today. Gossip travels around this town like wildfire.'

Mandy waited until the stranger had set off along the road, clutching the letter. Graham didn't look back and she wondered briefly what he must be thinking. She turned to Nick. 'Do you think this guy could really be your father? Are you sure your mum told you nothing about him? No clues at all?'

'Told you, she always says I don't have a dad. Am I Jesus or something? I mean, come on? Im … immac-u-late conception they call it in school assembly. This Graham Frankley man is news to me. Never heard his name before. Ever.'

Mandy smiled grimly. 'I guess we need to go and hear him out, see what this letter says and exactly what he wants from you.'

'Will you stay?'

'Of course I will. We don't know anything about Mr Frankley. I'm not going to leave you alone with a strange man. If we need to, we'll call the police.'

Mandy checked she had her phone in her handbag and that it had some charge. They left the drinks and the snack Nick had bought earlier on the counter in the craft centre. Mandy locked the door and they walked along the promenade to join the stranger at the café.

He stood up as they approached the table by the sea wall. 'Let me introduce myself properly. I'm Graham Frankley.' He took off his glove and held out his hand towards Mandy.

She just stared at his palm and he, eventually, withdrew his hand, wiping it self-consciously on the back of his jeans.

'Right, erm, what can I get you both to drink?'

Nick answered without hesitation. 'Berry smoothie, please. Seen it on the menu by the gate and always wanted to try one.'

Graham's gaze rested on Mandy and she had difficulty resisting the normal flirtatious flutter of her eyelashes when near to an attractive man. 'A skinny latte, please.'

He turned, dodged the tables and chairs in the outside seating area and went into the café. Mandy hoiked the neckline of her top to cover more of her cleavage, momentarily wishing she'd worn a scarf and her big coat, then looked at Nick.

He shrugged. 'Don't know what to think yet.'

'Me neither. Let's just listen to what he has to say. We can get up and leave at any time, remember.'

'Free smoothie anyway.' Nick grinned, but Mandy knew him well enough by now to glimpse the fear and uncertainty dancing in his eyes.

Graham came back, balancing a tray with three drinks and a plate piled with Danish pastries and croissants. He gave Nick his requested smoothie, Mandy her latte and put a black coffee down in front of himself. He positioned the plate of pastries in the middle of the table, smiling warily at Nick and then Mandy.

Once he was settled, Graham took out the letter he had waved about before. 'I received this letter from Sally Crossten. Is that your mum?'

Nick looked across at Mandy for approval before replying. 'That's Mum's name, yes.'

'In summary, she wrote to me to say she was going away, that I'm your dad and that you might need me.'

Graham handed the envelope to Nick and after glancing at the address, Nick took out a single sheet of thin blue writing paper. He flattened it on the table to stop the breeze blowing it away. Graham and Mandy were quiet while he read the letter. She thought Graham kept stealing glances at her. Nick's face gave no clue as to what he thought about the contents of the note. When he'd finished reading, he passed it and the envelope to Mandy.

'Is it your mum's writing?' she asked.

'Yup. Can't believe she wrote and sent this but said nothing to me.'

Mandy scanned the letter. It was short and matter of fact in its tone. Sally referred to a resort in Spain where Nick had been conceived. She stated that Nick was Graham's son, gave his date of birth, but made no apology or reference to the fact she hadn't told Graham about this for fifteen years. She merely said that she had the chance of a better life and was going to take it. The last paragraph stated that Nick might need Graham's help now that she had gone.

Mandy's heart contracted at the expression on Nick's face when she looked up. It was somehow a mixture of trepidation, shock and hope. She studied her coffee to give herself a moment to think, warming her hands on the cup, but decided to talk before she tried drinking it. 'So you didn't know about Nick before? I mean, how do we know you are genuinely his father?'

She folded the letter and put it back into the envelope before passing it across the table to Graham. She tried to ignore the spark that passed between them as their fingers brushed.

'I guess at this point in time, none of us knows anything for certain. I definitely don't, but in her letter, as you saw, Sally told me exactly where Nick was conceived.' Here he darted an apologetic look at Nick. 'And she sent a photograph of herself from back then.' He took his wallet from the back pocket of his jeans and pulled out a battered snapshot, which he placed on the table between Nick and Mandy. 'I do remember dating Sally for a while around the time she talks about. It was a holiday romance.' A reddish tinge coloured his cheeks.

Mandy examined the photograph more closely and then passed it to Nick. 'Forgive me, but I don't understand why you'd be bothered after fifteen years.' Mandy knew her tone was suspicious.

Nick passed the photo of his mother back to Graham quickly, bowed his head and sucked on his straw. Under the cover of his eyebrows, his eyes darted between Mandy and Graham as they spoke, as if he was watching a table tennis game. Mandy was very conscious that she was not including the youth in the conversation, but she felt responsible for getting to the bottom of this mystery.

Graham glanced at Nick briefly too and then focussed his attention on Mandy. He launched into a hesitant speech with lots of pauses while he thought. 'When I got the letter, I was shocked ... shaken ... didn't know what to think to be honest. But, as I'd only been discussing with my mother the night before the letter arrived, about the fact that our family line stops with me ... because I haven't re-married and I don't think I'll ever have any children now, I just had to investigate, had to find out the truth of whether I already had ...' He darted his eyes towards Nick. '*Have* a son.' He picked up his cup and drank from his coffee, wincing because the liquid was still far too hot.

'Nick says he's never even heard your name mentioned before.'

'Excuse me for asking this, but what exactly is your relationship with Nick? Sorry if that sounds a rude question.' Graham's eyebrows rose to disappear beneath the front floppy bit of his hair.

Mandy adjusted the neckline of her top again, which as usual showed too much of her ample cleavage. She pulled the edges of her jacket together self-consciously. 'I'm his friend. I sell his art in my craft centre and he came to me for help this morning after his mum left him and again when he realized you were following him.'

She ran her finger around the handle of her cup and then stared up at Graham. 'If he is proved to be your son, would you want to be part of his life?'

Almost in echo of her own clothing adjustment, Graham ran a finger around his shirt collar, as if it suddenly felt too tight and smoothed the front of his fleece. 'Look I don't profess to know all, or even any of the answers in this unique situation. I suppose we maybe need DNA tests to be sure of the relationship between Nick and myself, but beyond that ... I have no agenda, no idea. I guess I'm curious but I need to take things one step at a time.'

'You can surely see that this has been a big shock for Nick? Especially, as his mum has just left him to cope alone.' Mandy glared at Graham but wasn't quite sure why she was suddenly feeling so angry with him.

Nick reached the end of his drink and the straw made slurping noises at the bottom of the glass. It alerted the two adults to his presence, as he sat listening quietly, taking everything in. Mandy turned to him. 'Nick, what do you make of all this?'

'Not sure really. Never had a dad. Haven't got a mum now either. I want to stay with you, Mand.' Despite sounding very matter of fact, Nick's bottom lip trembled and she was reminded that underneath the bluster, he was still young and scared.

She reached a hand across the table towards Nick but stopped short of touching him. 'Don't you worry. I'll make sure everything's okay for you.'

Could she fulfil that promise? She couldn't even take care of herself properly, so how could she help a vulnerable young adult? A lad to whom she had no blood, or legal relationship and therefore no real right to have a say in what happened to him. She studied the patterns in the milk foam on the surface of her latte, as if they would give her some insight into what to do or say next.

Graham's voice cut through her thoughts. 'Look, I didn't come here to make any trouble. If I'm honest, I wasn't sure what to think when I received this letter, or what I'd find here in Borteen. I just felt I should come to investigate.'

Mandy looked up and locked eyes with Graham, trying to gauge if he was genuine, searching his expression to try to work out exactly what he wanted. He didn't look as if he was pretending to be someone he wasn't. He actually looked nice and friendly, but then she wasn't very good at assessing men and had been deceived many times before for that very reason. You couldn't necessarily tell by what someone portrayed on the surface ... books, covers and all that. 'Have you any ID on you, to prove you are who you say you are?' Her brusque manner came from the realisation that staring at Graham had again produced a quiver of attraction inside of her.

Graham raised his eyebrows, but quickly took out his wallet again and proceeded to place credit cards and his driving licence photocard on the table. They all confirmed the identity of Graham Frankley and the image on the driving licence was definitely the man sitting in front of her.

She nodded. 'Thank you for that. So where do we go from here? Nick is worried he might get taken into care if it becomes known that his mother has gone AWOL. I was hoping she might only be away temporarily and that he could stay with me until she reappears.'

'Unfortunately, her letter, as you've read, seems to suggest she is going to be gone rather longer than that.'

Nick took a sharp noisy intake of breath and they both looked at him.

'To be honest,' continued Graham. 'It almost feels as if she thought she was handing responsibility for Nick over to me just by sending this letter.'

Mandy had a sudden thought. 'What does it say on your birth certificate, Nick?'

'Don't know. Have I got one?' He was frowning uncertainly.

'Maybe we should see if we can find it, or else try to get a copy.'

Nick shrugged with a puzzled expression on his face.

Mandy knew she needed time to think. She'd have to ask for advice from someone about this situation, but she'd no idea who could help. 'Look Mr Frankley, this has been a shock to all of us. I promise, Nick will be safe staying with me for now. What if we exchange details so that we can keep in contact and talk more when we've had time to decide what to do?'

Graham pulled a business card from his wallet, then put away his credit cards and driving licence. Mandy scrabbled in her bag for an Owl Corner Crafts card. Its three bright owls looked too jovial given the serious nature of the previous conversation.

Graham took Mandy's card, glanced at it briefly and stood up. 'I'll be in touch.' He pushed back his chair, nodded at Nick, hesitated and then walked away.

Nick stared after his retreating back for a moment, before pouncing on the plate of untouched pastries. Mandy couldn't help but grin.

She turned over Graham's business card. It read "Frankley Gins" with a fancy "FG" logo. The address was somewhere near Manchester, so Graham Frankley had come a fair distance all the way over to the east coast to investigate Nick's mum's claims.

A gin distiller? She'd never met one of those before.

Chapter Two

On his drive home, Graham had plenty of time to think about his meeting with Mandy and Nick, as Borteen to Manchester wasn't exactly an easy journey. He wondered what the wary blonde – he didn't think that was her natural colour – and the moody-looking teenager, who might, or might not, be his son, had thought of him.

He'd always had a desire to see the world through someone else's eyes. Did others see the same colours, the same shapes? He liked to think deeply about things, should have been a philosopher his mother said. Maybe he was just too serious and perhaps he'd been doing too much soul-searching of late.

Mandy was a very attractive woman, if you could see through the veneer of too much make-up, processed hair and the clothes that displayed too much of her body – for his taste anyway. It was obvious that she viewed him with great suspicion, evidenced by the constant pulling up of her neckline, rather than wanting to display her assets. She'd been on high alert the whole time. Well, who wouldn't be? He'd not handled his introduction to his possible son too well, had gone blundering in with his excitement and curiosity, clutching the letter from his old flame – a *very* old flame – and expecting ... expecting what exactly? To be welcomed with open arms? To already be known about? He'd been a bit of an idiot albeit with the best of intentions, he realised belatedly.

His liaison with Sally Crossten in what felt like the distant past, even another lifetime, had been a holiday romance. He'd been just twenty years old, bowled over that a girl had noticed him, let alone wanted to kiss and be alone with him. They'd skirted around each other for the best part of a week and then, when they finally became brave enough to be intimate, they'd sneaked off at every opportunity to make passionate, but inexperienced love over the last week of their holidays. They'd never met again after those two weeks in Spain, but they had written to each other by post for a little while afterwards. *By post*. Graham decided that made him sound old. These days it would be email or some form of social media chat. People didn't seem to write letters any more – they'd been quite old-fashioned even then.

The thing Graham was struggling with was why Sally hadn't told him she was pregnant back when it had happened. Has she felt she couldn't trust him? Had her parents interfered? She hadn't even given him a chance to help her, or to be part of his child's life. It left a lingering doubt over the truth about Nick's parentage and a whole heap of regret, that is if he *was* proved to be Nick's father after all.

Thinking about it and trying to second-guess what had happened all those years ago, Graham reckoned that Sally's letters had probably stopped around the time it had become clear she was expecting Nick. Either, she'd been too scared to tell him, had gone off him, maybe met someone else, or else the child wasn't his after all. Who knew?

How would he have reacted back then to a girl telling him she was having his baby? Sure, he'd have been scared, but he liked to think he'd have done the decent thing and supported Sally in whatever way he could, maybe even married her to give the child his name and Sally security. But, of course, as they'd been young, hadn't found their way in the world, didn't know each other too well either, that could have been a huge mistake.

Why get in touch now? Somehow it didn't make any sense at all. It was one of the things that didn't ring true in the letter, a letter that might never have found him, had his parents not still lived at the same address as when Sally and he were writing to each other. The letter seemed such a feeble gesture to get help for her son, one that might never have reached its intended recipient. He didn't understand Sally Crossten's thinking, but then, he had no way of knowing her current state of mind, or how desperate she'd become. Maybe she hadn't thought too deeply about any of it.

Nick was real enough. He looked decidedly neglected with his dirty and much too small clothes. His hair needed a good cut too. However, even with all of his questioning and misgivings, if Graham wasn't fancifully imagining it, Nick had the Frankley nose just like his late father. He himself took after his mother's side, ginger-haired and green-eyed – a good smattering of Irish genes that had come from his grandmother.

He could, of course, be deluding himself completely, because he'd been recently regretting that he would be unlikely to have a son … or a daughter. It was possible, maybe even probable that he had no connection to Nick Crossten at all. Maybe it was all some sort of scam, designed to get money out of him. If it was, he pondered, then Nick wasn't in on the scheme. The lad had looked bewildered and shocked, both about the disappearance of his mother and the appearance of a supposed father, about whom he seemed to know absolutely nothing before today. Unless Nick was an extremely accomplished actor, he'd been genuinely surprised, poor lad.

Even with his suspicions, Graham was intrigued about the possibility of a son, especially now that he had begun to despair about ever having children. He hadn't hesitated to come to Borteen to investigate. The thought that he might already have produced an heir made tingles run up his spine, as if he'd drunk a very cold drink much too fast.

With a business to run and a disabled mother to support and care for, he'd got out of the habit of dating and if he wanted children then that was a necessary step.

Somehow, after his ex-wife Trisha's betrayal, he didn't feel able to risk putting his heart and livelihood on a plate to be sliced up yet again. Better to be alone, even if that meant he was lonely and childless.

Graham shivered at even the thought of Trisha's name. The hurt of her infidelity still dug deeply into his guts and the pain didn't show any sign of abating with the passage of time. The damned woman had left a scar the size of the Grand Canyon through his life. Would he ever get over her treachery? Could he ever learn to trust a woman again?

He reached the outskirts of Manchester much quicker than he'd anticipated, mainly because he'd been focussed totally on his internal dialogue. As he pulled down the long drive to Frankley Gins, he began to worry about whether he'd had his full concentration on the road for most of the journey.

These thoughts fled as he found his small group of employees all standing in the courtyard outside of the old farm sheds they used as a gin distillery. He'd only intended a quick visit to check on the production plans for the week and how the bottling had progressed that day. His workers, who were mostly part-time due to the nature of the business, apart from Big Al and Wendham, should have gone home by now; they'd only come in to bottle the batch of raspberry and blueberry flavoured gin that had been made as an experiment.

At first, he imagined a fire alarm, or some other emergency. His sense of foreboding grew as he parked and got out to approach the group, each individual turning to face him.

'Hey! What's up?' He tried a bright tone, even though he imagined broken bottles, spilled gin, lost keys, fire, flood ...

'Hey, yourself Graham. Where've you been all day?' yelled Big Al, who did most of the heavy work.

'Had to go to the coast on an errand.' He was deliberately vague.

'Daniel Jacobs has been over,' said another.

Jacobs was the man Graham rented the buildings from. He paid part of the rent in gin – that always made Graham and Jacobs smile.

'Okay and what did he want? Did he cause this stir?'

'He's retiring and … he's … he's sold the farm to a property developer.' Wendham stepped forward from the rest.

Graham felt the cogs in his brain slow down as he struggled to assimilate what his production manager, Wendham, was telling him. 'Selling up?'

'Sold … sold up.' Wendham frowned.

'But surely, he should have given us some warning, that's if this means what I think it does. He should have told me first.'

Graham would rather have had this vital conversation away from his employees, but it seemed the farmer had announced his news in general hearing. Ripples of worry and discontent were already circulating uncontrolled and unchecked.

'Jacobs said it all happened very quickly. The developer approached him and made him an offer he couldn't refuse. The developer has already been talking to several council members about their plans apparently so expects a green light for two hundred houses on the farmland.'

A cold shiver passed over Graham and not just because of the air temperature. 'I'd better go and see Jacobs straight away.'

He turned to the assembled small group. Concern was written on their faces. 'I promise I'll let you all know what's happening as soon as I know anything myself.'

Senses reeling, he made for the office door. He could hear outraged mutterings behind him. First day he'd been away from the business for absolutely ages and there was a crisis.

Graham's hurried meeting with Daniel Jacobs hadn't filled him with much hope. The man looked old and wizened after a lifetime spent working outdoors. He deserved a comfortable retirement, but it looked as if that was going to happen at the expense of Graham's business, just as it was beginning to take off.

Frankley Gins was a small concern, born of a change in distilling laws, which permitted smaller scale production of spirits. Prior to that the production of gin had been only for the bigger businesses.

His father had helped him to set up the gin distillery five years before, a short while before he died. Graham had been in a bad place mentally after losing his wife Trisha to another man and, as a result, surrendering his business and home in the same week. The small gin distillery was the chance for a fresh start. A good healing distraction.

They'd cherry-picked Wendham, a recent graduate of the prestigious Brewing and Distilling course at Heriot-Watt University in Edinburgh, and set up the gin production with their fingers firmly crossed for luck. The rapid success of the craft gin business had been a surprise. Then his father had died suddenly and his mother had been diagnosed with multiple sclerosis, leaving her most of the time confined to a wheelchair. Graham had begun to wonder if bad luck was destined to follow on his heels forever.

Daniel Jacobs was terribly apologetic. He gave Graham all of the contact details for the developer and handed him an official solicitor's letter, giving him, what Jacobs said was the required twelve months' notice from his lease to vacate the buildings used by the distillery. Jacobs did say, however, that the developer might give Graham an incentive payment to move out more quickly if he could, but that wasn't up to him, it was just something the developer had mentioned in passing when the deal was being forged.

Graham voiced his dismay about not having been consulted and Jacobs apologised profusely, saying that everything had happened so quickly. Graham curbed his anger; he could see this was the best option for a comfortable retirement for the farmer.

'You'll miss my gin payments,' he joked as he left the farmhouse. He'd always been on good terms with Jacobs and despite the blow this news had given him, he was reluctant to part on an argument.

Graham's thoughts were going around and around in no particular order. What to do about Frankley Gins? Did he want to carry on as a gin distiller? If he didn't, how could he help the people who worked for him to get new jobs? If he did, where could he move the business to and how long would it take to get it set up and running again? He'd learned so much in the five years that the business had been operating, that it could be an opportunity to take a new broom to the company. His head began to hurt with all of the possible permutations for rescuing his livelihood.

Graham felt perplexed, but as the seed of a different idea began to grow inside of him and wouldn't let go, he grew suddenly excited. If Nick Crossten was indeed his child, maybe he could move the business to Borteen, or at least live there and have the business nearby ... and the sea air might suit his mother?

Doubts immediately began crowding in. Moving to a different part of the country could be a logistical nightmare, perhaps business suicide. If he took this radical step, would Wendham, who was so vital to the business, come with him? With the twelve month notice period he'd have time to help those who worked for him find other employment options, although the time would unquestionably pass quickly. A friend he'd been at school with ran an employment agency. He added contacting her to his action list.

First things first – was Nick Crossten actually his son?

Chapter Three

When Mandy and Nick had returned to the welcome warmth of the craft centre and Mandy finally opened Owl Corner Crafts, she decided the best thing she could do was to distract Nick and keep him busy for the rest of the day. Mainly, if she really admitted it, to give herself time to think. She started dusting the display shelving, getting Nick to help her move the items on the shelves as she worked.

She was touched by how much care he took over moving the fragile and pottery items. There was no need to remind him to be gentle.

Just before lunch, when they had worked their way around a third of the shelving units, Louise Stevens turned up. Her shy, freckled face peeped through the door, as she almost slunk into the room.

'Teacher training day,' she announced. It sounded like an apology for being there.

'Yes.' Mandy nodded over to where Nick was re-arranging craft books in size order on a recently dusted shelf. Nick grinned over at them both.

Nick and Louise attended Borteen High School and were in the same year, but Louise had once told Mandy that they were in very different class sets. Louise was academic, whereas Nick was often in detention for his behaviour, or else for not doing his homework. The only apparent common link between the two teenagers was their love of art.

Louise painted watercolours of the local area and Nick portraits and street scenes in his own particular modern style, but the pair were often sharing art studio space at school. Mandy displayed Louise's pictures at the craft centre for sale, as well as Nick's.

Mandy liked Louise. She'd promised the quiet girl a

Saturday job at Owl Corner Crafts when the tourist season began – she already gave her a bit of pocket money here and there when she popped in to help out. Mandy also had two regular part-time assistants, Romana and Peggy, but neither were working that day.

Louise Stevens spent far too much time in the craft centre as it was, but Mandy knew she liked to use her as a sounding board. Louise's parents were a little old-fashioned and staid, so she valued Mandy's opinion.

After the two teenagers had reached the finals in an art competition at the school, Mandy had decided to dedicate a section of Owl Corner Crafts to the work of local young craftspeople and artists. The idea was that the sale of any artwork would help to support the youth of Borteen in their artistic ambitions. So far, the results were encouraging and the items on display ranged from pictures, pottery, whittled animal figures and even hand-knitted sheep brooches. The latter were very popular with the tourists.

Mandy had used the youth initiative in the advertising for Owl Corner Crafts and had even successfully placed an article about the centre and the youth work into a national countryside magazine. Mandy proudly displayed the article in a frame hung next to the local artwork section of Owl Corner.

Louise and Nick were always polite to each other, but not over familiar. Mandy didn't imagine for one minute that Nick would want to confide his troubles to Louise, but she discreetly left them alone together just in case he felt the need to get some peer sympathy for his current situation.

At least the additional presence of Louise seemed to diffuse the tension that had built since the events of the early morning. Mandy had clean shelves and beautifully ordered displays by the time Louise announced she was going home.

It had been a slow afternoon with just a few locals coming to the craft centre, so Mandy suggested to Nick that they close early and go to his mother's house to collect his things.

As she had walked down to work that morning, she left him sitting on a bench on the promenade while she went home for her car, picked him up and then, following his directions, drove to the address he'd been living at with his mother.

The house in a cul-de-sac at the other end of Borteen to her own home looked very neglected. It was just as she would have expected, judging by Nick's appearance. They had to fight their way through the bushes overgrowing the path. The paint on the front door was peeling and the doorbell had a sticking plaster taped over it.

A thought crossed Mandy's mind. 'Does your mum own this house?'

'Nah, rents it.'

'Have you been here long?'

He shrugged in his habitual fashion. 'As long as I can remember.'

Mandy knew she would complain loudly if the landlord let any property she was renting get into this state of disrepair, but maybe Sally Crossten didn't have the funds to be picky about where she lived.

'Hmm. I guess if the rent isn't paid the landlord won't be too pleased. You'd better bring any valuables and your school stuff.'

Nick gave her an odd look. She decided it meant he didn't feel he had much of value.

Inside, the house was freezing and had a strange smell: damp combined with something else. Mandy couldn't decide if it was cheap air freshener or rotting vegetables. The rooms were sparsely furnished, but surprisingly tidy, almost as if Sally Crossten had deliberately cleaned before she went away. Mandy shivered – there was an eerie feeling about the house. She would be glad to get out of the place and not just because of the smell.

It didn't take Nick long to pack. He put a battered holdall, a rucksack, a big winter coat that looked at least two sizes too big and two partially finished paintings into the boot of Mandy's car.

'That's all my stuff.'

'Everything?'

'Pretty much.'

'School stuff?'

'Yup, it's in there.'

Mandy didn't ask him any more questions, but she wondered about his life up to now. Perhaps she could find out more over the next few days. It struck her as weird that she'd never even hesitated to offer him shelter. It had just seemed a normal and natural thing to do.

When they arrived at Mandy's house, her black cat was mewing on the doorstep. The neat, clean semi was in stark contrast to the run-down terraced house in which Nick had been living with his mother.

'You've got a cat?' exclaimed Nick, with more animation than she'd seen from him all day, apart from when he ate the pastries at the café.

'Meet Merlin. He doesn't always like strangers though, so beware of his claws ...'

Nick sat on the doorstep, his belongings at his feet and fickle Merlin welcomed the new member of their household enthusiastically with purrs, as he rubbed his sleek body against Nick, to the lad's obvious delight and Mandy's surprise.

'Never been allowed a pet.'

'Well it looks as if Merlin has adopted you already.'

She gulped at the words she had just used, but thankfully a glance at Nick suggested that he hadn't registered their meaning and what the situation Nick found himself in could mean. Would Nick have to be found a new home? Would she be allowed to care for him? Would his mum come back? So many questions and unknowns loomed in their future but she had no wish to alarm Nick any more than he was already.

She knew there were quite a few hoops to leap through

before you could legally adopt a child. Why was she even contemplating that? How did they choose who was suitable? How did they match a child to prospective parents? They were questions she'd never allowed herself to dwell upon before today. Too painful. She scratched distractedly at one of the silvered scars on her arm.

Mandy led Nick up the stairs to her bright, clean second bedroom. It was decorated in shades of blue, with crisp white bed linen, edged with a blue trim. He bounced tentatively on the edge of the bed and grinned up at her.

'Your house smells nice and it's warm.'

To Mandy, it just smelled normal, so she was surprised he'd commented, but then the contrast to the air quality at his mother's house was vast. 'Thank you and this is your room for as long as you need it.'

'Thanks, Mand.'

Merlin had followed them up the stairs and jumped up onto the bed to settle down by Nick. The youth reached out a hand to stroke the cat's sleek back and Merlin purred again.

Mandy felt momentarily annoyed with the normally choosy animal, but then grateful he'd chosen to comfort Nick.

'Why don't you unpack your bag. There are plenty of drawers and lots of hangers in the wardrobe. Then have a look around the house, find the bathroom. I'll go and rustle up some food. Is there anything you don't eat?'

'Nope.'

Mandy left him stroking the cat and went downstairs to the kitchen. She prepared a simple meal for the two of them of bacon, cheese and vegetables tossed through pasta. Nick had explored the house by the time she called him to come and sit at the kitchen table. Mandy had another go at probing the disappearance of his mum.

'Are you sure your mum has gone completely? She hasn't just stormed off for a while in a huff?'

'You read that letter and she took two cases.' Nick began

to shovel pasta into his mouth, as if he feared Mandy might take the food away from him before he'd finished it.

'Have you any other relatives?' she asked.

Nick stopped with a forkful of pasta in mid-air. 'Had a nan, but she died.'

'Oh! I'm so sorry.' Mandy worried that she'd upset him, but Nick shrugged.

'She was old. And ill,' he said, matter-of-factly. 'She didn't like me much.'

'Anyone else? Any other relatives or close friends?'

He shook his head. 'Don't think so.'

Mandy chewed her food thoughtfully. 'Any idea where your mum went? She didn't give any clues in that letter. Only, I have a suspicion that we'll need some sort of approval from her for you to stay here with me.'

Nick looked up, sudden fear appearing in his eyes. He gulped down his latest mouthful of pasta. 'Why do we need permission?'

'You're only fifteen. There are rules.'

'Sick of rules. If I can't stay here, I'll just go live on the street then. I'm not going to one of those children's homes. Seen 'em on tele. I'm not going to one!'

Mandy realised that she would have to tread very carefully, or Nick might just take off. 'Hang on, young man. We'll sort this out, but we must do it properly. You don't want me to get into trouble, do you?'

''Course not.' The fear was back in his wide eyes.

'Then let me try to sort this out. Okay?'

He shrugged his shoulders.

She thought of little else that evening and resorted to making notes about her thoughts, worries and questions, while Nick watched the television.

Who could she ask about this? She must know someone who could help. It would surely be better to get informal advice before alerting the authorities, but she didn't want to leave it too long, or it might look suspicious in some way, when all she was trying to do was help Nick.

Nick's choice of programmes was a revelation. She could see that her viewing would be very different while he was staying. She normally watched arts programmes and property makeovers; Nick seemed an expert on soaps and reality TV. She stifled a groan.

Chapter Four

Graham was wary about telling his mother that Frankley Gins might soon be homeless and the future of the business in danger. In truth, he hadn't yet got his own head around it all. He understood why the land had been sold and he couldn't blame his landlord for wanting to safeguard his old age, but the repercussions for his own business could be catastrophic.

He rang the number of the contact from the development company that Daniel Jacobs had passed to him and when there was no answer, left a message requesting an urgent meeting to find out the developer's plans for the buildings he rented. At the moment he was only speculating and worrying, when he didn't really know for sure if the new landlord would change anything at all. They might just continue to allow him to rent the buildings, but in his heart of hearts, Graham had the nagging feeling that the entrance to the farm buildings used by Frankley Gins would make an ideal access road into the planned housing estate and he was kidding himself that everything could continue unchanged.

When they had originally leased the buildings, they'd had no idea whether the business would take off. His father had dealt with the negotiations, as Graham had been in a dark place. With his father dying so suddenly on top of everything else, his mother falling ill, and trying to keep the new business going, Graham hadn't revisited the terms of the lease until now.

When he found the document in the desk drawer in the study, the lease specified a twelve month notice period if either Frankley Gins or Daniel Jacobs wanted to pull out, so that was correct, even though Daniel Jacobs had implied that the developer would try to buy Graham out sooner with a financial settlement. If he could find the right location quickly that might suit both parties.

His mum had enough to contend with given her ongoing health problems and Graham was unwilling to add to her burden until he knew something more concrete about what was to happen. He decided to talk to her instead about his visit to Borteen and the possibility that Nick was his son and thus her grandson.

She'd read Sally's letter and knew where he'd been that day but her reaction to his report of his time in Borteen was cautious. 'Graham, love, please be sure he really is your flesh and blood. You hear of so many scams these days.'

'Don't worry, Mum, I'm going to arrange for a paternity test, so I have proof that he's my son.'

His mother had watched an awful lot of daytime television since becoming ill, so he knew that her suspicions were born of those dreadful, in Graham's eyes anyway, morning programmes where people accused each other of unthinkable things each and every day.

'I promise I'll make sure. If these basic paternity tests show a positive result, I'll get something more sophisticated and some legal advice. At the moment, it all seems like a dream, so I'm trying not to take it seriously until I know for sure.'

His mother winced as she moved her position in the chair. 'If he genuinely is your son, I'm sure I will grow to love him. But ... I'll say it again, make sure there's no mistake.'

'I know all that, but if there's a chance he's my son, how can I just turn and walk away, especially when he's vulnerable and needs my help? I'm sure when you get to know him, you'll love him. I just have this inner feeling that it's true – you'd say *a feeling in your water* that he's mine. I can't wait to get the tests underway.'

'We don't want a cuckoo in the nest.'

'Mum!' Graham couldn't help the image popping into his head of a large ungainly cuckoo being fed by a tiny blue tit.

'Well it happens I'm afraid.'

'I think when you meet him, you'll realise he has certain family resemblances.'

'You just want him to be yours and I do understand that, but be careful, please.' His mother's face softened. 'So tell me about him.'

'I don't know a lot yet. He's fifteen, looks like he could do with some new clothes and a few of your stews with dumplings. It seems he's an artist like you.'

'Really?' Ann was smiling now.

'The woman, who seems to have appointed herself as his protector, Mandy her name is, she said she sells his art at her craft centre.'

'Now that does sound exciting. He must be yours.' Ann smiled fondly at Graham. 'Just be sure.'

'I will. I promise.'

Why did he need to pursue this? Many men would walk away, have nothing to do with it, after all Nick was fifteen. It was what his mother had hinted he should do when he had first shown her the letter from Sally, but he just couldn't.

The thought of someone out in the world with his genes, his flesh and blood, intrigued and excited him. It seemed especially important after the death of his own father. He'd had no choice but to follow up the letter. No choice but to go to Borteen.

His dad had always been so honest, so keen to do the right thing, often to the detriment of himself. He'd encouraged Graham to get Frankley Gins up and running, tried to give his son purpose again after the disaster his life had become, had promised to help him, but what none of them had known was that his father had an underlying heart condition. His collapse and sudden death had been a shock to everyone, especially Graham.

He knew that if Nick was his son, he'd missed his early years, but maybe it wasn't too late to help and influence the young man as he moved into adulthood. Nick seemed a little wayward and would definitely need a decent haircut and some new clothes, but Graham would be proud to call him his son. Nick appeared to be a survivor.

Mandy couldn't sleep. It was something about having another person in the house. Although Nick wasn't a stranger and she'd sold his work for a while, she still didn't know him all that well. Also, the events of the day kept repeating themselves on a continuous loop in her head. She wondered if she'd taken on too much taking Nick in.

That evening, she'd discovered that Nick didn't own a toothbrush, or if he did, he hadn't viewed it as an essential item to bring from his mother's house. She'd given him her spare one and a tube of toothpaste but had secretly wondered if he knew how to use them. People lived in such different ways depending on their circumstances, background and parental influences.

Merlin had decided to sleep in the spare room with her visitor and that unsettled her too. She was used to the weight of the animal on the bottom of her duvet. Fickle cat. Mandy wasn't quite sure why she was annoyed, because in a way she was pleased that the cat had given Nick a warm welcome and sensed that he needed extra support.

Nick seemed to have made himself at home and if he was in any way uncomfortable, he wasn't showing any signs of it. He hadn't said a word about his mother since their first conversations or questioned any further Mandy's desire to get proper approvals for him to lodge with her.

Mandy knew that the simplest way would be to get Nick's mother's consent, but how did you go about finding someone who had left intentionally and not supplied any clues about their destination? Especially someone who seemed to have planned to disappear? Mandy couldn't help her thoughts straying to how it seemed as if Sally Crossten had cleaned her house before she left. Her actions seemed premeditated and yet, she hadn't made any proper arrangements for the care of her son, unless you counted that letter to Graham, which might never have arrived and had almost reached him by chance. If Nick was Mandy's child ... but maybe she'd better not go there or judge so harshly.

The clean house played on her mind and so she asked Nick casually about it. 'I think your mum was tidier than I am judging by her house?'

'Real nightmare, Mum. Hated anything out of place. OCD or something. Prefer it here. Better not to always feel wrong for moving things.'

Well that answered that one.

Chapter Five

Graham met a representative from the housing development company at their office in central Manchester.

Even though they would be unlikely to break ground to begin building the houses until the following year, it was clear that, as Graham had suspected, the area where his distillery was situated was intended for the grand entrance to the estate. He wasn't shown the plans but caught site of an artist's impression of the development that appeared to make a feature of the lake from which they drew water for making their gin. He realised at that point that any negotiation to extend the lease for the buildings was a non-starter.

Instead he turned his attention to Daniel Jacob's comment that the developer might pay him an incentive to move from the buildings more quickly than the year's notice allowed. He left the offices having gained an assurance that he would be given a sliding scale of incentive offers to give up his lease more quickly just as soon as the outline planning permissions had met council approval.

As he got the impression that these approvals might be gained sooner rather than later, Graham called a meeting back at Frankley Gins for later that afternoon, to fulfil his promise about being honest with his workers – but first he needed to update his mother.

Surprisingly, Ann Frankley was quite sanguine about the whole thing and indeed her thinking echoed his own thoughts.

'I'm sad in a way that you'll have to move out of that barn, because your father helped to set it up, but I suppose you've learned so much more about the production of gin as you've gone along and maybe you'd do things slightly differently next time?'

'Quite true. Certain pieces of equipment would benefit

from being in different positions to make the processes more efficient.'

'Well make sure you make a record of what you'd change, so you remember for the new place. Now you've got that look on your face that you used to have as a child ...'

'What look?'

'I think you know. The one when you want to say something else but aren't sure whether to.'

'It's not a fully formed thought yet.'

Ann shifted her position in the chair. 'Just say it. I think I can probably guess anyway.'

'I'm wondering, if Nick is proved to be my son, whether you and I might move to the seaside ...' Graham held his breath for his mother's response.

'Love, please be careful. I don't want you to get hurt badly again like before.'

'I'm stronger now, Mum, but I promise I'll be cautious.'

'Well, you know that at one time I'd have said I never wanted to leave this house, but now your dad has gone ... some sunny days at the beach might do me the power of good.'

'So, if everything works out and there are quite a few variables *to* work out, you would come with me to Borteen?'

'As long as Nick is yours, yes.'

Graham left the house with a smile on his face, feeling as if one hurdle had been vaulted.

At Frankley Gins, Graham didn't see any point in being anything other than as honest as he could be.

'We have to leave this barn, that is now a given, I'm afraid. But, from today I want to up production. We need to build up some stock to keep our customers supplied during the move to wherever Frankley Gins finally lands. So, a positive is that I can offer all of you extra hours for the time being and I promise to update you as soon as the longer term position becomes any clearer and I know more.'

'Fair enough,' said Big Al, who always seemed to be the self-appointed spokesman. 'Only thing is, what with the uncertainty, I've already got wind of a new job for myself and possibly one other.'

'With everything up in the air I can't blame any of you for looking for jobs elsewhere. I can only promise to let you know more about future plans as soon as I know anything else.'

There was no point setting any more hares running until he had things clear in his own head. He needed those DNA test results. Meanwhile he would sound out Wendham about possible future options.

Mandy and Nick seemed to slip into living together quite easily. During the February half-term school holiday, Nick spent most of his time helping Mandy with jobs at the craft centre and in her home.

He was surprisingly helpful around the house and didn't have to be asked to wash up after meals. He seemed to view washing the dishes as a normal task. As a bonus, he greeted each plate of food Mandy served up with enthusiasm and interest, asking her if she'd teach him to cook his favourites.

She found she was actually enjoying having someone to cook for. It stopped her grabbing snacks or ready meals and made her think about providing tasty dishes instead.

Nick also kept his room tidy and made his bed each morning. Mandy wondered if it was the fear of being told he couldn't continue to stay with her that motivated his tidiness or his mum's way of being. Her thoughts strayed back to that tidy empty house he'd lived in with his mother.

However, she found it difficult to relax completely, somehow fearing a visit from the police or social services, because she hadn't yet formalised any arrangements for the care of the teenager. It seemed pointless to do anything just yet, as she still wondered if Sally Crossten would reappear, but when that week passed by too and there was no knock on the door from an outraged Sally wishing to reclaim Nick, Mandy began to wonder. Maybe she would come back after two weeks? After all, she told herself, a two-week holiday was quite a normal length of time. But was she deluding herself?

The next time she heard from Graham was by post. The parcel was addressed to Mandy but contained a DNA testing kit for Nick to use. It somehow seemed a rather clinical approach and at first her hackles rose, but the note inside made it clear that he felt he had to keep things *businesslike* until he could be sure of an actual blood relationship with Nick. He acknowledged his uncertainty and embarrassment at sending the test in the post and added his best wishes for a resolution for somewhere suitable for Nick to stay in the interim period, hoping it was with Mandy.

Trying to put herself in Graham's shoes, she could see that this was a really big deal for him and potentially also for Nick. A positive match of DNA could be life-changing for them both. She appreciated that Graham would want to be careful about raising the hopes of either of them. She did, however, wonder how Graham would have reacted if he had reached Borteen that day when he'd come over to investigate the truth of the letter he'd just received and found Nick with nowhere to stay and no one to look after him.

Mandy tried to convince herself that Nick would surely benefit from a steady male influence in his life, particularly if his mum never came back, but how did Mandy approach the need for the troubled teenager to take the test? She turned the box over in her hands and tried to compose an introduction to the subject of genetics.

As it was, she needn't have worried. Nick came home from school that afternoon in a quiet, thoughtful mood, eating his tea, barely looking up.

'Shall we watch TV tonight?' she asked, trying to reach out to him through the silence. She felt a little unsettled by this new mood.

'Homework first, I suppose.' He grinned before visibly gritting his teeth. Mandy had stressed the importance of not drawing attention to himself when he returned to school after half-term, until she had everything sorted out regarding him living with her. Part of the deal had been to keep up with his homework, although she secretly thought this might draw even more attention to him as she knew from her conversations with Louise that it was out of character for Nick to do the work, let alone on time.

'What subjects have you got tonight?'

'Only history. Hate it, but Mr Hodgekiss is evil if you don't meet his deadlines, so better get on with it.'

'Need any help?' She made the offer hoping it would be something she knew something about.

'Nah.'

She started to clear the dishes away and Nick went to fetch his school rucksack. However, he made no attempt to get his books out of the bag.

'Mand ... will we see that man again?'

She paused before replying, knowing exactly who he meant. 'Graham?'

'Yes. Could he really be my dad do you think?'

'It's possible, but we won't really know for sure unless you both do a test to prove it.'

'Blood test?' His eyes widened with a horrified expression.

'No. It's a simple test actually. You just collect some saliva in a little tube.'

'Is that all – spit?' He physically relaxed in front of her eyes.

'Yes, a DNA test.'

'Ah, I know about those, they do them on that TV programme Mum used to watch.'

After a moment of indecision, she handed him the packet and the note she'd received from Graham.

He looked at her quizzically.

'Graham Frankley sent it. Arrived this morning in the post.'

He turned the box over in his hands, then read the note carefully. 'Mand this feels scary, but could be good, right? Graham seems a decent bloke, doesn't he?'

'Yes, he seems a genuine person, but if I'm totally honest with you, I'm not sure what to think at the moment. But then, if you don't do this test, you will never know for sure and I think you will always wonder what the result would have said.'

'No choice really. Keeps going around my head. Is he my dad? Not my dad? And I feel angry with Mum for not telling me more.'

'I can understand that. Don't hesitate or think about it too much then, just do the test and we'll send it off.'

Nick nodded and ripped open the cardboard box.

Chapter Six

The craft centre was housed in an old Methodist chapel not far from the Borteen promenade. Mandy had chosen this building to rent because it was natural for tourists to walk up and down the seafront. She counted on them seeing the sign for Owl Corner Crafts right in front of them and, hopefully, coming in to browse the crafts on display, particularly if there was a cold wind from the sea and they needed to warm up, or a sudden rain shower. It seemed to work; the craft centre was popular with both tourists and locals.

She'd decided when she opened the business that she would only stock tasteful local craft items. Maeve at the gift shop often joked that she sold the tat in her shop, just off the high street, and Mandy the posh stuff at Owl Corner Crafts. Mandy had shelves full of mainly art, cards, scarves, pictures, jewellery and ornamental objects, with a few items of clothing and furniture. She often had the exhibiting artists visiting the craft centre to talk to the tourists about their work. It seemed to add authenticity to the items. Mandy had tentatively begun to allow some of the exhibitors to run workshops in the space at the side of the centre, which she'd originally intended for a café.

Her two assistants were Romana and Peggy. Romana, as her name suggested was from Romania. Her boyfriend, Olavan, had instigated their move to England. He was a barista with an impressive beard and worked in the upmarket café halfway up the high street. Romana was very willing to work and never objected to covering for Mandy, as her boyfriend put in such long hours at the café. Romana was so stylish that Mandy often felt like a frump in contrast. The young woman's hair, make-up and nails were always perfect.

Her other assistant, Peggy, was a grandmother who had lived in Borteen all her life and knew Mandy's parents. She had to leave each school day at three in term time to pick her grandchildren up from school.

At this time of year it didn't really matter, but in the tourist season it was a constant juggling act to ensure enough staff cover and sufficient stock of the right type.

Mandy unpacked a box of fabric angels. It went against the grain to have items in the craft centre that weren't from local artists, but she'd decided she needed a section aimed at the children who inevitably accompanied their parents into Owl Corner. She wanted to try an alcove dedicated to cheaper things that might appeal to these younger visitors, in an attempt to get their parents to buy more, but also to distract small fingers from reaching for expensive delicate items on the display shelving. She already had a policy of putting really expensive things higher up on the shelves, but even that didn't always work.

She'd also decided to try to theme the displays and to introduce elements relevant to each season as it came around. It was a constant job to keep the displays fresh and appealing but one Mandy usually enjoyed.

Many artists and artisans approached her for display space, but these days she was very selective, only taking on goods she was sure would sell and which she herself believed in. Most of the time Mandy loved her business.

Peggy was helping her today and had just told her she thought some things had gone missing from the shelves during the morning. A shoplifter had been at work in the centre and a clever one. Mandy felt disheartened as she and Peggy tried to remember the people who had been in. He or she had worked out the coverage of the security mirrors and only taken small items out of range. Each item missing reduced takings and was annoying. Mandy vowed to investigate CCTV again, although it had been too expensive last time she'd researched it. Without that it would be difficult to prove anything against the few people who had visited them that day.

In truth, she'd been distracted even before Peggy had mentioned the shoplifter. She was having increasing difficulty concentrating on anything. She paced aimless and unseeing around the craft centre, trying to get everything into perspective surrounding the situation with Nick. She didn't seem to have the focus for even dusting. Sally Crossten had now been gone for just over two weeks and Mandy's theory about her returning after a two-week holiday was thus looking less and less likely.

This whole saga with Nick had unsettled her. She needed to get something resolved about his care, so she didn't keep feeling that she could be accused of wrongdoing. She'd had the best of intentions taking Nick in, but anything could be misconstrued, you only had to look at the news reports every day.

As it approached lunchtime, Mandy kept a look out of the craft centre window. The weather had turned unseasonably mild as March had begun and the sun was out. If he was on shift, PC Ethan Gibson, her long-time acquaintance, often went to get his lunch from the fish and chip shop.

Her watching paid off and she ambushed the policeman as he came out of The Borteen Cod with a cone of chips and something else, which, when he unwrapped it, turned out to be a saveloy.

'Ethan! Are you sitting on the seafront to eat those? If so, can I join you?'

'Sounds ominous. You can do, as long as you don't steal my chips. I get the impression you want to talk to me about something serious?'

'In confidence, if possible.'

He waved his cone of chips and was in danger of losing some of them. 'You know I can only promise that if it doesn't involve a crime or someone being placed in danger.' His face was serious.

'Of course.'

They walked over to the edge of the sea wall and took up residence on one of the benches. Even though the sun was out, it wasn't particularly warm. Mandy felt suddenly nervous.

'Come on then, try me. I'm going to eat this before it gets cold, so you talk and I'll answer when I've finished chewing.'

He proceeded to munch his way through his lunch. Mandy preferred to look out to sea while she was talking rather than watch him eating.

'Okay. Scenario. Someone leaves home without trace, but it's not suspicious as they leave a note giving some instructions about their wishes while they are away. If it was suspected that they went abroad, would you, the police, as in you, be able to find out if they did?'

'*Hmmm actcha kloo dor.*'

'Pardon?'

Ethan swallowed. 'Sorry, shouldn't try to speak while I'm eating. So, who exactly has gone missing and do I need to know about it?'

'Sally Crossten.'

'Young Nick's mum?'

'Yes. He's staying with me while I try to sort things out.'

'How long's she been gone?'

'Just over two weeks now.'

Ethan popped another chip into his mouth and chewed thoughtfully. 'Have you told the school what's going on?'

'Not yet.'

'Can I suggest that it would be a good idea, if for no other reason than to register that you're looking after him? You don't want it to all seem like a secret, do you? I'm afraid if you don't, I will have to now anyway because I'm aware of the situation.'

'You're right, I'll get that sorted. But I need to tell Nick what I'm doing first.'

'If I hear anything about Sally Crossten, I'll let you know. You do think she went away voluntarily? There isn't any suggestion that she might have been abducted?'

'I don't believe so. She spoke, not very kindly I might add, to Nick before leaving.'

'Okay.'

'Was she at school with us?'

'No. I think she moved here when Nick was small. Southern accent I believe.'

There was one more lead for Mandy to follow up. The previous evening she'd asked Nick if his mum had any particular friends and about any work she'd been doing.

'She does a bit of cleaning. Maeve's gift shop, the solicitor's office, sometimes the public loos, but she hated that one according to Nick.'

'Not surprised. Friends?'

'Not as such, kept herself to herself from what Nick says. I'm hoping she might have talked to Maeve when she cleaned. I'll pop in and see her to find out.'

'Right. I'll see if any reports about Sally Crossten have been logged. Keep me in touch with developments, if nothing else to cover yourself.'

'Thanks, Ethan. See you soon.'

Mandy smiled and left him to finish his lunch in peace. She went back to the craft centre feeling as unsettled as before, if not more so.

It was a quiet day, Peggy had gone to collect her grandchildren, so Mandy locked up early and headed up the high street. Maeve's gift shop was in one of the alleys off this main road.

Brightly coloured windmills vied for space with blow-up boats and beach mats outside her shop. Maeve was sitting behind the counter, knitting at breakneck speed when Mandy opened the door. Plump and rosy-cheeked, Maeve had run the same shop with seemingly the same stock ever since Mandy had been a young girl. She looked the same as she had then too, apart from the tinge of grey in her mousey hair.

'Well, if it isn't Mandy. How's business, girl?'

'Not too bad, could always be better, couldn't it? But it's that time of year when things are slow.'

'Tell me about it. Now what can I do for you? Come to suss out the competition, have you?' Maeve winked.

She decided to get straight to the point. 'Maeve, I understand Sally Crossten cleans for you?'

'She does. When she can be bothered to turn up, that is. It's rather hit and miss. I think I've cleaned the shop more often than she has lately.'

'Did you know she's gone away?'

'What! Without giving me any notice? The minx! That's why she hasn't been answering my texts.'

Mandy had left messages on the answering service of the mobile phone number Nick had given her too. There had been no response, or acknowledgement. 'Sally went without giving anyone any notice, least of all her son.'

'Poor Nick, what's to become of him? Poor lamb.'

'I've taken him in for now. At least you've answered my questions, which were whether you knew she'd gone and if so where?'

'No. I sure didn't. Not even a subtle hint.'

Another dead end thought Mandy. Sally Crossten had done a pretty good job of disappearing. 'I'm beginning to think she didn't tell anyone. Would you have any idea where she would go? Nick seems to think she could be with an Australian she met. Did she ever mention him to you?'

'She never really said much at all and definitely didn't discuss her love life with me. No idea where she would go, I'm afraid. I'm hopping mad she's left me in the lurch.'

'Please let me know if you hear anything, either from Sally, or anything about her on the grapevine, anything at all. I could really do with having a word with her about Nick.'

'Sure I will and can you let me know if you hear of anyone wanting a cleaning job?'

'Of course. And Maeve, I know it's hard, but could you keep all this to yourself please?'

'You can count on me.'

Mandy hoped so, as Maeve wasn't known for her discretion. This added weight to the argument that Mandy should talk to the school about the Nick situation urgently.

Chapter Seven

Mandy waited until Nick had finished his homework that evening, packed up and plonked himself on the chair he had now claimed as his own territory in the lounge.

'What's on?' He yawned, as Merlin jumped up onto his lap purring.

In answer, she clicked off the television. The cat jumped off Nick's lap as if the animal sensed the atmosphere in the room had suddenly changed.

'Nick. I think the time has come to tell the school and social services what's been going on.'

'No! They'll take me away. They'll put me in a children's home.' He leapt up and ran his hands repeatedly through his unruly hair as he paced up and down.

'I've done some research and it appears because of your age, they are less likely to take you into care, that is, if we can prove you are safe here and that I'm a suitable person for you to be with.' Mandy was trying to fight down the panic at Nick's reaction and was desperate to pacify him.

'I've never felt safer.' Nick stopped pacing and his face radiated hope again.

'I'm hoping they will see your opinion as important. It's a risk, Nick, but I think it's better to be up front about all this. The longer we go on without saying anything, the more it looks like some sort of deception. I'd rather not get into trouble, so if it's all assessed properly and approved, I'd be much happier.'

Nick sat down on the settee with his hands over his face for a little while. Mandy waited patiently. He eventually looked up, his expression much older than his years. 'Okay then. I'm just freaking that it could all go wrong.'

'I know. I am too, that's why I wanted to explain to you what I was about to do, just in case.'

She clicked the television back on and watched as Nick visibly tried to relax as one of his favourite soaps came up on the screen. Merlin snuggled down next to him.

Mandy made the appointment to see the head of Borteen High School with her heart in her mouth. She didn't know Karen Brookes. Mandy couldn't decide if not knowing the woman was better or worse. For someone used to being acquainted with most of the locals it was an alien experience to have no knowledge of the woman's character or past to guide her approach.

The heart in mouth feeling, accompanied by a seeming washing machine full of butterflies in her stomach returned as she walked up the school drive. She really didn't know what to expect.

'Good morning, Ms Vanes.' The handshake was firm, suggesting no nonsense. Mandy felt her heart lurch in sudden fear. Karen Brookes was neat and trim in a navy-blue suit with incredible high heels on her shoes.

'Mandy, please.'

Mandy fought down memories of being in the headmaster's office, this very room, when she was a teenager on that fateful day when she'd prematurely left the school. The furniture was different but somehow the room smelt the same. But, she reminded herself, this wasn't about her.

Karen nodded warily. 'So, how can I help you, Mandy? I understand you run a local business, but, as far as I'm aware, you don't have a child at the school?'

The school secretary had obviously been filling Karen in on her background. Mandy wondered how much of her past had been discussed. She felt her face colour at the thought.

'That's right, but I've actually come here today to talk about one of your pupils.'

Karen's eyebrows arched in question.

'Nick Crossten.'

'Oh dear, he hasn't been causing trouble again, has he?'

'Trouble?'

Karen looked sheepish. 'Sorry. I must have the wrong impression, please go on.'

Mandy was more than a little annoyed at the woman assuming Nick had done something wrong but she was careful to hide it.

'I run the craft centre near the beach, Owl Corner Crafts, and I exhibit some of Nick's paintings for sale. It was all approved by your predecessor, Harry Dixon.'

Karen looked stunned. This aspect of Nick's background couldn't have come to her attention before. 'Really? He paints? What does he paint?'

'He's an extremely talented artist. He paints his observations of life, usually street scenes and people, in monochrome colours that have proved very popular with my customers. He's now getting really good at portraits in a similar style too.'

'Well I never. I wouldn't ever have believed it. He always seems so disinterested in his studies.'

'We've become friends since he's been selling his pictures through my shop and … I'll get to the point: his mum has gone away suddenly and left Nick to fend for himself. I thought that you should be aware of that fact and might be able to point me in the direction of the right people to speak to about his care.'

'Of course, how awful for the poor young man. How on earth is he managing? Social services must be alerted right away.' Karen reached for her phone.

Mandy could feel her heart rate accelerating. This situation was in danger of spiralling out of control just as Nick had feared. 'He's fine. He's been staying with me, just until we could establish whether his mother was returning or not, but now that's not looking very likely.'

'I see.'

Was that disapproval in the headmistress's eyes? Mandy

realized that the woman was only trying to establish whether Nick was under any threat or danger. Her suspicion wasn't personally directed at her. There were, after all, some strange people in the world. Despite her innocence and good intentions in this situation, it didn't stop a bead of sweat running down Mandy's back.

'I have no problem with Nick staying at mine, but now it seems clear that his mum has abandoned him, I would rather have the necessary checks and approvals done – to have it all out in the open and above board. When I told him he could stay with me, I'd imagined Sally would return after a week in the sun, but it's been over two weeks now and there's been no sign, or word of her.'

'Okay, we need a meeting with social services. I'll ring and set it up now while you're here.'

Mandy thought it was considerate of Karen to make the call while she was in the room, so that she could hear exactly what was said. As the social worker was already visiting the school about another pupil that day, the meeting was set up for two o'clock that afternoon. Mandy made her goodbyes and wondered if Karen would be right back on the phone to the social worker, Harriet Drew, as soon as she had left the room to talk about her. She pondered again what the school secretary could have told Karen about her own history. She was quickly becoming paranoid.

She returned to Owl Corner Crafts, but somehow couldn't face the sandwich she'd bought for lunch on the way down the high street. Her day became an exercise in nervous clock-watching.

When she returned to the school in the afternoon, Harriet Drew proved to be a small bird-like woman, with a pointy nose and bird's nest iron-grey hair. She began by praising Mandy. 'I understand you have been very kind to Nick Crossten and kept him safe when his mother went missing?'

Mandy fought not to stammer. It felt as if she was on trial. 'I, somehow, thought Sally Crossten would return quite quickly, after a holiday, but it's looking less likely now.'

Harriet paused to make notes in her folder. 'Mmm, okay.' She sighed. 'Nick has been on our "keep an eye on" list for some time. I know his mother has had difficulties for a while, but I never imagined she'd abandon him completely.'

Mandy thought it was time to get everything out in the open. She hadn't realized just how all the stuff surrounding Nick had been weighing on her shoulders. It was as if the knots unwound as she spoke. 'I have absolutely no problem with Nick staying with me. I've been enjoying his company. To be honest, he's absolutely terrified of being sent to a children's home.'

'I can well understand his fears. If you are willing to provide a home for him, at least temporarily, you do understand that from a child protection point of view we need to carry out some background checks on you and also, we'll need to visit you at home to – and I'm sure it's just a formality – to ensure the environment is suitable and safe for Nick?'

'I'll co-operate fully with any checks you want to do. No problem at all.'

'Has Nick any other relatives that you're aware of, ones who might step in?'

'As far as I've been able to find out, Nick's grandma died last year and she was the only family he had left ... or so we thought.'

Harriet looked at her expectantly, eyebrows raised. 'Go on.'

'A man, Graham Frankley, came to visit Nick from Manchester. Thankfully, Nick was with me when he appeared on the scene. He claims to be Nick's biological father, even though Nick's mother had never told him anything about his dad. It appears that Sally Crossten wrote to Graham before she went away to finally tell him about Nick. Mr Frankley was not even aware he had a son and bearing in mind Nick is fifteen it was a big shock to him. Mr Frankley let me read the letter Sally Crossten sent which told of her intentions to leave Borteen.'

Harriet was scribbling lots of notes in very looped handwriting. 'This man didn't make any attempt to take Nick away with him, did he?'

'No. I was careful to be there for the whole time. Graham was as shocked and bewildered about Sally Crossten's revelations, as Nick was to be abandoned and discover the identity of his supposed father. I have Mr Frankley's contact details here to add to your file.' She passed over the business card that Graham had given to her.

'Right, this is getting curiouser and curiouser.' Harriet copied down the details from Graham's business card in careful print totally in contrast to the rest of her notes. She handed back the card. 'You understand that my main concern is for Nick's safety and that he is being cared for, and it sounds as if you are looking after that aspect of this unfortunate situation very well. I will arrange as a matter of urgency, one, to speak to Nick and see how he feels about all of this.' She glanced at the headmistress at this point and Karen nodded her agreement. 'Two, I'll arrange for the necessary checks on yourself and your home as soon as I can and three, I'll speak to Mr Frankley.'

'Sounds like a plan.' Mandy at last felt unburdened now she had voiced everything but her nervous tension was lodged in her stomach as she asked the next question. 'Is it okay for Nick to continue staying with me until all of this is cleared up?'

'I can see no reason why not, providing both Nick and you are happy. The situation will have to be reviewed, of course.'

'Great. When you see Nick, could you please make sure that you reassure him? I have a horrible suspicion that he might run away if you mention children's homes or moving him elsewhere.'

'With Mrs Brookes's permission, I'll see Nick before the end of the school day and then I'll get the ball rolling on the rest of our *plan*.' She smiled and Mandy felt herself relax a little bit more.

Mandy walked back down the hill to the seafront feeling pleased that all of this was in the right hands now, but she still had a niggling worry that Nick wouldn't be allowed to stay with her and might run away in fear.

When she'd made herself a cup of tea and calmed down a little, she gave Graham Frankley a quick call, to warn him to expect contact from social services about Nick.

Initially, he sounded rather alarmed and somewhat annoyed.

Mandy found herself defensive. 'I had to tell the lady from social services, Harriet Drew, everything. It's over two weeks since Sally Crossten disappeared, it was starting to feel as if I was doing something wrong by not telling anyone that his mum had gone away and abandoned him.'

Graham's tone changed. 'I can see that. No, it's fine, I agree it's best to have everything in the open.'

'I just thought you should know.'

'Thank you. Can I ask what Nick thought about the test I sent?'

'All done and posted.'

There was relief in Graham's voice. 'Wow that's wonderful. It won't be long until we know then.'

Mandy had a sudden chill pass over her body. 'Nick is really excited about having a father, no, about having *you* as a father. I do hope his dreams aren't dashed by the test results.'

'I'm hoping for a positive result too, as I've kind of got used to the idea of being a dad.'

'Fingers crossed for both of you then.' Mandy crossed her fingers and sent out a silent prayer for the best result.

She didn't say anything yet, but she'd applied for a copy of Nick's birth certificate. Nick had had no luck in finding the original when she'd asked him to look for the document at his mother's house so, deciding that Nick would need a copy of the certificate at some point anyway, they had filled in an application form online.

Later that afternoon, Nick arrived at Owl Corner Crafts in his school uniform. He loitered patiently by the door, while Mandy wrapped one of the pottery dragons for a customer.

'Good day?' she asked him, after the man left, holding his package carefully.

'Yes. Got a great mark for my history homework and a lady, Mrs Drew came to see me about you and Mum.'

'And?' She was alarmed by his serious face.

He broke into a huge grin. 'Teasing! She seemed cool about me staying with you, for now anyway. I told her about Merlin and my posh bedroom. She wanted to know if I found Graham scary. I told her, I like him and that I'm hoping he's really my dad. Told her about the DNA test thingy, too. It'd be so cool if he's my dad, Mand.'

'We'll take everything one day at a time, but I for one feel much better now we've spoken out about your situation. Shall we get fish and chips on the way home to celebrate?'

'Yeah!'

They high-fived.

She would never have imagined that having a fifteen-year-old's approval would make her feel quite so good.

Chapter Eight

Early the next week, Mandy received a visit from Harriet Drew at Owl Corner Crafts. At first, she didn't think Harriet was going to say anything about the Nick situation, as she wanted help buying a present for her sister's wedding anniversary.

'I thought twenty years was worth celebrating. Not many couple's get that far these days, do they?'

Mandy asked her budget and then guided her around the craft centre, pointing out suitable items. Harriet was taken with a watercolour painting by a local artist and settled on that. Mandy wrapped the gift in some of the special paper she kept for gift-wrapping.

'I always worry I'll leave the price on the present when I do this.' She laughed and checked for the umpteenth time that the price tag was on her table and not still attached to the picture.

Harriet waited until she had paid for the present and then smiled at Mandy. 'Thank you for your help with the present. I just wanted to say that so far everything has checked out okay. It's now on record that Nick is staying with you. Just the home visit left to do, but I'm sure it won't be a problem.'

'That's wonderful. To be honest I don't know what I'd do without him. He's enjoying living with me too, I think.'

'He did say that in his interview and lots of other lovely complimentary things about you, in his gruff teenage way of course.' She laughed. 'He also mentioned his possible father and how excited he was to get to know him, even though he lives so far away.'

'I'm not sure how that one will work out yet, but I'm hopeful for Nick.'

Mandy felt her body begin to relax. Everything regarding

Nick was now open and on record with the right people. They could take their time getting to know more about Graham and whether he was Nick's dad.

She helped Harriet get through the door with the picture and held it while she opened her car. As the social worker drove away, Mandy took the time to go and peer over the sea wall and take a cleansing breath of sea air. The tide was out and Borteen beach looked huge in the sunlight. Maybe things would be all right after all.

It was the first time Mandy had been out for an evening since Nick had moved in. He was happily ensconced in front of football on the TV, quite excited about having a night in on his own. Pippa, who ran Rose Court Guest House and Jenny, who worked in Sowden and now lived at Tree Tops at the top of the hill, had both been at school with Mandy. They insisted she join them for a night out, but she didn't feel she wanted to be out too late. Her new sense of responsibility was strange. Had she become an adult at last?

As she sat in The Ship Inn with the girls, she was aware that a guy had been making eyes at her for a while. Eventually, he got up from the bar stool he'd been perched on and came over to the group. He sat in the spare seat opposite Mandy and ignored Pippa and Jenny.

'It's hot in here. I'm Zand.'

'Mandy. Sure is warm tonight.'

They clasped hands in greeting, then she released his palm right away.

Somehow, she felt different. Where was the usual excitement inside of her at meeting a new man? Where was that buzz of the chase? Could she even be bothered to talk to this person? He wasn't particularly attractive to her, but when had that stopped her before? She had a wistful vision of the sofa at home and sharing banter with Nick about the football. What was happening here? Maybe she was getting old, or perhaps she hadn't drunk enough. She took a slurp from her wine glass, hoping it might change how she was viewing this situation.

She glanced at her friends and then forced herself to smile at the man. 'So, Zand, what do you do?'

'I'm a treasure hunter.'

She had to make a real effort not to spray her mouthful of wine all over him, as she tried not to laugh. She didn't dare make eye contact with her friends, as it was, she could feel Pippa's leg next to hers shaking with suppressed laughter. The look on Mandy's face must have echoed the disbelief she felt, because Zand felt the need to repeat himself.

'I'm a treasure hunter ... really.'

Was it just a line to charm the girls? She definitely hadn't drunk enough for this. 'Wow!' She only said that because he obviously expected her to be impressed. *Play the game, Mandy. At least for a few moments.* 'What sort of treasure do you hunt?'

'I've searched for all sorts over the years.'

She had an irreverent vision of him with a metal detector pulling a horseshoe from a farmer's field.

Zand was just warming up to his subject. 'Panning for gold, pearl diving, opal mining, even dinosaur bone hunting. I've had a go at all of them.'

'And you make a living doing that?'

'I've made fortunes, lost them and made them again. It's really addictive, like a drug.' He had a wistful look on his face.

'Do you do drugs?' What was she saying? She'd lost the plot.

He looked shocked. 'No, no. Well an occasional cannabis joint.' He scratched his stubble noisily. 'Goodness, you're a difficult girl to talk to.'

Mandy found her smile was much wider than his comment warranted. At least this was evidence that things were indeed changing. In the old days, she wouldn't have asked as many, if any, questions, or delved to see if a man's story was true, but then in the old days she'd have been drunk by now anyway and not cared whether he was feeding her a line, just whether he fancied her enough for a snog or a "tumble in the hay".

Being "a parent" had certainly stopped her drinking too much. She'd saved a fortune at the supermarket already.

The guy opposite to her looked rather sulky after her questions and lack of adoring responses. Zand obviously wasn't used to an inquisition before a girl would agree to even dance with him.

'So, a girlfriend of yours would be decked in diamonds, pearls and gold?' said Mandy, having to school her face so as not to laugh.

His expression was definitely sheepish now. 'Maybe next time I find some. I'm at a low point of discovery at the moment, trying to decide what my next move might be. Where to go, what to do? So many choices. The world is rich in treasure.'

'I'm sure.' She knew her tone was sarcastic. She almost felt sorry that she'd burst his bubble of exuberance. He'd obviously been more honest with her than he'd intended.

'Hey, Zand. That's what you said your name was, right? You look like you need cheering up. I guess a treasure hunter won't make a fortune in Borteen, but how about I buy you a drink and we have a dance?'

It was a strange experience, but somehow liberating, to be sober enough to call the shots. After a drink and a couple of chaste dances on the small dance floor in the pub's conservatory, she said goodnight to Zand and her friends and left the gold digger to try his luck elsewhere.

She giggled all the way home. Yes, she was changing and, although it was a little bewildering, it felt really good.

It was unusual after a night out to not even have a slight

hangover. Mandy was just analysing how she felt about this difference and contemplating what to have for breakfast when her distinctive Take That "Giants" mobile phone ringtone sounded. Graham's name was emblazoned on the screen. She accepted the call and closed the kitchen door so as not to disturb Nick, who as far as she was aware was still asleep.

'He's mine!' Graham Frankley sounded breathless on the other end of the telephone line. 'He's my son.'

'100 percent sure?' Mandy couldn't help but ask that question.

'Ninety-nine point nine percent is what the report actually says.'

'Wow!' She sat down on one of the kitchen stools and pulled the clip out of her hair.

'If it's possible, I'd like to be the one to tell Nicholas.'

'He hates being called Nicholas. Call him Nick if you want him on your side.'

'Good job you told me that. Has he heard anything from his mum?'

'No, nothing at all. From what he says, it seems they didn't get on too well, but I know it's upset him terribly that she's just ... gone, seemingly without trace.'

'You were very kind to take him in.'

'He's a lovely young man and getting even nicer now he's settling down and beginning to relax with me. I can't imagine leaving him behind like Sally did, whatever the circumstances.'

'I still can't believe he's mine. My flesh and blood. I've missed out on fifteen whole years of his life.'

'It's unbelievable.' Mandy felt a sob rising up her throat and gulped to stop it. Much longer for her ...

A note of anxiety crept into Graham's voice. 'How do you think he'll react to the news?'

'He'll either run off or hug you and I can't second-guess which. It will depend how you tell him, what you tell him and exactly what you intend to do for the future.'

'I haven't quite worked that out yet. I'd better think about it some more before I come over. I know I have to go through the proper channels if I want contact with him. Harriet Drew outlined the stages and checks that need to be completed when she spoke to me. And there's the added complication of me living so far away from Borteen.'

'Can I suggest you're sure of your intentions before you tell Nick the news. He's had enough uncertainty recently. He'll need definites rather than more questions, I think.'

Mandy felt the huge lump return to lodge in her throat. She was going to have to take advice about Nick's future too. A call to Harriet Drew to confirm Nick's parentage would be one of her first moves. Even if Graham was his father, there were surely legal processes to prove it properly. She was pretty sure she shouldn't leave Graham on his own with Nick until she was certain everything was settled. Although it was a big responsibility, she'd become quite attached to the wayward artistic child and wanted to do her best by him.

Graham was clearing his throat on the other end of the line. She'd lapsed into reverie and hadn't been speaking or listening.

'I'm going to book a room at the guest house by the seafront for this weekend. Will you be around?'

'That's my friend, Pippa's place – Rose Court Guest House. I usually work part of each weekend, but I'm sure I can get cover.'

'I'd welcome your help.'

'You do realize you have a potentially famous artist for a son?' She blurted the words out to cover her confusion over the paternity news and the thought of seeing Graham again. It really wouldn't be a good move to fancy Nick's newly found father, would it?

'Is his art that good? I can't wait to see some of it.'

'He won a competition at the high school and his canvases sell really well at my craft centre.'

'Wow! Is Sally Crossten artistic?'

'To be honest, I have absolutely no idea.'

'My mum is. She's had her own exhibitions in the past.'

'Family trait then. Those Frankley genes have been working away in the background.' She thought Nick would be pleased about this snippet of information, that was when she could share it with him. How was she going to keep quiet about all this when she was already bursting to tell Nick?

'I can't wait to hear more, see some of his pictures. There are a few things going on with Frankley Gins at the moment, so I'll confirm I'm coming to Borteen first thing on Friday morning, if that's okay?'

'I won't mention anything to Nick until you're sure. Although, I won't pretend it's going to be easy keeping such a huge secret.'

'I can appreciate that. I'll do my best to come over on Friday, so we can tell Nick the news together.'

She rang Harriet Drew next and explained what the paternity test had revealed. Harriet noted the information but confirmed further approved tests and investigations would be necessary before Graham had any legal say in Nick's future.

Mandy found it hard to concentrate for the rest of the day with so many thoughts whirling around in her head.

Chapter Nine

Mandy checked her phone every few minutes for a message from Graham on Friday. The suspense began to build from the moment she opened her eyes to her alarm at six in the morning and she fervently hoped Graham would message her before Nick left for school.

When Nick came downstairs, his hair standing at weird angles after his shower, she told him to get some breakfast before school and pondered what she could give him in his packed lunch.

Nick must have picked up that something was different, as he stood staring at her. 'Okay?' he enquired tentatively.

'I'm fine.' She forced a smile. 'Tuna and mayo sandwich for lunch?'

'Great, thanks.' He continued to look at her with curiosity.

She'd just buttered the bread when a message pinged on her phone. She scrabbled to reach it, before Nick noticed the name appearing on the screen. *Too late!*

'Is that Graham, Graham?'

'You are too quick young man and nosey too.' She prodded the phone and read the message. 'Yes, it's a message from Graham.'

'About me?'

'Sort of. He's coming over tonight and staying for the weekend at Rose Court. He wants to talk to us both.'

Nick's face closed down for a moment. 'He's got the results?'

'I'm not sure what he's coming to say.' She knew her tone sounded false but was at a loss as to what else to say to Nick.

Nick shoved some more cereal in his mouth, a trickle of milk running down his chin. He spoke through his chewing, something Mandy hated and hoped to discourage.

'Do I have to go to school today?'

'Most definitely. Graham won't be here till much, much later. He might not even see us this evening. He has a long way to come, remember? The traffic could be heavy.'

'I can't concentrate on lessons. This weekend will change my life won't it? Whether it's yes or no.'

And mine too, thought Mandy.

'My mother always told me to put things out of my mind until they happen. If you do that, you'll be able to concentrate at school. Come on, try it. Put your thoughts about Graham and the test in a box over there.' She pointed towards the far side of the room.

'I'll try.'

'Great. Now finish your cereal and get to school.'

She knew that Nick had been making a real effort at Borteen High since he'd come to live with her. For the first time for a while, she wondered if he would bunk off for the day, as he set off with his school bag hoisted over one shoulder. She could hardly blame him; his mind must be racing with possibilities and permutations of what Graham would or wouldn't say and how his life would pan out from here. There'd still been absolutely no contact from his mother, which to Mandy seemed beyond belief.

Graham sent Mandy a further message around five o'clock that afternoon, to say that he was comfortably installed at Rose Court and eager to meet up with her and Nick that evening.

She ducked into the garden to ring him, so that she could speak without Nick overhearing.

'Shall we meet up for food? Or do you think, with what we need to discuss, it would be better for you to come here?'

'I kind of think neutral territory might be best. What type of food does Nick like?'

'Food of any type as long as it's not too spicy hot.' She laughed and was aware she sounded nervous.

Graham laughed too. He sounded even more nervous than she did.

'Recommendations? It's your patch after all.'

'We could go to the pizza place in Sowden, but that would mean we'd both have to drive and you wouldn't be able to have a drink.' She realised as she said the words that her statement made several assumptions, that he'd want a drink and that they should travel separately just in case.

Thankfully, Graham seemed to keep up with her thinking.

'You're right, of course. It would be better if we travelled separately. I don't think I'll want a drink tonight anyway. Just because I make gin, doesn't mean I always have to have alcohol.' He laughed which suggested he'd noted her comment, but hopefully not taken offence. 'I'm a connoisseur rather than a guzzler by the way. Is this pizza place easy to find?'

'Yes, right opposite the cathedral with a car park next door.'

'Sounds like a plan then. Do we need to book?'

'I'll do that. Is seven okay?'

'See you then.'

It wasn't until she went back into the house that Mandy began to feel shaky.

They'd agreed that Graham would tell Nick the test results this evening. She was terribly nervous about the boy's reaction and guessed Graham would be too.

Mandy was already anticipating the revelation ahead and wondered if she should make herself scarce when it came to Graham telling Nick the news. Mandy and Nick arrived at the restaurant first and Nick went off to look at the art in the entrance hall while Mandy waited outside.

As Graham came around the corner from the car park, Mandy couldn't help her heart speeding up. He was wearing smart chinos, a checked shirt and a casual jacket. His copper hair shone and his smile felt all for her.

She quickly asked her question. 'Do you want to agree a signal for later? I could disappear to the ladies while you tell Nick the news?'

'Definitely not. As far as I'm concerned you're part of this. I'd like you there. If nothing else to help Nick if he needs it. As you said before, we have no way of knowing how he'll react.'

She led the way through the double doors, collected a very quiet Nick and they were soon seated at a round table with menus large enough to hide behind.

'Are we doing starters?' Mandy asked brightly peering around the big menu and trying not to reveal her nervousness.

'I'm not really hungry,' said Nick, scowling as he looked up and down the choices on offer.

'Well that has to be a first,' joked Mandy. 'Graham, you're going to have to put him out of his misery.'

Graham lowered the menu he had so obviously been hiding behind and looked directly at Nick. 'I'll come right out and say it – the test confirmed that I am ninety-nine point nine percent likely to be your father.'

Nick seemed to freeze for a few seconds as the news sunk in, then he surprised both of them by throwing down his menu and running from the restaurant. Mandy leapt to her feet, preparing to go after him, but then saw he was just outside on the cathedral green. He was pacing from tree to tree, seemingly talking to himself. As she and Graham watched, standing next to each other at the window, Nick punched the air, his face more animated than she'd ever seen it.

Mandy felt a rush of relief flood through her and her huge grin was echoed by Graham's.

'He's coming back,' said Graham, pulling her away from the window.

When Nick re-joined them, they were studying their menus as if Nick had merely paid a visit to the toilet.

'I'd like dough balls and a meat feast pizza, please,' declared Nick, grinning from ear-to-ear.

'Got your appetite back then,' said Mandy.

The waiter looked a bit alarmed when he came to take their order and found three people laughing uncontrollably. They made an effort to calm down sufficiently to order their food.

'Look, Nick. I've no idea what this will mean yet,' said Graham. 'We'll have to work it out together and one step at a time.'

'It's fine. At least I have a dad. Can you imagine how odd it makes you feel to be told all your life that you haven't got a father?'

Mandy chose that moment to take an envelope out of her handbag. She passed it to Nick. 'This is your copy birth certificate. It came in the post today.'

Nick took the single sheet of paper out of the envelope and unfolded it with care. 'It's blank where it says father!' His eyes widened and he looked at Graham. It seemed to take a moment for the realisation of what the document recorded to sink in. 'So this is what Mum has meant all of these years, but she's never shown me this before.'

'Sally couldn't put Graham as your birth father, because this is a legal document and as your mum and dad weren't married ... weren't even together, she wouldn't have been able to include him without his consent.'

Graham took the certificate and scanned the details. 'At least no one else is recorded as Nick's father.'

'That's why I wanted to check, just in case she'd got together with someone else while she was pregnant and they'd agreed to be on the certificate.'

Nick was silent.

'Well now we know for sure I'm your father, I'll see if we can get this changed.'

Nick's face brightened.

'I asked about that and Nick's birth can be re-registered if the court declares you his father.'

'Well I'm going to go through all the proper channels to prove I'm his dad any way, so we'll see what we can do.'

Nick and Graham high-fived across the table and Mandy found moisture collecting in her eyes in response to the happy looks on their faces.

By unspoken agreement the trio talked about anything other than Nick's parentage for the rest of the evening. Graham told them a little about his business, Mandy talked about Owl Corner Crafts and Nick explained the inspiration for his latest paintings, showing that he was a real observer of other people.

Whatever the future held, Mandy could tell for this evening at least, Nick was happy.

When Graham had driven off to go back to the guest house, Mandy turned to look at Nick in the passenger seat next to her.

'How do you feel about all this?' she asked.

'Scared and excited at the same time. I like the thought of it, but don't know anything about this man who now says he's my dad.'

'I get that.' She smiled in what she hoped was a reassuring way.

He put his head on one side and she could almost see the thoughts tumbling around in his head. 'If he's my dad, then it means he must once have been Mum's boyfriend and I've met a few of those who were evil, so how can I be sure about Graham? Mum doesn't have much taste when it comes to men.'

Mandy couldn't help but giggle at this teenage insight into his mother's dating history.

Nick's face was, however, serious. 'What if they say I have to go and live with Graham in Manchester? I want to stay here with you. At least you're nice and live in Borteen where I belong.'

'The answer to all of this is that we have to take each day at a time and make the best choices we can with the knowledge we have at that point. We just have to cope with the here and now and move on into the future. Sorry that's my favourite saying. Whatever happens, Nick, you'll be fine.' She took off the handbrake and set off for home.

'Wish I knew that, Mand. Could we both go live with Graham?'

Now wait a minute, Nick was lumping her and Graham together? How did that happen? 'Nick, I can't go and live with Graham.'

'But you'd be cool together.'

'What on earth made you come to that conclusion?' She felt her face glowing red with sudden heat.

'You seem chilled when Graham's around.'

Did she? Out of the mouth of babes and all that. She liked Graham, was attracted to him even, but she hadn't really had chance to form a proper opinion of the man and had been trying to keep her distance in any case, due to his link with Nick. 'Look Nick, this fantasy about Graham and I isn't going to happen. You need to get those notions out of your head, I'm afraid.'

'How good would it be if Graham was my dad and you were my mum?'

'I'm flattered, very flattered, believe me, but you already have a mum.'

'I'd prefer to live with you and Graham. I want to be a gin maker when I leave school – I'm not just saying that. Graham says putting the ingredients together for a special gin is like painting a picture, and I get that. I want to paint "taste pictures" and in my spare time, paint canvases.'

'It sounds like you've got your life sorted out.' She smiled at the serious expression on Nick's face as she glanced over.

'I hope so, Mand. Really do.'

Mandy fervently hoped that things would work out too.

Chapter Ten

Graham had asked Mandy to meet him for a drink when she got back to Borteen, so that they could discuss the fallout from the evening and maybe decide a way forward with Nick. Mandy had been totally open with Nick about where she was going and why.

She made sure he was ensconced in front of one of his favourite television programmes, where individuals arrived for blind dates arranged by the production company. He had Merlin on his lap and a bowl of crisps on the table next to him. Then, she walked to The Ship Inn, where she'd agreed to meet Graham.

As she went through the familiar door with its stained-glass window of a galleon in full sail, her heart leapt a little at the sight of Graham sitting at the bar. He was smiling at her. She was trying so hard not to be attracted to him, because of the complications with Nick and also his comments about the pair – but was failing miserably. She imagined for a few moments how she would feel if this was an actual date.

However, after his initial welcoming smile, Graham's facial expression had become serious and it brought her right back down to earth. None of this was about her.

Ordering a glass of white wine, she clutched it like a security blanket and tried to get her brain in gear to make conversation.

'You must be thrilled about the paternity result.'

Graham looked at her, his green eyes full of trepidation. 'Both thrilled and terrified.'

'What do you think it will mean for you and Nick going forward?'

'I'll consider everything carefully, of course, but I'm still not convinced I can take him on. I have no experience of being a dad, especially not to an adolescent. I'm carer to my disabled mother at the moment too. Then there's the fact we live so far apart.'

'I don't know anything about being a mum either, but I've been trying. He's a decent kid, a talented artist. He deserves a chance. He didn't get on with his mum lately, but it's been such a shock to him her disappearing like that and he's so excited that he finally has a dad.'

'Don't get me wrong, it's fantastic you feel this way, but can I ask why you're so protective of a child that isn't even yours and has no family link?'

She took a deep breath. She wasn't about to tell Graham the real underlying reason for her actions. That reason was buried deep in the past, along with her feelings and she didn't dare lift the lid if she was to remain sane. She fudged a reply about supporting the youth of Borteen with art and it being a natural extension to take Nick in. Then she made her excuses and went to the ladies' toilets to recover her composure.

The reflection looking back at her from the mirror seemed haunted. She didn't really know what to say to Graham. How could she advise him about Nick when she'd made her own poor life choices?

She was more than a little alarmed when she returned to the bar to find Graham talking to an unpleasant reminder of a poor past choice: Andrew Jenkins. He was with a couple of other guys she recognized from Borteen. Given her nasty experiences with the sleaze, she ducked behind a pillar and strained her ears to hear what was being said.

'No, no. She's just a friend,' Graham was telling them.

'That's what they all say.' The men laughed in unison.

'Watch her is all I'm saying. *Randy Mandy* gets through men faster than most women get through cups of coffee,' declared Andrew with that smirk Mandy recognised all too well.

'Right slapper,' added another.

Mandy couldn't believe what she was hearing. The derogatory words made her freeze on the spot. How could she face Graham now? She knew that her cheeks were flaming with anger and embarrassment. She could challenge the men, but what was the point? It would just be her word against theirs and after all there was some truth in their remarks. Instead, she went with her gut reaction and fled for the exit.

Graham had seen her run; she knew he had. Just for one brief moment their eyes had connected across the room before she turned for the door and bolted.

Moments later she was in the car park, sobbing uncontrollably.

The door behind her swung open again.

'Hey, wait.' It was Graham's voice.

'Why should I?' She turned to Graham but couldn't stop the tears pouring down her cheeks. 'What exactly did they say about me?'

'Hmm … this and that.'

'That one guy, Andrew, he virtually raped me when I went out with him on a date once. He's not a nice guy and he has a grudge because I fought him off. He did exactly the same to one of my friends a few weeks later too.'

'Hey, hey, Mandy, I make up my own mind about people, okay? I don't care what they said. I could tell they were being malicious and mean. They thought we were on a date and were trying to spoil things for you … for us. Maybe I'll go back in there and put them right.'

He made to go back to the pub but Mandy grabbed his arm to stop him. He tried to pull her closer, but she backed away, her hands held up in front of her to fend him off. Graham would never see her as attractive now. Of that she was absolutely certain. But why did she care so much about that?

Meeting up at The Ship had been a bad idea. She wasn't sure she'd ever be able to face walking into the pub again.

'I've lived here too long.' She took a long shuddering breath. 'Look, Graham, I'm working at the craft centre tomorrow. Maybe you'd like to see some of Nick's art? I'll say goodnight now. You do see why I have to say goodnight right now don't you?'

She didn't wait for him to reply. She walked off into the darkness and was grateful he made no attempt to follow her.

Graham watched Mandy as she walked swiftly up the road. He was at a complete loss over how to make things better. He hadn't invited the comments of the men in the pub, they must have seen him with Mandy and decided to pounce. Was she really as bad as they said, or did the guy called Andrew just have a grudge as Mandy had suggested, because she'd rejected his advances?

The Mandy he knew, albeit on a very short acquaintance, was kind and supportive. What hurt the most was that she thought he would listen to the barbed comments in the bar, rather than making up his own mind. After all, different relationships brought out different things in people.

He knew enough about Mandy to understand that underneath all the bling and short skirts was a confused young woman seeking approval, desperately wanting to be liked. Maybe that desire got out of control sometimes.

The thought he kept coming back to was why she'd been so concerned about what he thought of her. Did she think he'd complain to social services about her reputation, maybe claiming she wasn't a suitable person to care for Nick? Or could she be worried about what Graham thought about her for another reason ...

Chapter Eleven

Mandy groaned. Her alarm was sounding and she couldn't find her phone in the gloom of her early morning bedroom.

After a frantic scrabble, she silenced its insistent tone and flopped back onto the pillow. Tears immediately began to seep out of the corners of her eyes. It was time to leap out of bed, jump in the shower, dash for breakfast and zoom to the craft centre to ensure all was well. She would have to meet Graham again. There was really no choice, but all she wanted to do was dive back under the duvet and submerge into her black feelings. What a total mess. Maybe she was the one who should move to a different area and start again. A clean slate seemed very appealing at the moment.

It didn't seem to matter that she was the owner of a successful craft business. Her personal life was a disaster. How could she move on from last night? The only way was up. She surely couldn't sink much lower.

Graham must think so badly of her. She'd been condemned by the men of Borteen as little short of a floozie.

Curling into a ball, she couldn't help the loud sobs that wracked her body.

'Mand?'

OMG, Nick! She'd forgotten in her misery the lost waif of a teenager in the bedroom across the landing.

She unfurled, mopping at her face with the edge of the duvet.

'You okay?' Nick was peeping around the edge of the door, silhouetted in the light from the landing.

'Sorry. I didn't mean to scare you.'

'You didn't. Mum cried a lot. I think she was so unhappy living with me. You're not crying because I'm living here?'

Mandy jerked to full awareness and out of her self-absorption.

'No! No way. You mustn't think that. I'm crying because I've messed up my own life, or so it felt for a moment when I woke up.'

She pulled her hair away from her face and tied it back with the ever-present scrunchy on her wrist.

Uncharacteristically, Nick took tentative steps into the room and sat on the end of the bed. He looked ready to bolt at a moment's notice. 'Serious though, would you like me to go?'

'No, of course not. Please believe me. This is nothing to do with you, not caused by you at all. Adults get fed up sometimes.'

'Mum was fed up all the time. That's why she went away.'

He looked so incredibly sad that Mandy felt her own problems sinking to the bottom of the cesspit of life. Here was a reason to get up. A reason to shake off her black mood. If only she could wash off the mask of her reputation and go out of the door newly cleansed, not feeling she was being laughed at as the town's loose woman.

'Let's have a cooked breakfast to cheer us up, eh?' Even as she said the words, her stressed stomach protested at the thought of bacon and sausage, but she would cook for Nick at least.

He nodded a little forlornly.

'I'll meet you downstairs. I'll just have a quick shower and dress first.'

He smiled and left her room.

After last night, how could she ever face Graham again? He was Nick's father, so she would have to, but, how could she? Her cheeks coloured at the mere thought.

It dawned on her that even though she'd been trying to deny her feelings, it had never mattered this much before. Graham was a decent guy and she was attracted to him more than she'd been to anyone for a long time – *dammit!* Not that she intended to show him that and after last night, she vowed that she never would. Best to put a lid on those feelings and keep everything firmly battened down.

Just when she'd seen the door open on a glimmer of possibility, a decent life, a decent man, a decent relationship, then that door had been firmly, unceremoniously slammed in her face by her past.

Hadn't that past just been her attempt to discover who she really was? Searching for validation. Searching for acceptance. She'd always wanted the approval of others, particularly men and that she believed had been her downfall.

She kept coming back to the fact that all of this was secondary to Nick's needs. Surely, she should strive to give him the best chance so that he wasn't screwed up and going through angst like this later in his own life?

If she'd been in the house on her own, she might have declared this a duvet day and snuggled back under the covers of her bed, abdicated from her normal life and sunk into the black depths of despair. Instead of that, she scrubbed herself viciously in the shower, dried her hair, dressed and went downstairs to ask Nick if he'd any weekend homework as she cooked their breakfast.

Graham had said he would meet her at Owl Corner Crafts at ten thirty that morning. Mandy went down to the craft centre early and didn't allow herself time to dwell, busying herself with the perpetual task of tidying the shelves. She turned exhibits carefully to show them to their best advantage, hiding price tickets beneath the objects so that people had to pick them up to see how much they were and maybe buy them.

She'd just lifted a pottery dragon, one of her bestsellers, when Graham came striding through the door. She suddenly had difficulty balancing the expensive ornament, so she couldn't run into the staff kitchen and hide the rush of redness to her cheeks. She took time repositioning the dragon carefully on its shelf to compose herself and then turned, looking at Graham's feet in preference to his face. He was wearing smart navy trainers with a light blue trim.

'Mandy, please look at me.'

'I can't. I'm too embarrassed after last night.'

His hand came into view and grasped her arm gently. 'Look, last night must have been awful for you. I really felt for you as those guys were well out of order.'

She risked a glance at his face. His serious expression didn't suggest he was making fun of her. His skin was clear and freshly shaven. As she couldn't yet bring herself to meet his eyes she focussed on his lips and then wished she hadn't as an unbidden spark of desire reminded her she found this man attractive. She had an overwhelming, and totally inappropriate, given the conversation, desire to kiss him.

'I wanted to take them all outside and thump them one by one and I haven't felt like that for years, probably not since my school days.'

She took a deep breath. Now she wanted to kiss him even more, but instead she brought herself back to earth. 'I'll admit I've dated a lot of guys as I've never wanted to get serious about anyone, but I assure you I don't sleep with all of them.' *OMG, why hadn't she stayed silent? That sounded absolutely awful!* She made an effort to steer the conversation back to safer subjects. 'What have you decided to do about Nick?'

Her attempt to divert the conversation felt odd and clunky, but she didn't want to talk about her dating habits any longer. She never wanted to date another man in her life.

She chanced a look at Graham. There was now a glint in his eyes. Was he trying not to laugh?

His face contorted for a moment and then he gave in and chuckled, immediately looking embarrassed. 'Sorry, sorry, inappropriate amusement.'

Despite herself, his chuckle was infectious and before she

knew it, she was laughing too. 'Obvious change of subject, eh?'

'Look, no one gets to our ages without past history. Today is a new day, let's reinvent ourselves.'

'I've been thinking along the same lines as that for quite a while.'

'As for Nick, I need to consider the next step very carefully. I will have to go to court or something to get custody, if I want it, but I'll take legal advice on that. It depends if Sally is ever coming home or is gone for good.'

'You can't *un*know that you're his dad though, can you?'

'No. He's my son and I want to be part of his life whatever happens in the future, it's just what form that should take. I'm just concerned because I don't really know how to be a dad, how to be with Nick. It's a bit overwhelming to be honest. But ... I was so touched by his reaction yesterday.'

'I know, it was absolutely lovely, especially when he punched the air in joy. Look, Graham, he's only been staying with me a little while and I'm overwhelmed too. Unsure as well, but the bottom line is that he's a great kid and one that hasn't been looked after very well lately ... if ever. It's worrying how much he knows about this town and its inhabitants. He must have spent most of his time wandering around the streets away from home.'

'I can't help being seriously annoyed with Sally. One for treating him like that, two for abandoning him and three for not telling me about his existence before now. I mean fifteen years for goodness' sake. I could have at least contributed money for clothes and haircuts – which he most definitely needs.'

'From the bit Nick's said, I think Sally must have got to desperation stage. I've been getting a picture of a person who was rock bottom unhappy, possibly very depressed.'

'I wonder if we can find her. Things would be so much simpler with her consent to everything. The letter she sent isn't quite enough.'

'I don't think she left many clues behind. When I went to their house with Nick, it was sparse and neat, almost as if no one lived there. It broke my heart how few things Nick had to bring with him too. He's hardly any non-school uniform clothes. His painting things are the only things he values.'

'I feel I should at least try to find Sally, if nothing else to make sure she's safe, especially if she's as depressed as you fear.'

'My policeman friend is keeping an eye out for any news about her, but there has been nothing so far. Nick and I tried ringing her mobile, but the number said it was not in service.'

'I'll see if I can come up with any more ideas to find her.'

'That would be great.' Mandy smiled at him.

'Coming back to my son – it's still so surreal to say that – there is the distance problem too. I can't see Nick very easily if he's in Borteen and I'm in Manchester.'

'That's true, but not impossible.' Mandy felt her heart rate speed up again at the thought that Graham might take Nick away. Was it simply that or the belief that if that happened she wouldn't see Graham again either?

'There are a few problems with my business lease at the moment. Big decision time. But if you believe in fate, and I think maybe I do these days, it may well mean I can move the business nearer to Borteen.'

'Wow that's a radical thought. How easy is it to move a gin distillery?'

'I guess I'll find out. Besides the practical moving of the equipment, which shouldn't be too hard, I'd need my expert gin creator to move with me. And can I find a suitable house for Mum's needs? If I move areas it would mean letting staff go. Most are part-time but many of them have been on this journey with the gin production since the start, so I'd feel personally responsible for helping them find alternative work.'

'I can see that's all complicated and a challenge, but I'm sure you could do it. You'd be able to offer a stable home life for your son. You run a successful business, own property, care for your mother. Surely you are an ideal candidate to look after Nick.'

Mandy was discussing Graham having paternity rights over Nick as if it didn't matter at all to her, but beneath the surface, her stomach churned with the anticipated pain of losing Nick. She had to rationalise that she was just projecting other meanings, other situations onto Nick and his presence in her life. It was important that she separated the real and the imagined. Of course, she knew that the best outcome for Nick would be living with his natural father. A male influence could make all the difference to the teenager's life.

The other ghostlike figure in her mind had already been through these teenage phases, grown into a man ...

At least Mandy had begun to feel calmer about her own past history after this conversation. Graham hadn't viewed her as *unclean* after all, maybe she didn't need to feel so bad about the past. 'Why don't you come for tea this evening at mine and we'll try again to find out what Nick knows about his mum's disappearance? Try to piece together where she might be. I warn you though, Nick will be defensive, but if we explain the importance of finding Sally, hopefully he'll try to help.'

'Do you think Nick might find it all too difficult?'

'Hmmm maybe. We'll have to take it very slowly. I'll be honest, my greatest fear is that if everything gets too much for him, he'll run away and live rough. He's sort of hinted that's what he'd do before.'

'That would be a disaster. I have no wish to lose him just after finding him.'

'I agree. At all costs that must not happen.'

They both stood in silence with their own thoughts for a moment. Mandy decided a change and lightening of conversation was needed. 'Anyway, the whole reason for me asking you to come to Owl Corner was so that you could see some of Nick's artwork.'

She led Graham over to the far wall and pointed to three large canvases. 'These are Nick's.'

His jaw dropped. 'Really? Wow!'

Graham walked nearer to the wall and examined the pictures more closely.

Mandy looked at the pictures with fresh eyes. The colour palette used was minimal, the brush strokes bold. They looked more impressive at a distance but would make an instant statement on any wall.

'Wow, I can't believe that Nick painted these.'

'They are good, aren't they?'

Graham nodded, pride in his son written all over his face.

After a while, he trailed around the centre looking at the things on the shelves; Mandy watched him closely. She loved the way he flicked his hair back when it fell into his eyes. Finally, he turned back to her.

'I'd love to come to tea, but I'll have to go back to my business soon and sort out the problems with our distillery site.'

'Gin's not my favourite drink, I'm afraid.'

'You haven't tried my gin … yet.' He grinned broadly and winked.

Mandy knew from how her body reacted that her heart was completely lost.

Chapter Twelve

Mandy felt especially nervous about having Graham over for an evening meal. It was something about him seeing her in her own environment, with all her personal things around her – exposing herself to him is how it felt, even if she kept telling herself he was really coming over to see Nick and get to know his son better.

However, when he arrived, with a huge box of chocolates as an offering, he was so easy to be with that he felt like a close friend already. He sat on one of the kitchen bar stools, his long jean-clad legs dangling, watching as Nick sketched things around him for a homework project with Merlin trying to sit on his work.

Mandy stirred the Bolognese sauce and put in the spaghetti, her standard visitor dish, and kept the conversation light and general.

The spaghetti caused a few laughs between the trio, as they struggled to loop up the pasta without splashing their clothing, or the table. Graham proved to be an expert, but Mandy and Nick were less successful. Maybe not such a wise choice, thought Mandy, dabbing at her shirt with her napkin.

It wasn't until they were sitting in the lounge after the meal, Mandy and Graham with a coffee and Nick with a fruit juice, that Mandy gently turned the conversation to Sally Crossten.

'Nick, I know you find the subject difficult, but Graham and I need to try to find your mother.'

'What for? She's gone.'

'I know that, but it would make it so much easier for you and for us if we could find her and get her permission to look after you.'

Nick shrugged and sighed loudly. He began picking at a thread on his jumper.

'If we can't find her and get her permission, it will probably mean we'll have to go to court to get legal approvals for your care,' said Graham.

'Don't see how I can help. No idea where she went.'

Graham leaned forward. 'What about this new man? Do you know his name? What he does? Where she met him? How long she's known him, maybe?'

Nick drew back into his chair against the barrage of questions. 'Saw him once. Tall, dark curly hair, older than Mum. Think he had an Australian accent. Didn't like him. But I never like the men she sees. Mum had known him three, maybe four weeks when they went off together.'

Mandy and Graham exchanged a look.

Mandy had a sudden thought. 'Has your mum got a passport?'

'Got a new one. She hated the photo. I haven't got one – never been abroad.'

He twisted his face in an expression that Mandy couldn't decide meant that he felt hard done by because he hadn't travelled, or that he couldn't care less. So, it looked likely that Sally had gone abroad. It would make any search inevitably more complicated.

Nick emptied his glass of juice. 'I don't want to find Mum. It's better living here.'

Graham and Mandy shared another look.

Later, when Mandy and Graham were alone, Nick having gone to his room to do his homework, or at least that was what he said, and the washing-up had been done, they sat down with another coffee. Mandy took out a notebook to jot down some more ideas about searching for Sally Crossten. She didn't comment, but was surprised when Merlin settled next to Graham.

'Social media?' suggested Graham, reaching out a hand to stroke the cat's dark fur.

'You mean an appeal to find her?'

'Maybe, but initially we could search to see if she has social media accounts.'

Mandy grabbed her phone and began to search, but there were no obvious Sally Crossten accounts on Facebook, Twitter or Instagram.' She looked up at Graham. 'I'll have a better look later, but nothing obvious showing after a quick search.'

'Can we perhaps get a photograph of her?'

'I'll have to ask Nick.'

'The only photo I have is the one she sent with her letter, but that was her sixteen, maybe seventeen years ago.' He took the grainy photograph out of his wallet and showed it to Mandy again.

'I'm not sure that's going to be much use, I'm afraid.'

Graham shook his head and Mandy was mesmerised for a moment by the floppy piece of chestnut hair on his forehead.

'We need a private investigator maybe?'

'Could be expensive though. I'll speak to my police contact again and see if he's heard anything, although if he had I'm sure he'd have been in touch by now.'

'Is he a friend?' Graham's face had a strange expression.

'Old friend. I went to school with him and no, I've never been out with him.'

Graham's eyes widened with alarm. 'Did I say anything?'

'Didn't have to!'

He sipped his coffee thoughtfully for a moment. 'By the way, who's Ellie?'

'What made you ask that?'

'Nick said that it was someone called Ellie who first recognized his art and gave him a prize.'

'Yes, he won an art competition at the high school run by my friend Ellie. She was the one who persuaded me to exhibit Nick's canvases and to sell them to help support his studies and practically, so that he could buy things like new shoes and clothes for himself.'

'I'd like to meet Ellie, so that I can shake her hand and thank her.'

Mandy was surprised at the huge lump that appeared in her throat. 'She doesn't live in Borteen any more and we've ... lost touch. It's a long story, but she had to go away for her own safety ... I still miss her.'

'Pity.'

They sat in silence for a while and Mandy managed to get her emotions under control.

'By the way, I've had an initial chat with my solicitor about Nick,' said Graham.

'Since this morning! Does he work on Saturdays?'

'Old friend, so he made an exception.'

'And?'

'Solicitor urged caution, of course. I'll need to arrange for recognized DNA tests, rather than the quick cheap ones from the internet we did.'

'I suppose that makes sense, even though the results will be the same, anyone seeing you two together can tell you're related.'

'Really?'

'Yes. The way you move, certain expressions and your hands are the same shape.'

'I'm still not completely sure what to do. I need some time to decide whether to commit big time to Nick's life, move my business over here, or take him back to Manchester ... or even just to let social services take over.'

She was shaken by his last words. 'You can't! You can't let him be taken into care. It would destroy him. If you don't want him, I'm going to apply to be his guardian and I hope you would support me in that.'

'Sorry, I was thinking out loud. I didn't really mean that last statement. It's unknown territory, scary unknown territory. It feels so surreal, to think I could have fathered a child and not known anything about it up to now. I mean I might never have known if Sally's plans hadn't changed.'

'Fathers can do that though, can't they? It's the woman who very often has to face the consequences of a moment of pleasure.'

He looked puzzled, probably unsure about the bitterness she knew was obvious in her statement and her tone. She scanned his face and wondered if those eyes were completely trustworthy. It sounded harsh and twisted, but could you ever trust a man?

After Graham left to return to Manchester and Nick was in bed, Mandy sat for a long time in the lounge, in darkness. She went through every permutation she could think of for the future of Nick – Going to live in Manchester with Graham and Graham's mum, living with Graham and his mum in Borteen if they moved over here, living with her as a foster child, being fully adopted by her, being given to another family as a foster or adopted child, going to a children's home or hostel, his mother returning …

By the time she went up to bed, her thoughts had exhausted her and her head was spinning.

Chapter Thirteen

Life quickly fell into a pattern. The home visit to check out Mandy's house had gone successfully and she was now Nick's official temporary foster mother. They lived quite happily together. He began to appreciate some of her television programmes and she his. Graham came over to Borteen each weekend and continued to build bonds with his son.

Mandy could tell that Nick looked forward to when his dad appeared on Friday evening and, even though she didn't really want to admit it, so did she.

In terms of her personal life, she was becoming like a nun. No more clubbing or hanging out in the pub. She became an expert on the soaps on TV and had begun making cards to sell in the craft centre. Nick showed an interest and designed his own. They spent many evenings companionably increasing their pile of stock.

This wasn't quite how she had envisaged her new life to be, but, hey ho, for some strange reason she was happy and content ... for now.

Ahead of one weekend when Graham was due to visit, she had what felt like a bizarre conversation with Nick.

'Ever been married, Mand?' he asked as he scrubbed at a saucepan in the washing-up water.

'No way! I've never even lived with anyone, just flitted in and out of boyfriends' lives really.' She took the pan and wiped it vigorously with the tea towel.

'Surprising.' He had his head on one side and looked wise beyond his years. Even though he was now getting better grades at school, Mandy had noticed how much more relaxed Nick seemed to be now they were entering the Easter holidays. She was glad that he wouldn't be doing his GCSEs until the following year. Just think what improvements could be made in his learning before then.

She smiled.

Nick went to fill a glass with milk. 'Has Dad been in touch yet?'

'Not yet.' She glanced at the clock. 'I guess he'll ring me when he's in Borteen later.'

'Can we go to Sowden for pizza tonight?'

'Let's see what Graham thinks. He might be tired after the long drive, or even fancy something different to pizza to eat.'

'Suppose so.' Nick looked disappointed.

'I guess I can always drive.'

That brought a smile to his face again.

'How are you feeling about Graham these days?'

The smile became broader. 'Great. He's cool.'

'I'll grant you he's a nice guy – pity he lives so far away.'

On route to put his used glass in the sink, Nick, unusually, laid a hand on her arm and looked at her intently. 'You know, I know I've said it before, but you could do worse than dating my dad. How cool would that be? You and Dad together!'

Mandy's insides somersaulted. It was as if Nick had read her inner thoughts and musings. 'Oh, Nick. We've already talked about this. Please don't hold out hope for that.' She knew that she didn't hold out any hope herself.

'Why not? You two would be the best parents.'

Was Nick going to keep on about this? Mandy didn't think she could stand him reminding her constantly about an unfulfillable dream, so she spoke sharply in an attempt to silence him. 'It's not going to happen, okay?'

'Whatever.' Nick swilled out his glass and put it into the washing-up water a little more roughly than was ideal. He was lucky it didn't break.

As it was now the Easter school holidays, Nick was off to Sowden that day to have a look in the art shops. Mandy had given him some money to spend on sketch books earlier that morning. He grabbed his backpack and waved vaguely as he went out of the door to catch the bus.

'Be safe,' she yelled after him.

Her mobile rang almost as soon as he'd left, leaving her feeling that Graham had somehow observed her conversation with Nick.

Graham sounded happy. 'How are things?'

'Fine, no problems.' She crossed her fingers behind her back at the slight fib. 'Are you staying in the guest house again?'

'Yes. I'm becoming quite a regular. Pippa even gives me my favourite room.'

'Which one?' Mandy found her cheeks colouring even though Graham couldn't see her, at the intimacy of asking where he was sleeping.

'The one at the top of the house facing the beach. It's the attic room so I have to duck in places to avoid hitting my head, but I just love the view and the sound of the waves with the window open.'

He laughed and Mandy smiled at last, even though he couldn't see her expression.

'Nick asked if we could go for a pizza in Sowden this evening. I'm happy to drive.'

'Sounds good to me. I'm happy to pay, but pizza again?'

'That's really not necessary, Graham, but thank you. Nick's pizza mad I'm afraid. How about lunch on Saturday too? I can get my girls to cover the lunch period. After that, maybe you could take Nick for a game of crazy golf on Sunday or something.'

'That all sounds good. Sorry, I'd forgotten you'd be working. It would be great if you can manage Saturday lunch. Thank you, Mandy.'

'We look forward to seeing you. Nick will be so excited when I tell him our plans.'

Graham went quiet at the other end of the line and she had

the distinct feeling that he wanted to say something else. She waited patiently.

'Does he talk about me?' Graham's voice sounded strained as if he feared her response.

'Of course he does, although like you he doesn't really know you all that well yet, so he has a lot of questions in his mind. You both need to keep working at that connection.'

'I'll be in Borteen a bit earlier today. I've a meeting with Harriet Drew for some advice on how to proceed regarding confirming my paternity.'

Mandy felt a little lurch in her body but told herself sternly that this move could be important for Nick. 'Thanks for telling me. She's very direct and helpful and will point you in the right direction I'm sure. Could you possibly drop by the craft centre afterwards and keep me up to date with what she suggests?'

'Sure. I don't suppose there's been any news of Sally?'

'No, zilch – nada. She seems to have vanished off the face of the earth. I did a more thorough search of social media, but found nothing and Ethan – the policeman – hasn't come up with anything either.'

'I still find it unbelievable she simply left Nick.'

'Me too. Maybe she was waiting until she thought he was old enough to fend for himself.'

'But he isn't though, is he?'

Mandy thought about that question a moment before she answered. 'I think he would have given it a good go, but money would have undoubtedly been an issue. He's quite streetwise, but more vulnerable than anyone would ever suspect underneath the surface quietness.'

'I'm enjoying getting to know him and, hopefully, I'll be able to provide some much needed security and stability in his life.'

'See you this afternoon.'

She was aware that she'd shut him down in mid flow, but

the emotions his words were provoking were beginning to get painful. Was she about to lose Nick too? Wasn't *she* trying to provide security and stability? It took a long while to settle down after the conversation.

While she was looking forward to Graham's visit, possibly too much, Mandy couldn't shake a niggly feeling that if he was pursuing his claim to paternity this might mean Nick had to go and live in Manchester. How would the sensitive teenager cope with moving to a different area? But it could be the making of him and maybe her concern was really for herself and how *she* would feel being on her own again. She'd got used to Nick being around and had noticed a real change in him. He was becoming less jumpy and nervous, seeming more confident and even, at times, cheeky.

Unquestionably, it had also been good for her to have someone other than herself and her own perceived shortcomings to focus on too.

If Nick moved to Manchester, Graham would no longer have the excuse to visit Borteen ... and that troubled her more than she would care to admit. She let herself daydream for a moment about what she found attractive about Graham and why, if the worst happened, she would miss him. She came to the conclusion that it was the way she felt when he was nearby, almost trembly inside – that plus the flick of his hair and flash of those malachite eyes.

Stop this, Mandy! You must NOT fall for Nick's dad. But in her heart of hearts, she knew she already had.

Chapter Fourteen

Her heart was in her mouth every time the door to the craft centre opened that afternoon, but it wasn't until she was about to close up that Graham came through the door. His hair was tousled and there was a sheen of raindrops on the shoulders of his khaki-coloured jacket. He looked like the hero in a romantic film Mandy had watched the previous evening – too much so ... Her heart performed a somersault that took her breath for a moment.

'Sorry. I'm much later than I imagined. I found myself needing a long thinking-walk on the beach after meeting Harriet Drew.'

'Not bad news?' Mandy braced herself. Anything that affected Nick now affected her too.

Graham smiled. 'No, no. Good actually. It's reasonably straightforward, just might take some time. I've other things on my mind too ... Mum and my business.'

'I do hope your mum's health isn't any worse.'

'Well it's not going to get much better, but it's not that. The three subjects, Nick, Mum and the business are linked. I *will* have to move business premises in the near future and thoughts keep going around and around in my head. You know, those circular thoughts without end?'

'I know them well.'

'I have to find new buildings to house my gin distillery and the obvious thing would be to find them near my current home with Mum, near my experienced workers, my established business links ... but ... if this *is* fate – relocation to Borteen or Sowden is on the cards. That's when the circular thoughts start – should I move Mum? I can't let my workers down, I have to find them jobs, it's easier to stay where we are, but Mum and I could move to Borteen and *argghh* ...!'

He'd mentioned the possibility of this before but this time he sounded more sure. Mandy couldn't help her sharp intake of breath. Her mind began to freewheel. Maybe this was the answer? She'd hardly allowed herself to believe this option possible. She would still be able to see Nick ... wouldn't lose contact with Graham.

'Not a word to Nick yet.' Graham had a finger over his lips.

'Of course not.'

'I still have a lot to think through.'

Unlike the last time they'd been for pizza in Sowden, they went in one car. Mandy couldn't help but think that to any onlookers they would appear a family unit, just an ordinary family, one man, his partner and their child. Nothing could be further from the truth, but no doubt it was the conclusion anyone in the pizza restaurant would draw too.

Nick was full of news about a new art teacher at school. Mandy supposed he must have praised Nick's work for the lad to be so enthusiastic about the man. She was pleased.

Nick sketched the waitress when she came to take their order. When she'd finished scribbling on her notepad, she leaned over to have a look at what he'd drawn.

'Wow, that's amazing. Can I buy it?'

Nick carefully ripped the page from his notepad and held it out to her. 'Yours. Cheeky sketching you without asking.'

'Thank you. My boyfriend will love it.' She plonked a kiss on Nick's cheek and he turned the colour of beetroot.

Nick immediately took refuge in another sketch. Mandy jumped out of her skin when a man's voice boomed behind her. 'Did you just draw me, young man?'

She turned to see a smartly dressed elderly gentleman who had left his seat and was standing behind her chair. Nick looked ready to bolt.

'Well, did you draw me?'

'Ye-e-s-s,' stuttered Nick.

'Can I see?' The man walked to Nick's side of the table and the lad reluctantly showed his sketch.

'That's amazing.' The man was smiling and patting Nick on his back. He turned to Nick and Mandy. 'You have a real talent here. Your son is gifted. Does he paint too, as well as sketch?'

Mandy exchanged a look with Graham, but both seemed to decide not to say anything about their unusual family set-up.

'Yes, he won an art competition at Borteen High School,' Mandy said proudly and Nick nodded.

'I'm Michael Bryant. I live at Lucerne Lodge on the Borteen side of Sowden. I already have a very formal stuffy portrait of myself, but if you would be agreeable ...' His glance took in all three of them. 'I'd like this young man to paint a large modern version of me to hang opposite the stuffy one. I'd pay, of course. You can name your price young man.'

'Really?' Nick looked shell-shocked.

'How wonderful,' said Mandy. She fished her business card out of her bag and gave it to Mr Bryant.

'Ah, yes, Owl Corner Crafts. A friend bought me a wonderful pottery dragon from your shop for my birthday.'

'Oh good. The dragons are very popular.'

Their pizzas arrived at that moment.

'I'll leave you to eat and I'll be in touch very soon about my new portrait.' Michael Bryant nodded to Nick and went back to his own table. A tall younger man joined him moments later, who Mandy decided had to be his son.

Nick was positively buzzing for the rest of the evening and Mandy could see that Graham was as proud of Nick and his artistic talent as she was.

On the way back to Borteen after their pizza, Mandy asked Graham about his plans for the rest of the weekend. 'You're having lunch with us tomorrow, I know, but Nick and I had already discussed going to the beach tomorrow evening. There's a band playing on the promenade. You are welcome to join us.'

'Sounds great, but what sort of band?' His voice was wary.

'Do I take it you don't like certain types of music?'

'I'm not into shouty, loud, modern stuff, punk rock, that sort of thing.' He screwed up his face.

'You're in luck then. The band is known for playing 80s and 90s songs.'

'Phew! Relief! And yes, I'd like to come with you.' There was a definite smile in his voice now and it made Mandy smile too.

Graham lay in his room at Rose Court, listening to the unfamiliar sounds. His mind was full of Mandy. He felt guilty as it should be Nick he was concentrating on – his son! Somehow, he couldn't stop thinking about Mandy though. Was it her eyes, her cheeks, her chin or just her overall energy that intrigued him? He normally went for quieter women, as he didn't like fuss and was really quite shy.

Being taken with Mandy didn't seem like a very smart idea. It could really mess things up with Nick. His son thought so much of Mandy and she was Nick's guardian for now. Then there was her supposed reputation given what the guys in the pub had said about her. If he was going to move to Borteen, he needed Mandy on side, not antagonised by any failed pass on his part.

He tossed and turned until his thoughts had exhausted him and by then all was quiet in the rest of the guest house around him.

He was mildly annoyed that his thoughts were circular again, particularly when Mandy's beautiful grey eyes drifted back into his mind. He buried his head under the pillow.

Chapter Fifteen

The weekend seemed to be zooming by. Graham, Mandy and Nick met for lunch at the beachside café. Nick demolished the selection of sandwiches that Graham ordered and made them all laugh with the deliberate slurping noises he and his straw made as he finished his berry smoothie.

The fact he was confident enough to do this told Mandy he was relaxing with the two of them at last.

The three of them were definitely becoming easier in each other's company and they didn't seem short of things to talk about. Mandy left Graham and Nick in order to return to work at the craft centre. Nick had promised to take his father for a tour of rock pools at the far end of the beach. It was hard to leave them, but Mandy knew that it was vital the two build a bond between them that didn't include her – especially if Graham were to take Nick to live in Manchester when he inevitably gained custody.

Despite his seeming earlier enthusiasm, Graham looked as if they were taking him to a funeral rather than a music gig when they collected him from the guest house on Saturday night. He was dressed in a black shirt and black jeans with a padded gilet slung over his shoulder for when it got colder later in the evening; April was still unpredictable temperature wise. His clothes emphasised how tall and trim he was, his copper hair was slicked back – but his eyes looked decidedly guarded.

Mandy couldn't help noting his attractions but laughed at his expression. 'You don't look as if you're looking forward to this at all.'

'I'm open-minded … I think,' he said.

Nick was a tiny bit shy to begin with, but his eyes were bright with excitement.

The three of them set off on the short walk to the beach, a slight gap between each of them as none of them appeared to know how else to walk together. Nick positioned himself in the middle.

Mandy could hear the band warming up as soon as they were outside the guest house. The gig promised to be loud. As they got closer, she was hailed by several people she knew and waved or returned their greetings.

They made their way onto the sand and faced the makeshift stage at the edge of the promenade.

'Oh, goodness. It's Suzi Meadows.'

'In the band?' asked Graham.

'Yes, we were at the same school together. She's younger than me, interesting character, even more interesting background. She used to have a band even when she was at Borteen High.'

'Which one?' Graham gestured towards the stage.

'The drummer.'

Graham looked at the drummer, a tiny woman with jet black straight hair, cut short on one side and left long on the other. The short side of her hairstyle displayed an ear bedecked with an array of silver earrings. A nose stud glinted in the stage lighting. She didn't look like anyone he'd ever been to school with, but then she wouldn't – he'd been to a small private all boys school.

A fish out of water could be a term to describe him this evening. He hadn't ever really got into the music scene and was terrible at dancing at discos. He'd once been described as a "knee-bender" and that had put him off entirely. He hoped Mandy didn't ask him to dance. He wouldn't be able to refuse, but to say yes could lead to horrific embarrassment.

Now they were here, Nick looked just about as enthralled about the event as he did but had taken refuge as usual in his sketchbook and was producing drawing after drawing of the band and people on the beach. Graham marvelled once more at the skill his son showed, with his minimal strokes producing maximum impact.

Graham was alarmed to see a sketch of himself and Mandy talking together, their heads close. The expression Nick had caught on Graham's face clearly showed the attraction he was feeling towards Mandy. Would she notice that look in his eyes, either in person, or on Nick's sketch? Had Nick noticed?

Graham looked again at the drawing and wondered if he was imagining an echo of his own feelings on Mandy's face. Surely he wasn't her type? He was deluding himself and seeing what he wanted to see ... or was Nick somehow able to capture the essence of people? It was as if he saw through any façade people were trying to hide behind.

When he turned away from Nick's sketch pad, he became aware that Mandy was jigging away next to him, getting carried away with the music and singing along with familiar songs. Graham wished that he had her freeness of spirit, or was that just another façade? It fascinated him that the image people presented to the world was often very different to the emotions and opinions hidden deep inside of them. He was so absorbed with his thoughts that he jumped when she spoke to him as he'd almost transported himself out of the scene and become an observer.

'How can you stand so still and not want to groove to this music?'

'I've never been any good at dancing, and got teased at school.'

'Maybe it's time to lay those demons to rest then. Follow my lead, let yourself go. After all, who do you know here in Borteen?'

Graham thought *I'm seriously considering moving here!* He actually replied, 'Just you and Nick.'

'Exactly.' She laughed. 'I'll be gentle with you, but Nick

might sketch you.' She winked and fluttered her eyelashes alarmingly.

If this was meant to make him relax, it was having the opposite effect. She linked his arm through hers and began pushing his side rhythmically with her hip in time to the music to force him to move slightly too. He held himself rigid, not least because certain parts of his anatomy were reacting to her closeness and the warmth of her body.

Oblivious to his predicament, she persisted in her swaying and, eventually, he gave in and let her dictate his movements. He tried to relax, tried to focus on the music, anything but the woman next to him. It was a while later that he realized she was no longer shoving him with her hip, that he was now absorbed in moving to the music of his own volition. He smiled and noticed Mandy glancing sideways at him.

'See, it's not that hard. Tell me you're not enjoying yourself.'

He grinned in a sarcastic way and she laughed.

The next song was one he recognized and with a sudden impulse he grabbed her hands and swung her round. Nick was sketching like crazy. Graham tried not to think about that.

He began to recognize a strange feeling, one he hadn't felt for a very long time; he suspected it might be enjoyment, or even happiness. He smiled again and swung a laughing Mandy around and around.

When that song finished, Mandy and Graham were both face to face and red faced. Not renowned for noticing things, even he could see that she was as embarrassed as he was. If this had been a different situation, he might have taken a chance and leaned in to kiss her. Lord knew he wanted to. But this wasn't just a simple "boy dances with girl" situation, there was a lot riding on the relationship between him and Mandy remaining sweet, so instead of giving into his first impulse, he pulled away. Going over to Nick, Graham gave himself a moment to recover by examining Nick's sketches.

When he turned back to Mandy, it was as if nothing had ever happened and they were back to their warily friendly way of being. He couldn't help feeling that a moment had passed that might never return.

All too soon it was Sunday afternoon. Graham walked Nick back to Owl Corner Crafts after crazy golf and he asked if he could have a word with Mandy privately.

'I didn't want to broach this in front of Nick in case you were dead against it but I'd like Nick to meet his grandma and to see what I do for a living. However, with nothing agreed about my parental status, it is of course reliant on you being willing to come to Manchester with him.'

Mandy seemed to pause for an infinitesimal second. 'No problem. A trip away would be great.'

Graham breathed out. He hadn't realised that he'd been holding his breath for Mandy's response. 'I will of course pay for your petrol or train tickets and arrange suitable accommodation for you both. Would this coming weekend be any good?'

'I'll have to make sure I have cover for the craft centre and someone to feed Merlin, but I don't see why not. We'll come on the train. Maybe stay Friday and Saturday night and travel back on Sunday?'

'Sounds good. We'll look forward to it. Can I tell Nick?'

She nodded.

'Hey, Nick.'

He came striding out of the far room of the craft centre.

Graham continued. 'How do you fancy coming to see where I live, the gin distillery and most importantly to meet your grandma?'

Nick came over to high-five Graham, joy written all over his face.

When Graham got home and had caught up with his mother's

weekend news, he took a deep breath and explained what he had in mind for the coming weekend.

'How exciting. It will be lovely to meet my grandson, especially if we might be moving to be near him.' She paused and Graham knew she was going to say more. 'So, who is this woman coming along with Nick?'

'She's the kind person who took Nick in when his mother abandoned him. Mandy Vanes. She owns a craft centre called Owl Corner Crafts in Borteen. She sells paintings, including Nick's, so you should have something in common.'

'You fancy her, don't you?' Ann Frankley had good intuition and despite her illness, her wit and her tongue were as sharp as razor blades. He could only hope that they always would be.

'Mum!'

'You've got a little twinkle in your eye when you speak about her.'

'Don't you dare say anything when she's here.' Graham could already imagine his embarrassment if his mother did. 'She's very attractive, but not the type I normally go for and I hardly know her yet.'

'It would be nice for you to have some female company though.'

'Don't you dare say anything to Mandy, or Nick. I'm warning you, Mum.'

His mother smiled and patted his arm. 'I'm just looking forward to meeting my grandson.'

His mum struggled with mobility, the MS she'd suffered with for five years had been a late onset type and it had made its initial appearance in the months following her husband, Graham's father's death. Her legs were so numb some days that they refused to obey her and her hands so clumsy, she dropped everything. More distressing for Ann was that the disease had begun to affect her eyesight too. It made her favourite pastime of watercolour painting rather tricky, but she'd persevered and taken up abstract acrylic painting in place of the precise landscape and portrait painting she'd done before. Graham was aware that she didn't get as much satisfaction from producing art in this style but at least it kept her painting.

It was only a matter of time before he needed to employ a full-time carer. There was only so much he could do himself with a business to run and now a son living a fair distance away.

He felt incredibly protective of his mother, particularly because of how she'd stoically and calmly supported him through his personal crisis. At least she was positive about meeting Nick. Graham just hoped she wouldn't say anything too embarrassing when she met Mandy.

Chapter Sixteen

Mandy's excitement about the coming weekend lasted until she'd seen Graham walk away. The more she thought about it, the more nervous she got. In Borteen, she knew who she was and recognised her past mistakes, even if she didn't like herself a lot of the time. In Manchester, she would have to meet Graham's mother and work colleagues. In Manchester, she would feel vulnerable, inadequate ...

Nick, still on school holiday, left the house to go and sketch on the beach on Monday morning with a cheerful *bye*. Shortly afterwards, the doorbell sounding broke into Mandy's reverie about the forthcoming weekend away. She glanced through the peephole in the front door. A stranger. Maybe he was selling something. She put on the security chain and opened the door a crack.

'Mandy Vanes?'

Maybe not an anonymous salesman. 'Depends who wants to know.'

Was this something about Nick? A shiver of fear snaked through her.

'My name is Jonas Fraser and I work for an independent adoption contact agency.' He held his identity badge, a laminated card with his name and the agency details on it, up to the crack in the door. She made a show of reading it to give herself time to calm down.

An adoption agency? She'd just been thinking about Nick and adoption. How could this person know that from her thoughts and arrive at her door?

'And ...?'

'Could I come in?'

'Err, no! I'm not in the habit of letting strangers into my home.'

'I appreciate that, but what I have to say may be better said with you sitting down.'

It was as if her heart had dropped down in a lift too fast with the sudden realization. OMG this wasn't about Nick! Heat rushed into her body, to be immediately replaced by cold and her head began to swim.

'You'd better come in. I think I might just have twigged what this is about.'

Her hand shook as she took off the security chain and opened the door. She closed the door when he was inside and had to make a real effort to walk down the hallway. Leading Jonas to the kitchen table, she desperately tried not to allow the black dots that had appeared in her vision to multiply.

'It looks as if you've guessed why I'm here.'

'Maybe, but I'd like you to tell me anyway?'

'I'm working on behalf of a client who was adopted at birth twenty years ago. He recently accessed his adoption papers, as he is legally entitled to do when over eighteen and I believe the birth mother's name contained in the file may be yours.'

Mandy couldn't speak past the huge lump that had appeared in her throat. Tears began to gush down her face. Jonas produced clean tissues from a pocket; he was obviously used to needing them in his line of work.

'Does ... my ... sssson want to ... fffind me?' She was shaking all over.

'The son given for adoption by one Mandy Vanes at birth does indeed want to find and, if possible, meet his birth mother.'

It took all Mandy's willpower to talk through the sobs that were wracking her body.

'I ... did ... not give him ... for adop ... tion. I was forced to give him away. There hasn't been one moment since that I ... haven't thought of him. My baby ... my son.'

'You were very young when it all happened. I come across this so often.'

'Fifteen. My father was adamant he had to go. Is … is he well … happy?'

'He's fine. A lovely, tall young man. He has a desire to understand the circumstances of his birth and why he ended up being adopted.'

'Oh God. He's going to hate me, isn't he?'

'I don't think his desire to know more about his roots is motivated by needing to place blame or launch recriminations. More a need to understand his origins, background and birth.'

'Oh.' She couldn't think of anything else to say, was struck dumb as her thoughts cartwheeled around the situation and imagined different versions of a meeting with her son.

'Look, can I make you a hot drink? You've had quite a shock.' Jonas's concerned face was kind.

'I'll do it. What would you like?' She got to her feet, hoping that her legs would support her despite feeling as if they were made of jelly.

'Black coffee, please.'

She went through the motions of getting the drinks, as if it was someone else's hands and arms performing the task. They didn't speak again until she returned to the table. Jonas waited until she'd sipped her coffee.

He'd been right. She needed the drink. She could feel the colour returning to her face.

'Does everyone react like this?'

'Not quite. Some people slam the door in my face. Others hear me out and then tell me to go away, and that's the polite version by the way. Many make me promise to tell my client I couldn't find them. A fair proportion react as you did. Tears. Worries about recrimination. Worries about everything really, especially about the questions they might get asked.'

'And he really does want to meet me?'

'Ideally, yes.'

'Wow. He's twenty. Grown up. You never forget their birthday, you know.' A lump reappeared in her throat.

'Yes. His adoptive parents have unfortunately both passed away recently, so I suppose he felt it was a good time to seek you out.'

The black dots were back. Mandy rested her head on her arms on the table, until her vision cleared.

'Would you like me to leave you alone now? I can give you my contact details and let you think about this for a while. You can ring me when you've reached a conclusion.'

'Yes, I mean no. I want to meet him, I most definitely do, but I'm absolutely terrified.'

'It's a very natural reaction. I usually advise to get the initial meeting over with as quickly as possible, before you've overthought everything.'

'I can see that. Less time for the mind to go mad.'

'Did you ever imagine this might happen?'

'Yes and no. You think about it. You dread it. You want it. You see television programmes about it. If you let a child go, I believe you never have total peace of mind, you always wonder if they're okay, what they think about what you did, why they think you let them go. Anniversaries are the worst, their birthdays, Christmas. You wonder over the years what presents you would have bought for them, what they might look like now, where they are, even whether they are still alive.'

Jonas nodded. She could tell he'd heard all this before many times. He took a business card out of his folder and placed it gently in front of her.

'I'll go back to my client and tell him you're willing to meet him. Are any days better than others?'

'I run the craft centre near the beach. I can pretty much arrange cover on any day as long as I have enough notice.'

'I'll be in touch soon then.' He slurped the rest of his drink and stood up.

'What's his name? I never got to give him one, only had a moment to hold him, one chance to look at his face, before he was taken away.'

'Paul.'

'Paul.' She took in a shuddering breath as she tested the name and a tear escaped and ran down her face.

It didn't matter how much of a shock it had been, this felt right. She had to meet her son. Her flesh and blood. The subject of so much anxiety, worry, guilt and the signal for the destruction of her relationship with her parents.

They'd never forgiven her for getting pregnant in the first place and she'd never been able to forgive them for making her give away her baby. Her father had gone to his grave with the barriers still erected between them. She'd not even been able to cry at his funeral, even though she felt duty-bound to attend for her mother's sake. The hatred and anger had gone with her even there. Her mother had moved away to live with her sister in Brighton. They spoke four times a year: her mother's birthday, her aunt's birthday, Mandy's birthday and Christmas Day.

'I can see what you mean about it being best to meet up quickly. It's tormenting me already. I don't think I can stand to wait long.'

'I'll get onto it as soon as I get back. Paul will be anxious for news in any case, remember he's nervous too.'

As soon as Mandy shut the door, yet more tears began to fall in a never-ending shower. After the deluge, she felt bruised, but strangely lighter, as if the heavy burden she had carried for the last twenty years had been lifted. Her son. She was going to meet her son. She looked out of the window and there was a rainbow over the beach after a shower of rain. It felt like a sign of a new beginning.

Catching sight of herself in the mirror, she gulped. It was time for that makeover she'd been promising herself, but what should she change and what should she change first?

The possibilities rushed around her head all day at Owl Corner, making her slower and more clumsy than normal. At least the day went quickly and before she knew it she was back home, distractedly wondering about what to cook for their evening meal.

She turned to Nick, who was busy gathering snacks to eat in front of the television. 'I think I need a new image.'

Nick glanced up from delving in the kitchen cupboard and looked her up and down. It was most disconcerting.

'Longer skirt, less boobs?'

Her mouth fell open in shock. 'You cheeky pup.'

His face fell. 'Thought you wanted suggestions.'

'Sorry, Nick. I did ask and you are more than likely right.'

Nick's face reddened and he seemed to be trying to decide whether to say something or not. Taking an obvious deep breath, he spoke. It was one of those rare times he said more than the bare minimum. 'You could do with a nice guy like Graham and nice guys like things a little more ... subtle.'

'And you are an expert on all this then?' Despite herself, she could see the funny side of his observations.

'I watch people. It's what I do. I watch and learn, and then I draw and paint.'

She had to admit that his paintings spoke of an extraordinary perception. Should she listen to fashion advice from a fifteen-year-old boy? He was right though. She pulled at the material of her top to cover a little more of her ample cleavage – nice guys liked women who made them use their imagination, not ones who displayed their wares for all to see. How had she become this person? This person who even she didn't respect any more?

Before leaving for work the next day, Mandy rang her hairdresser and unbelievably she had a cancellation. Obviously fate, she decided. Now she just needed to get Romana or Peggy to cover the craft centre for the time of the appointment. That too proved easy and Mandy once again thought that her change of image was fated.

However, when it came to it, she sat in front of the huge salon mirror with her heart rate accelerating. She was on the verge of losing her nerve and almost ran for the door.

She met the hairdresser's curious gaze in the mirror and took a deep breath. 'I want to return to my natural colour. While it's growing out, I want a much shorter cut and darker streaks in the blonde.'

Chantal, who had been her hairdresser for over eight years, stood open-mouthed, frozen like a statue for a moment. 'You're absolutely positive, Mandy? I mean you've been long and dyed blonde all the time I've known you ... years. I can't stick it back on if I cut it short and you don't like it.'

'Aren't there those charities that use hair for cancer wigs?'

Chantal nodded, looking more like a goldfish as the conversation progressed.

'Well that's what I'd like. I want to donate my hair.'

'How short is short then?'

'Very short. I want to grow out the colour as soon as possible.'

Chantal put one hand on Mandy's shoulder. 'I almost want you to sign a disclaimer. Are you sure you're not having some sort of crisis? Had you better come back tomorrow?'

'I'm perfectly sane. I know what I'm doing. I don't want to be "this" Mandy any more.'

Chantal moved over to pick up her scissors. Mandy tossed her hair in the air, watching herself in the mirror. Then, she ran her fingers through the long dyed blonde tresses for the last time. Symbolically, she removed the scrunchy from her wrist and placed it on the shelf in front of her. She wouldn't need it again.

'Do you want to look through the style books?' Chantal was still looking worried.

'If it will make you happier to cut it, then yes.'

She flipped through the short styles and pointed to an elfin layered look.

Chantal gasped. 'That's really short.'

By now Mandy was getting exasperated. 'Look, would you prefer I went somewhere else to have it done?'

'No, no. I'm sure that style will look absolutely amazing on you. It's just so different to what you normally have. I'm genuinely shocked, but as long as you are certain, we'll get going.'

Mandy locked eyes with her in the mirror. 'I'm sure.'

Chapter Seventeen

Nick declared that he'd never been on a proper train before, just the miniature railway that was set up on the promenade in Borteen sometimes. He looked unusually smart in the new jeans and the jade hoodie he'd picked out when Mandy took him clothes shopping in Sowden during the week – and more grown up too with his shorter neat hairstyle.

Mandy had carefully selected items from her wardrobe for the weekend away that were less revealing. She wanted to choose a new style, but there'd not been time before their trip to Manchester. She couldn't help running her hand down the back of her hair. It was such a different look, but so far anyone who commented had been complimentary including Nick.

Nick's excitement had him jigging from foot to foot as they waited for the train to arrive at Sowden railway station. Mandy was amused by his excitement and thankfully it distracted her a little from her own nervousness about the weekend ahead. She kept reminding herself that this trip was for Nick and that she was just the means by which the youth could meet his grandma. She was superfluous and not important, so why did she feel so jittery?

They had discussed at length what to take as a present for Nick's grandma. Nick had paced around the craft centre with a furrow between his brows as he tried to decide what was best. In the end, Mandy steered him towards the seaglass jewellery case. He picked out a dark blue seaglass pendant on a silver chain. He'd looked across to Mandy with sudden doubt in his eyes, which disappeared as soon as Mandy smiled reassuringly at him. It touched her heart. She wrapped the gift in a sparkly box with a matching ribbon and Nick placed it reverently in his weekend bag.

Peggy had thankfully agreed to feed and spend a little time with Merlin while they were away. Mandy suspected the cat would miss Nick as the animal was always glued to his side when they were at home and had slept on Nick's bed since that first night.

The train was busy and Mandy was pleased she'd reserved seats. Nick took her holdall from her and put it next to his own on the rack above where they were sitting. She had a moment of feeling really proud of him for showing such maturity and kindness, especially when he did the same for an elderly woman who came to sit across the carriage from them.

They settled into their seats. Mandy took out her Kindle but found herself mesmerised by the passing countryside rather than reading the words on the screen. Nick had his sketch pad as usual and spent the whole journey drawing train passengers and impressions of the train and the track.

Mandy made renewed efforts to concentrate on her book, but found her eyes straying to Nick's sketch pad more often than the page she was trying to read. They'd caught a late afternoon train and had to change twice, much to Nick's delight. One of the changes meant they had to climb up a set of steps, cross the bridge over the train line and down another set at a very fast pace that left them breathless and laughing.

Graham met them at the station looking even more nervous than she felt. His eyes widened when he saw Mandy's new look, but he didn't comment. Mandy exchanged embarrassed air-kisses with him and Nick shook his hand. Mandy noted that the father and son weren't quite at the "pat each other on the back", or "man hug" stage.

Graham took Mandy's bag and led the way to his car. He drove them through the busy streets in his large black vehicle with the Frankley Gins logo on the doors. He explained he had to have room to transport cases of gin if necessary. She wasn't sure if she was pleased or disappointed that he hadn't mentioned her new hairstyle.

Graham had arranged for them to stay at a small, spotlessly clean bed and breakfast about five minutes from his own home. There were only two letting rooms at the B&B so they were the only guests.

The owner obviously knew Graham and showed a great deal of curiosity about his link with her weekend boarders, but Graham cleverly managed to evade any questions without telling the absolute truth or an outright lie.

He made sure they were happy with their rooms, before leaving them to freshen up after the journey and agreed to come back in half an hour to take them out for a meal. He told Mandy it would be just the three of them and he would introduce them to his mother on Saturday morning. He explained that his mum got progressively more exhausted as she went through a day, before needing to recharge her energy batteries with sleep.

The landlady tried a few more questions to get information about Mandy's relationship with Graham, but Mandy was as evasive as Graham himself had been.

Nick bounced on the bed in his room and declared it very soft.

Mandy left him looking through the sketches he'd made on the journey and went to change out of her jeans and boots and into a dress with a sparkly thread cardigan. The dress had one of the highest necklines she possessed. In keeping with the start of her image transformation, she didn't want to display lots of cleavage this weekend.

She chuckled to herself at her new way of thinking. What was happening to her? She'd had a particular way of dressing for quite a few years and had already been questioning if that style was still her before she met Graham. Since he had come into their lives though and particularly since she'd had the visit from Jonas Fraser about her son, the questions were louder and more prominent in her mind and she was certain that her old image was no longer how she wanted to portray herself to the world. The sense that it was time for big change was growing.

She shook herself. The half hour until Graham returned for them was going fast. She went into the tiny ensuite to touch up her make-up ... and frowned at her face in the mirror. Her make-up style would need to change too. She wiped off the pencil she'd applied to her eyebrows and then reapplied it more lightly. She added new make-up to her mental transformation list.

Graham took them to an Italian restaurant, which had cosy booth seating. Despite the extensive menu, Nick chose pizza.

'Don't you want to try something different?' asked Graham.

Nick grinned. 'I love pizza. I'd have it every meal if Mand would let me.'

Mandy raised her eyebrows and exchanged a look with Graham.

'Can I call you Dad instead of Graham?' asked Nick suddenly.

'I'd be honoured,' said Graham. Mandy was sure that he bent down to mess with his shoe in order to wipe a tear away and she felt quite watery-eyed herself.

When Graham had composed himself, and they'd ordered their food, he outlined tentative plans for the next day. 'I'll pick you up about ten. I'd like to show you both my distillery. You can meet Wendham who works with me. He's an expert on flavourings. Then, Nick, we'll all have lunch with your grandma.'

Mandy was aware that Nick hadn't been a great fan of his late grandma on his mother's side and wondered what he thought about the prospect of a new one. The expression on Nick's face wasn't giving her any clues about his thinking. It wasn't until Graham left them for a moment to go to the gents that a Nick with an anguished face turned to her. 'Mand, I'm bricking it.'

'What about? You were excited earlier.'

'That's before it hit me. I've got to meet a real person, a real grandma.' His eyes widened. 'She probably won't like me. And what if I don't like her?'

'Hey. What's brought this on?'

'It was just an idea before, something Dad wanted me to do, but now it's real.'

She did her best to reassure him, but that wasn't exactly easy when she was pretty frightened about meeting Graham's mother too.

Chapter Eighteen

The distillery was a much smaller operation than Mandy had imagined, and the first thing that struck her was the shininess of the surfaces; gleaming copper cylinders, stainless steel boxes and ducting glinted in the overhead lights. The floor looked clean enough to eat a meal from.

Nick's eyes shone, as much with curiosity as from the reflection of the lights. 'Whoa, what do these things do? What do those dials show? Can I taste some gin?'

Mandy could see the pride and delight in Graham's eyes in reaction to his son's enthusiasm and questions. It seemed like an alien world and even she couldn't wait to find out more. Who knew that this was how gin was produced?

Nick had already taken out the small sketch pad she'd given to him for the train journey and was sketching one of the copper vessels. She marvelled, as always, at how he could record an object accurately with so few strokes of a pencil. Whenever she tried to draw something it looked like a cartoon or nothing like the image she'd been attempting to capture.

Mandy was actually looking forward to finding out more about the production of gin.

'What is gin made from?' she asked.

Graham laughed. 'You would be surprised how many gin drinkers aren't aware of what they're drinking. The main ingredient is juniper berries.' He opened a container and gave both Mandy and Nick a few hard, round berries.

Nick examined them closely. He squeezed one and smelt it. 'I've seen some of these on Pink Moor above Borteen.'

'Yes, you will find juniper berries in England, but unfortunately we can't use those any more as they're too rare and the trees are protected. We have to buy stocks of berries from abroad.'

'There's a whole clump of them up on the moor. I like smelling the berries and leaves, but the trees haven't been looking too good this year.'

Mandy was surprised by this new aspect of Nick. She knew he wandered around the Borteen area, but would never have dreamed he would take an interest in nature.

'You're right, Nick. There's been a disease attacking the native juniper this year.'

'How awful,' said Mandy.

'It is. Makes it even less likely we'll be allowed to use them in the future. As we have to get the berries abroad, I try to source locally the other things we add, the botanicals.'

'What things are bot-botanicals?' asked Nick. He seemed more interested in the manufacture of gin than she'd dared to imagine.

'Well, as I think I mentioned to you before, it's almost like painting a picture. You start with a basic recipe and add things to change the taste albeit subtly. We love experimenting here, that's the fun of the job. We can use all sorts of things – lavender, lime, honey, herbs, leaves, fruits, spices.'

He pointed to a table with lots of different jars full of ingredients at the back. Mandy went over to have a look. 'I'll let you taste some different recipes in a while.' He turned to Nick. 'Only sips for you though as you're underage.'

Nick shrugged. He was now sketching in earnest, page after page in an almost frantic recording of his surroundings.

'I'm still confused about how the gin is actually made.' Mandy gazed around a little bewildered.

'I really don't want to bore you with too much detail.'

'No, no, it's fascinating. A world I know absolutely nothing about.' She wanted to touch one of the copper cylinders but was worried about leaving finger marks on the polished surface.

'The world I live in.' He looked pleased she was showing an interest but turned to Nick first. 'Can I have a look at what you've been sketching?'

Nick reluctantly handed over his sketch pad. 'Only rough.'

The drawings were far from rough. Impressions of the distilling coppers and depictions of both Mandy and Graham that somehow captured their essence and the fact that they kept looking at each other. 'Wow!' They both said the word at the same time and their eyes met over the book and lingered a fraction longer than normal.

Mandy was again struck by the unusual dark green of Graham's eyes and the way her body reacted to even a small meeting of their eyes.

'These are so good, Nick. If you could work them up into canvases, they'd be great, maybe for our new reception area, when we have one. I'd pay you for them, of course.'

'Really?' Nick's grin couldn't have been wider, but then his face fell. 'I haven't got anywhere to paint away from school and can't really afford the canvas and paints.'

'I can pay some money upfront for materials.'

Mandy was amazed at how this young man could make her heart contract. 'No worries, Nick. If Graham gives you an advance, we can go to Sowden to get what you need and we'll find somewhere for you to paint. Would one end of my conservatory do, or the workshop space at the craft centre?'

'Wouldn't want to mess up your conservatory though.'

'We'll have a look when we get back. We can put down some old sheets. It would be criminal to turn down a commission and you've got to paint Michael Bryant's portrait too.' She turned back to Graham. 'Now, Mr Frankley, give me the low-down on how to make gin.'

'Okay, a potted version. As I said, I'm scared of boring you.'

'I'm sure you won't. It's fascinating.'

Graham smiled, the laughter lines around his eyes crinkling. 'We choose the ingredients, which always include water, grain alcohol and juniper berries. Hard ingredients are bruised in this big pestle and mortar.' He rested his hand on the rim of a huge wooden bowl. 'Then everything is left to macerate.'

'Macerate? Not a word I know.'

'I suppose you'd understand it as left to soak, so that the flavours start to combine. Depending on the flavour we want to achieve, we leave it *soaking* for a minimum of fourteen hours but sometimes up to three days. Then, the liquid is heated in the still – he pointed to one of the copper vessels. When it gets hot enough to turn into vapour, it goes across the tubing into this baby.' He patted a tall column of copper with lots of dials along its length. 'Eventually, the vapour becomes a liquid again and that goes through this tube into the stainless-steel tank.'

Mandy still didn't totally understand the process but was mesmerized by Graham's animated face as he described it. She had an irresistible urge to reach out and touch him, which meant she had to firmly clasp her hands behind her back.

'Can you drink the gin straight out of that tank?'

'Lord no. It's too strong at that stage, ninety percent alcohol, so has to be diluted with water, hydrated as we call it, to bring it to bottling strength and make it ready to drink. Would you like to taste some?' He was so close to her now, she began to feel giddy inhaling his spicy aftershave. Their eyes locked and she thought she recognised an echoing desire in Graham's eyes.

'What's in here?' asked Nick.

Mandy and Graham leapt apart. Nick was pointing to a door beyond which there was a whooshing sound.

Graham went over to join Nick. 'That's the boiler room. We'll go in, but it's a bit hot, I warn you.'

Mandy hung back, but even so a blast of heat hit her as Graham opened the door. It was a smaller room with a big metal container on one side from which came the noise and the heat. Wood was stacked neatly against the other wall. Nick, not phased by the change in temperature, immediately began sketching again.

'We use mainly our own wood from the copse on site to fire the boiler.'

'A nice little self-contained operation.'

'Thank you, I'm glad you're impressed.'

Graham grinned at her and she bathed in the warmth of his approval. She was enthralled by the distillery, but also by him. There was nothing more attractive than someone who enjoyed his work. She wondered briefly what it would be like if this man looked at her with love. Where did that come from? Love wasn't a word in her usual vocabulary – lust maybe.

Graham shooed Nick out of the boiler room and shut the door on the heat. They left him sketching the copper vessels. Graham led Mandy over to a table with glasses already laid out and bottles of gin with the Frankley Gins logo on the label.

'We try to give each different mix a distinctive name.'

Mandy looked closer. The names included Heather Berry, Sage Elixir and Lavender Heaven. The subtle colours of the liquids looked intriguing.

Graham began mixing tiny drinks, just covering the base of a glass, part gin, part tonic. He had lots of different flavoured tonic bottles too.

'Now you don't need to swallow these tasters. Have a good smell of the glass. Just swill it around your mouth, let it rest on your tongue, then swill it around again. Either swallow or spit out the liquid. Here try this one, tell me what you smell and taste.'

Terribly self-conscious, Mandy followed his instructions, aware he was watching her, specifically her mouth, very closely to see her reaction. She had to concentrate hard not to splutter, dribble or choke on the gin. Managing to follow his instructions, she decided it was better to swallow before she spoke.

'It's like ginny-liquorice?'

'Super. Absolutely spot on.' He was pleased with her again, she could tell.

Maybe she could be good at this. He passed her another glass and she followed the tasting procedure.

'Orange and lime?'

'You could be a professional taster.' Their fingers brushed as he took the glass from her. Graham felt very close.

'Can I have a go?'

Mandy jumped at the sound of the young man's voice, realising that her fascination with Graham's eyes and the movements of his hands had made her forget Nick was even in the same room.

Nick picked up a sample glass and sniffed. He'd obviously been listening closely to what Graham had been saying. '*Eurgh*. Can't put that in my mouth. Sorry.' He held the glass away again, as if it contained deadly poison.

'Just sniff the samples then,' said Graham, trying his hardest not to laugh.

'Not sure I want to. It's making me feel sick just being near the glass.' Nick was pulling the funniest of faces.

Mandy and Graham gave in and both laughed out loud.

'In some ways I'm relieved,' Mandy said to Nick. 'At least you aren't going to sneak off and get drunk on the gin when we aren't looking.'

They were still laughing when a stranger to Mandy, tall and dark haired, wearing blue overalls entered the room.

'Ah, this is Wendham. Now, *he*'s the real expert on flavours and tastes.'

Graham introduced Mandy and Nick to the new arrival.

Wendham was a colourful character, who seemed to have made up for not having hair on the top of his head by growing an impressive moustache. Mandy was reminded of someone from the circus that had visited Borteen every year when she was young.

'He's an expert at flavours,' said Graham.

Wendham bowed and twirled the end of his moustache, further adding to the impression that he belonged to the circus.

Graham told Wendham he had his work cut out to make a gin palatable to the grimacing teenager.

'Is that a challenge?' said Wendham in a deep Scottish accent that took Mandy completely by surprise. His voice didn't seem to match his appearance somehow.

'At the moment, I'm happy he doesn't want to drink gin,' she said.

Graham was also relieved Nick hadn't guzzled the gin. He so wanted the approval of his son, he couldn't remember when he'd wanted something more. He scrutinised every change of expression on Nick's face. It made him think fondly of his own father and how happy he would have been to meet his grandson. Nick reminded him of his dad, right down to the little crease at the edge of his mouth that so obviously showed pleasure or displeasure.

His dad had been interested in distilling and had financed the business venture when Graham was at his lowest ebb, homeless, jobless, Trisha-less. His father had worked so hard to get Graham interested and on board with the business and gradually it had worked. Graham could see with hindsight that his dad had been desperate to jerk his son out of the awful lethargy that the circumstances of his life had led to. The gin business had literally saved Graham's life. Ironic, when back in history excessive gin consumption had been responsible for claiming the lives of so many.

The Frankley gins weren't the cheap, guzzling type, more drinks to be savoured and mixed with different tonics. Special, an art form. Graham was feeling proud today – proud of Nick, proud of his craft gin business.

He turned his attention back to Mandy, watching as she chatted easily with Wendham and sipped a few samples of different gins. Her face was expressive too and he could easily tell which drinks she preferred. As he observed the two discussing the merits of the samples, Graham realised something else too, well, several things really. One, he cared what Mandy thought and two, he was jealous of the easy way Wendham was talking to her, making her laugh, making her listen, making her face relaxed and animated. Did she react in the same ways when Graham was talking to her? He'd have to pay more attention. Her new hairstyle suited her, he reflected. He'd wanted to comment on it but hadn't found the right moment or the right words.

Mandy was aware of Graham's scrutiny and hoped that he thought the pink glow on her cheeks was because of the alcohol, not her reaction to him watching her closely. He seemed to be paying more attention to her today.

She told Wendham that these gins were more subtle than any gin she'd drunk before. The flavours were delicate.

Nick pulled another disgusted face. 'Still don't fancy trying them. I think I'll leave drinking gin till I'm much older.'

Graham seemed to find this amusing and Mandy liked it that he didn't seem to mind that Nick wouldn't try the drinks.

'It's a great set-up you have here.' She moved her stance to include Graham more easily in the conversation with Wendham.

It was Graham who replied. 'Yes, it works well. Unfortunately, we have to move from here. The landlord has sold his farm, including the plot the distillery is on for housing. It all happened very quickly. On one hand I can understand his decision as the deal is worth much more than the rent from us, but it does rather leave us in the lurch.'

'How awful, you did say there was some problem with the lease. Do just the two of you produce the gin?'

'No, we have a full-time operative, Big Al, mainly for heavy lifting. He pointed over to the huge box casks of grape alcohol.

Then there's a number of part-time staff, who mainly come in to help when there's bottling to do. Wendham is dedicated to the gin production and he lives close by – but you'd think he lives here if you saw how many hours he spends on site.'

Wendham playfully punched Graham on the shoulder.

Nick had wandered off to sketch on the far side of the room and Graham lowered his voice. 'I need to know how things will progress with Nick, as there is a real possibility I could set up again in Borteen. Wendham has already said that he'd move with me.'

Mandy knew then that Graham really was serious about being part of his son's life.

'Right, young man.' Graham went over to Nick. 'Have you got enough ideas for my reception canvases?'

'Loads.' Nick was smiling and appeared totally relaxed in Graham's company at last.

'Shall we go and meet your grandma? She'll wonder where we've got to.'

A surge of insecurity came from nowhere and Mandy pulled up the neckline of her top, even though this one wasn't particularly low cut.

Chapter Nineteen

Mandy adored Graham's mother from the outset. Ann seemed so serene, despite her obvious health difficulties and she was clearly overjoyed to have a grandson.

The older woman put her hands on either side of Nick's face and studied his features. 'You know, Nick, I wasn't sure about all of this when Graham told me about it, but looking at your face, I can tell you are truly my grandson. You have your grandfather's nose without a shadow of a doubt.'

Nick didn't seem very keen on the big hug and kiss she gave him next, but he put up with her attention and showed immediate signs of liking her too, especially after she admired the drawings in his sketchbook. Mandy was so happy that the two of them appeared to be forging a relationship.

Mrs Frankley sent Nick off into a corner of the room to retrieve several flat folders containing some of her watercolour paintings. They sat close together as she explained why she had painted each picture.

'I've started painting acrylics now, but I still hanker after the watercolours.'

'Maybe you could help me get better at watercolour painting?' There was a tentative note in Nick's voice as he asked the question.

'Nothing would give me greater pleasure.' Ann's face showed that she was full of love for her newly discovered grandson already.

Mandy went into the kitchen to help Graham prepare sandwiches for their lunch. There were also shop-bought lemon drizzle and carrot cakes, which she sliced onto a plate. When they returned to the lounge with the lunch food, Nick was just finishing a lovely sketch of Ann who was posed looking out of the window. Nick tore the page carefully from his pad and was enveloped in another close hug when he gave it to his grandma as a present.

When they'd eaten, Graham suggested they kick a ball around in the garden and Nick gratefully escaped his grandma's clutches.

Mandy settled down on the sofa next to Graham's mother and watched the two males bonding over a football. She was so absorbed with watching Graham's delighted face that she almost jumped when his mother spoke.

'What would you like to call me, Mandy?'

Was this a trick question Mandy wondered? 'What would you like me to call you? Mrs Frankley, Grandma or, I don't think I caught your first name.'

'It's Ann, but Grandma if it's easier. I'm quite enjoying the new title.'

Mandy made what she hoped was a pleased murmur.

'Now, I think we need to talk about my son.'

Mandy sat up straighter and turned to face the older woman. Ann's green eyes, so similar to Graham's, drilled into her. A shiver travelled down Mandy's back.

'Graham?'

Ann nodded. 'Can I ask what your intentions are regarding him?'

'Intentions? I don't think I have any particular intentions. He just happens to be the father of the child I have in temporary foster care.' Why did that sound like a blatant lie? What intentions did she have? Maybe not intentions, but a girl could dream, couldn't she?

Ann's lips drew into a firmer line. 'Well whatever happens, I would ask you to be careful with my son's feelings. He had a pretty rough ride a few years ago and I'd hate for him to have another setback.'

The football banged against the window and both women shifted their attention back outside. Graham made a sign of apology to his mum and kicked the ball back to a laughing Nick.

The gap in the conversation had at least given Mandy time to think. She stood up and collected the empty drinks mugs from the table before speaking again. 'Ann ... Grandma, I can't say I have any idea how this will work out, but I promise to be mindful of mine, Nick's and Graham's feelings. I can understand you being concerned. Graham is your son after all. My main role in all of this is as Nick's temporary foster mum.'

After saying that, she gave Ann no chance to reply, going into the kitchen with the mugs. She felt momentarily miffed that Graham's mother would think she would play around with Graham's emotions, but after taking her time washing up, she could see that the older woman would be protective of her own son, just as Mandy had learned to look out for Nick in the short while he'd been living with her.

When she returned to the sitting room, it was as if their previous conversation and Ann's warning had never occurred. Ann asked her about Owl Corner Crafts and in particular about Nick's pictures she had on sale.

Eventually, the boys came back in from the garden hot and red-faced. Graham's suggestion of ice creams from the freezer caused a whoop of delight from Nick. It was an illusion of a close family – grandma, man, woman and child – all co-existing happily. The thought set up a longing inside Mandy for a dream she hadn't allowed herself to have for a very long time.

As Graham drove Mandy and Nick back to the station for the return journey to Borteen, Mandy felt more comfortable in Graham's company than on Friday evening when they'd arrived.

'Your mother is lovely, but I get the impression she can be fierce if anyone threatens those close to her,' she said.

'Yes, she is. Thank you. I do hope she didn't give you a lecture about me.'

Graham must be well aware of his mother's protective instincts where he was concerned. She decided not to elaborate as it was clearly unnecessary. 'She misses your father.'

'I know. I do too.'

'Was his death sudden?'

Graham shifted his hands on the steering wheel. 'A heart attack.' He glanced meaningfully at Nick in the back seat.

It felt strange to leave Graham on the platform when they boarded the train. Nick and Graham high-fived and performed an awkward man hug. Mandy and Graham had an equally awkward loose hug, but their air-kisses were more enthusiastic than on Friday evening when they'd arrived.

Graham's parting words filled Mandy with a warm glow. 'By the way – I love your new hair.'

The fact that Nick waved for much longer than they could still see Graham on the platform, eloquently expressed his feelings about his newly found father.

Chapter Twenty

Mandy took further steps towards her transformation when she got home from the weekend in Manchester, encouraged by Graham's parting comment. She parcelled up the clothes she was no longer comfortable wearing and visited Suzi Meadows at the Cancer Research charity shop to drop them off. Suzi was pleased to see her and they put the world to rights for thirty minutes.

Mandy was very much an advocate of shopping local. She was loyal to Borteen shopkeepers who, particularly in the winter months, needed whatever trade they could get. She herself was very aware of the pattern of the year. Bank holidays were particularly significant as they not only attracted holidaymakers but also day trippers. The Easter Bank Holidays were the following weekend and from then until the autumn there would be more visitors in the town and Owl Corner Crafts takings would hopefully increase too.

When she had had her locks shorn, she knew the image transformation would not be complete without new clothes and make-up. Here she had a dilemma. Her normal clothes shop of choice was Polka Dot Paradise, a vintage and nearly new fashion shop at the furthest end of the high street from the sea. The owner, Sorrel was so used to Mandy's shopping habits that she even kept items she thought were suitable for her behind the counter. Mandy had thus far been amazed how well Sorrel had read her fashion needs, but of course, now those had changed completely.

Did she risk being tempted by her old style if she went to Polka Dot Paradise or did she travel into Sowden to new shops and break her golden rule of shopping local?

She decided she would be strong and explain what she was

trying to achieve to Sorrel and hope she could help her with her new style.

As Mandy entered the shop, Sorrel's eyes nearly popped out of her head when she registered Mandy's new hairstyle.

'Whoa, girlfriend. Is this really Mandy Vanes?'

Mandy hoped the reaction was favourable and that she didn't look like a mismatched character in a game she used to play as a child called Misfits, where mismatched parts of bodies were put together to make odd looking characters. After all, she may have new hair, but was still wearing her old style make-up and clothes. Both of those would have to change.

'Say hello to the new Mandy Vanes,' she joked.

'Wow! You look so different without the bleached hair. Grown up, sophisticated, classy.'

Was Sorrel just being kind? Did she just look old?

'Thank you. And now I need a new style of clothing to go with my new hair. I want to lose the daily cleavage and leave it behind with the blonde.'

'How exciting, no problem at all. I'm already buzzing with ideas just looking at you. First floor methinks.'

Mandy followed her up the stairs. Sorrel was wearing a dress made from white fabric with black polka dots to echo her shop name. Mandy had irreverent thoughts about joining up the dots as she followed her to the first floor.

Sorrel had such a good eye for shape and style that Mandy was soon trying on lots of clothes. It wasn't easy to find that elusive change she was seeking but then, with Sorrel's guidance, she'd suddenly found it. A selection of wide-legged trousers and colourful well-cut tops and dresses that flattered her shape but didn't show too much flesh joined the pile of prospective purchases.

The shop owner even produced some colourful camisoles to tone down some of the cleavage-showing tops and dresses that Mandy still liked and had kept. Mandy felt almost overwhelmed with gratitude, especially as Sorrel accepted what Mandy wanted to achieve without ever asking her why she wanted to make the change.

Mandy left the shop swinging pink polka-dotted carrier bags and smiling broadly as her new look came together in her head. She was now wearing a pair of cream flared trousers and a slit neck black top with tiny flowers in the pattern. Most importantly, she felt good. Great in fact.

Next stop the chemist for new make-up. This was fun.

It was even more exciting when she passed several people she knew well in the high street. Fred, the butcher didn't appear to recognize her at all and looked bewildered when she spoke to him. Olivia from the newsagents was standing on the shop doorstep and gave a low whistle when she saw Mandy.

'New look – I like it!' she said, smiling.

'Thank you,' Mandy replied.

Mandy swung her shopping bags more enthusiastically and said a silent thank you to the sky.

'Whoa.'

Mandy was pleased with the reaction when she came downstairs the next morning and the sound erupted involuntarily from Nick's mouth.

His eyes assessed her thoroughly. 'Much better. Sophisticated and classy.'

She smiled, tears dancing in her eyes. 'Thank you, Nick.'

The mulberry coloured dress hugged her figure, but was four inches longer than her normal clothes, both at the neckline and the hemline. It was a business dress and made her feel businesslike for work. Her new hairstyle felt sleek against her head. She'd toned down the shades and quantity of her make-up, filed her nails shorter and applied a quiet shade of nail polish instead of one of her usual riotous colours.

New Mandy felt so good as she walked down the hill to the

craft centre and the sun was shining as if to echo her mood. This had been the right thing to do. She was ready for the next phase of her life.

Graham had finally received confirmation from the site developer that approvals had been given for the development to go ahead and that the distillery would be demolished as part of the plan to build the housing estate.

It was somehow more daunting being presented with a reality, rather than a possibility and he found himself experiencing a whole range of emotions from sadness through to elation as he thought about the consequences of having to relocate.

He was pleased that he'd been open with the people who worked with him from the beginning, but was now having to live with the consequences of them finding alternative employment. The last bottling round had been quite fraught using temporary staff and Graham and Wendham had worked long hours to keep everything going.

He searched on the internet for some of the other gin manufacturers about the same size as his own and came to the conclusion that those that had woven a story around either their location or their brand of gin were the most prominent and successful. Graham knew this was what he needed to achieve to make a success of the move.

He sat back in his chair and allowed his imagination to work on a story around pink gin produced from botanicals sourced on Pink Moor above the seaside town of Borteen, maybe rosehips, rowan and elderberries; blue gin using seaweed and grasses found near to the seafront; maybe even an art lover's gin to honour his son and before he knew it, he'd convinced himself that a move to Borteen could work.

Mandy was in such a happy mood that she finished work early. Leaving Romana to lock up she took Nick into Sowden to buy the materials he needed to set up an art studio in the conservatory. Michael Bryant had left a voicemail to set the wheels in motion for his portrait too, so Nick was going to be busy.

Nick hugged her when she insisted on buying a sturdy easel.

'I'll phone Mr Bryant this evening and ask him when it would be convenient for us to visit him at Lucerne Lodge. You'll need sketches and maybe a few photographs so you can complete his picture.'

'It's proper scary, Mand. I've never done a picture to order like this. Dad's pictures are different.'

'You'll be fine.'

'But how much do I charge?'

'Let's find out exactly what he wants first and worry about the price afterwards.'

The pair moved the furniture around in the conservatory when they got home and set up the easel and an old table Mandy had in her bedroom for Nick to put his paints on.

Before Mandy could phone Michael Bryant, she had a call from Graham.

'I've hinted at this already, but I'm now all systems go for a move to Borteen or somewhere nearby.'

'Wow!' was all Mandy could think to say.

'My mum and Wendham are on board and ready to move. I've been agonising about the people who work for me, but it turns out Hazel, who I secretly think is sweet on Wendham, used to work as a carer and is willing to come with us too to look after Mum. Big Al has already left to go to a new warehouse job and I suspect he won't be the last. My job agency friend thinks she can place the last three, so I can relax about that a bit more. We've actually got several months before we have to get out, but I want to get things going, particularly now we're starting to lose experienced workers.'

He seemed to realise he'd been talking a lot. 'Everything okay over in Borteen?'

'Yes, everything is fine.'

'Only I wanted to enlist your help in looking for a suitable property. It isn't the sort of business I can move just anywhere and I need various permissions and the right environment.'

'What sort of place are you looking for?'

'Ideally, it would be a farmhouse type place with at least four bedrooms. There's Mum and I. Hazel will live with us too and I'll offer Wendham a room at least initially. Then buildings for a distillery and if possible, a natural source of water, maybe a freshwater spring. That's why we're where we are now – there's a small lake at the back of the building, fed from underground springs. The icing on the cake would be if the living accommodation was on the same site as the distillery ... but then that might make things too complicated since Mum doesn't do stairs any more.'

He seemed to realise at this point that he was babbling. 'Sorry, Mandy. I haven't given you time to get used to the idea. It's just that if I want to keep my existing contracts and clients, I need to get up and running quickly. Even though we've been stockpiling like mad.'

Mandy was a little overwhelmed but liked his enthusiasm and excitement. 'So, something like a farmhouse with barns?'

'Perfect, as long as there are ground floor rooms for Mum. A bonus would be an area of woodland. The still is powered by a wood-burning boiler. You'll remember seeing it.'

'Do you want to buy or rent the property over here?'

'I think having had my fingers burned with renting and being about to be thrown out of the distillery, my preference now would be to buy. Dad left me a substantial sum when he died and I'd like to put it to good use on something he believed in.'

'I'll keep a look out for sale boards when I'm out and about.'

'And I'll register with estate agents in the area and check online, but it would be good to have you watching for possibilities and keeping an ear out for things that might come on the market, if you don't mind? I gather the best properties go before they're even advertised.'

'I guess if you're meant to come here, you'll find things to do with the move will flow smoothly.'

'Yes, we'll find the right property right away and everything will be without obstacles or delays.'

'Let's hope so.'

'Did you just see the flying pigs go past?'

'Pessimist.'

Graham laughed but in a sarcastic way. 'Life often hands me lemons.'

'Then make lemonade gin.'

'Now there's a thought for a new recipe.'

'Are you over in Borteen this weekend?'

'No, as it's the Easter weekend, the guest house is full. I made a couple of other calls about accommodation, but came to the conclusion it might be easier to leave it till the following week. I'll look online, but is there any chance you could visit a few estate agents for me?

The words were out of her mouth before she'd censored them. 'You can stay with us if you don't mind the tiny box room.'

'Really? That would be great as I'd like to get going on this property hunt.'

'I love house-hunting. I've helped several friends in the past. Email me your criteria and the contact details you'd like me to give to the agents and I'll have a go. I have a friend in Sowden, another school buddy, who's an estate agent. Yes, Tam may be able to help you.'

'I was a bit worried about it all, but I'm beginning to get excited. Somehow talking to you, it all feels doable. So keep your fingers crossed for me and keep your ear to the ground.'

'Will do.'

'What do you think Nick will think about me coming to live in Borteen?'

'I think we'll *both* enjoy having you over here.'

'I'm looking forward to getting to know you ... *both* much better. I'll see you on Friday.'

She blushed, even though he couldn't see it down the phone.

The call ended and Mandy went to make a coffee and idly began to scan the property websites to see what she could find in the area. The search felt both exciting and scary. Was she about to lose Nick? On the other hand, it didn't sound as if he would be far away and interestingly neither would Graham ...

Chapter Twenty-One

Mandy headed for Sowden on her afternoon off, having already set up an appointment with Tam at the estate agents. She hadn't seen her friend for a while so they chatted about this and that before getting to details of Graham's house and distillery search.

Tam had always been the organised, serious one at school, the girl who could tell you which homework was due for which subject and when, without even looking at her planner. She brought those same skills to her job and, as Mandy described Graham's requirements, her brow furrowed in thought and her dark brown bobbed hair established a mesmerising rhythmic swing.

'Exciting search. Very different requirements to the norm,' she said, almost breathless as her mind worked over possibilities.

'But is it realistic? Graham says ideally the distillery and home would be on the same site, but he would consider separate options too.'

'It might be a challenge, but I can already think of a couple of combined site options and one split suggestion. You say he'll be in the area for viewings at the weekend?'

'Yes. I knew you'd be the best person for the job.'

Tam's expression changed and she looked directly at Mandy. 'So, this Graham, is he a love interest?'

Mandy felt her cheeks warm up. 'Not exactly ...'

'Not exactly, meaning you would if you could?'

'Maybe ...'

'It's just that if I'm looking for a property for you too, I might make different suggestions.' Tam laughed.

'Just stick to the brief for now, Tam. I'll let you know if things get even more complicated.' She put her hand up to cool her flaming cheeks. Why would Tam's suggestion affect her so much if there wasn't anything to it?

When she left the estate agent's, she resolved to do something she'd toyed with for a while. Someone had told her a girl at the supermarket in Sowden was clairvoyant and gave out messages with the coffee she made. Mandy wasn't sure she believed in such things, but she needed a clear steer, a sign …

The girl who made her coffee had auburn curls sticking out of the back of her supermarket uniform cap. Her eyes were bright and sparkly in the brash overhead lights. The latte she presented to Mandy had patterns all over the froth.

'Ooo interesting.' The girl's eyes widened when she realised she'd spoken aloud.

'Are you the one they talk about?' Mandy asked.

The girl glanced around her, suddenly seeming nervous. She looked more like a fairy from the book of fairy stories Mandy had avidly read as a child, than the witch someone had described her as when they'd been explaining about her "prophesies".

'Yes, it's me, but I'm not supposed to read coffees any more. My manager is already hopping mad. He's forbidden me to say anything to customers that isn't anything to do with their order, or their change. Sorry!'

'I don't want to get you into trouble, but I really need your help.'

The girl glanced nervously around her again. 'Look, I'm due a break. Go and sit at a table as far away from the counter as you can and I'll be over in a minute. If anyone asks, we're old friends. Oh, and don't touch your coffee yet.'

Mandy did as she was told. The seat she picked was near a balcony that looked out over the supermarket. She sat staring at her coffee. There were patterns on top of the milk, but she couldn't make anything out of them.

The girl behind the counter was making another drink, then she whispered to her colleague and left to walk over to Mandy. Mandy had thought about it and had positioned herself so the girl could sit with her back to the counter.

She sat down. 'I'm Becky Finch. If the manager asks, you've known me for years.'

'Mandy and okay.'

They both giggled conspiratorially.

'Your coffee's actually really interesting. I could hardly refuse to read it.'

'Tell me how this works.'

'I just see messages in the coffee I prepare.'

'What does mine say exactly?' Mandy almost wished she hadn't asked. She crossed her fingers under the table.

'I don't really get words.'

Waste of time, thought Mandy, feeling her anticipation performing a nosedive.

'I get more impressions, images and these are really complicated. A new house with two drinking glasses on the roof and a young adult ... no ... two – I think they're males.' Becky looked up from the surface of the coffee. 'Are you all right? You've gone awfully white.'

'Whoa ...' Mandy began to shake from head to foot and cold perspiration broke out on her forehead.

'Does it all mean something to you?' Becky had her head on one side and her blue eyes gleamed.

'Maybe ... can you interpret the images you see?'

'I'm afraid only you can do that.'

'Is there any way of telling if it's a positive or negative message?'

Becky still held her head on one side, studying Mandy. 'I gather it does mean something, even if the meaning isn't yet clear?' There also seems to be a baby.'

Mandy gulped. Was this just a load of rubbish or prophetic? It sounded like a new house for Graham, something to do with gin and were the two males Nick and Paul? But what about the baby?

'Anything else?'

'Only you can decide what it really signifies but it seems an image with a lot of light in it, which usually means something positive.'

'Would it help if I had another cup of coffee?'

'Not necessarily. Is it possible you're pregnant?'

'By divine intervention if I am. I haven't had sex in ages.' Mandy clasped her hands to her mouth embarrassed at what she'd just said.

Becky looked suddenly uncomfortable but not because of Mandy's words. '*Oops!* Here comes the manager. I'd better go.' She scurried off, wiping the next table as she went past.

Mandy sat at the table and sipped the latte, all the time trying to see what Becky Finch had seen in the froth. She couldn't seem to decipher anything. It looked like clouds in a coffee sky to her.

Chapter Twenty-Two

Having Graham to stay was nerve-wracking. She'd cleaned the box room thoroughly with Nick's help. Nick was of course very excited about having his father to stay. When she showed him into the room, Graham seemed too big for it and she knew that his feet would stick out of the bottom of the small bed.

'Are you going to be okay in here? An alternative would be sleeping on the bed settee in the conservatory.'

'I'll be fine. I'm grateful for you having me to stay at all.'

When he turned back towards her after putting his bag on the floor, they felt too close together in the small space. She smiled and scurried off to cover her unease at the feelings of desire that erupted through her body.

She let Nick enjoy the time with his dad. As she was cooking their evening meal, another safe option of quiche, chips and peas, she heard him relating the story of his first portrait sitting with Michael Bryant. Michael had come to the craft centre in the end, as he'd got another appointment in Borteen with Justin Sadler the solicitor.

'Mr Bryant looks scary but he's actually friendly,' said Nick. 'I took photos and made sketches. Come and see.'

Graham and Nick disappeared into the conservatory and Mandy could hear Graham making suitably positive comments about Nick's work.

At teatime, it struck her how they would again appear like a normal family to anyone looking through the window. They seemed to be able to talk easily about anything. After the meal, she suggested a game and Nick chose Monopoly. He said it was appropriate as his dad was looking for a house.

They all went to bed at the same time so there was no

time to spend alone with Graham and in a way Mandy was grateful.

She rushed down to Owl Corner early the next morning to make sure everything was prepared for the day. Romana was training Louise Stevens for her first Saturday as "the Saturday girl". Mandy assured them she'd be back after the property viewings that morning and left them to it.

By the time Mandy returned home to collect Graham for house-hunting, she had convinced herself she must stay detached and not get carried away with the romantic thoughts of a possible future with Graham after her encounter with Becky Finch. She'd given herself a firm talking to and told herself to just enjoy the house-hunting process with him and not expect anything else.

Graham was sitting in the kitchen when she returned to the house, an empty cereal bowl in front of him. He told her that Nick had gone into Sowden on the bus to buy a particular shade of paint he needed. Merlin came through the cat flap and mewed for his food. Mandy opened a tin, screwed her nose up at the fishy smell and put the cat's dish on the floor.

Then, Graham disconcerted her by mentioning her new style.

'Why the complete transformation by the way?'

She paused, hoping the heat in her cheeks would subside. Today she was wearing navy wide-legged trousers and a cream and blue patterned top with a high neck. She'd put a swing style navy jacket on top as the breeze was cold even though it was sunny. 'You're aware what my reputation's like in Borteen. I suddenly woke up to the fact that my image really wasn't me any more and so I decided it was time for a serious change of style.'

'Well, it really suits you.'

'Thank you. That's made my day.'

'I love to make someone's day.'

He smiled and despite her resolution, Mandy melted a little

inside. Graham smelled delicious with his freshly applied aftershave. *Keep it businesslike*, she reproached herself.

However, it seemed that the day wasn't going to go like that. Graham seemed in a very thoughtful mood as he sat at the breakfast bar. 'This move is really challenging me, even though I see the sense in it, even find it exciting.'

'Well it's a big step – new area, business, mother, son ... Are you sure it's the right thing for you?' She may as well play devil's advocate.

'I don't expect I'll be totally sure until it's happened and everyone in my life is happy with the outcome. It feels a huge responsibility. An enormous decision. And more than likely a huge investment too.'

'A chance to start afresh, maybe?'

'Yes. I've done it before, I can do it again ... I think.'

'Life has a habit of taking a different direction every now and then.'

'There's something you should know about me.'

Mandy felt her ears pricking up and her mind embroidering possible scenarios before he'd uttered any words. Prison record? Gay? Why did she think those?

'A few years ago, I had ... erm ... an episode, a breakdown, I guess some would call it. I fell off the planet for a while big time.'

His face was white, as if he feared her reaction. In her experience, it wasn't often a man admitted to something that could be deemed a weakness. Graham immediately went up in her estimation, not down as he obviously imagined he would from the look on his face.

'Do you know what caused it?' She smiled in what she hoped was an encouraging way.

'My wife told me she was pregnant.'

Mandy was terribly confused. He'd spoken the first time she'd met him about wanting to investigate if Nick was his son as he thought he would never have children. OMG had something gone wrong? Had his wife died in childbirth? Had the child died? She sat on the other stool next to him.

Graham had paused, maybe trying to decide what to say, or keep a lid on emotions, she couldn't tell. She remained silent, allowing him a moment, resisting the urge to reach out a hand to touch him as comfort and reassurance.

'I was overjoyed. For a moment, I floated up to the ceiling in bliss and then Trisha delivered the punch line ... It wasn't mine.'

Mandy gasped before she could stop her reaction. She was shocked, so goodness knows how he'd felt at the time. 'How devastating that must have been. Did she tell you whose it was?'

'Oh yes she did and it couldn't have been any worse. The baby had been fathered by my best friend and then business partner. They'd been having an affair behind my back.'

The shock increased. The poor man. 'Oh, Graham. I'm so sorry.'

They were silent for a moment and she finally put her hand over his.

'What did you do back then? Had you been married long?'

'Derek and I ran a health and safety consultancy business. We did surveys of business premises and procedures and then trained the staff to make any necessary changes. Derek was the best man at our wedding for goodness' sake. Trisha and I had been married three years.'

'The shock must've been awful.'

'Once Trisha admitted it, they took me to the cleaners. I lost half my house, couldn't face working with Derek any more, so my business went too. They run it together now. They walked off into the sunset ... a happy family ... and I really don't remember the six months that followed. I hardly left Mum and Dad's spare room. I think I scared them half to death, scared myself half to death too.'

'How utterly dreadful for you.'

144

Graham had turned his palm over and was now holding her hand, even though he appeared unaware of it as he spoke.

'It's a difficult thing to admit to, even now. When you've spent your whole life in control, trying to do well, the right thing ... and then, wham! It was as if someone had truly pulled the rug from underneath me.'

'Believe me, Graham, I understand all too well.'

His face was ashen by now and Mandy could feel he was shaking from reliving the memories.

'Look, we've got thirty minutes before our first house viewing, why don't I make some proper coffee before we go?' She tried to make light of it, but at the same time squeezed his hand. 'You look as if you could do with one.'

'Yes, please. Sorry about that. It somehow didn't feel right not to tell you. I'm hoping it doesn't affect any bid to be recognised officially as Nick's father.'

He let go of her hand and it was all she could do not to grasp on to it again.

'We all have ups and downs in our lives. I'm sure if you can show you have made a fresh start, can offer stability and a loving home, it will make a difference.'

'I'm hoping so.'

Graham seemed to recover after a strong cup of coffee. Mandy felt touched that he trusted her enough to make his confession. She wondered if he'd told her his story because of Nick or did he want her to know personally? She'd bitten back the urge to tell him about her own past.

Tam met them at the first property, a rambling and crumbling house on the outskirts of Sowden. Mandy could tell from the outset that although on paper the property fulfilled the brief – stream, outbuildings and house, it needed far too much work to be up and running in the timescales Graham was hoping for. They both left the viewing shaking their heads.

The second option was a dormer bungalow near the high street.

'I thought your mum might be able to go shopping from here,' said Tam.

Mandy felt dubious owing to the steepness of the streets around there. She had an awful vision of Mrs Frankley's wheelchair careering out of control down the hill. The house was fitted out for a disabled inhabitant though, with a stairlift to the upstairs bedrooms and various contraptions in the bathroom to make using it easier. Tam told them that the lady owner had recently died. Graham said he didn't discount this one, but it would mean finding a unit for gin production elsewhere and he was keen to have everything on the same site if possible.

However, Mandy did wonder if Tam had shown them the first two options to appear in contrast to the next offering. Had Tam been taking lessons from the property programmes on television where they saved the best until last?

Right at the top of the Borteen hillside, on the very edge of Pink Moor, this one was a huge bungalow with views across the bay. It had an outbuilding that was a hangar-like barn, which had been used to house the products for the owner's mail order business until he'd shut down. Mandy felt her disbelief multiply when Tam took them behind the possible gin distillery to show them a pool. According to Tam's information it was fed by a natural spring and there was a stream that headed over the ridge and down towards the town and beach. Graham's eyes showed his delight and surprise. He grasped Mandy's arm and squeezed his eyes tight shut. 'Trying not to get my hopes up.'

As they viewed the bungalow, Mandy couldn't help but imagine living there herself. The rooms were large and full of light. There was little furniture, as if someone had taken what they wanted and left the rest behind. Graham exclaimed over things he liked; the light-filled lounge, the large sociable kitchen and the things he wasn't quite as sure about; the size of the main bathroom, the arrangement of the bedrooms off a long corridor.

The barn, a short distance from the house, he declared a perfect size for the distillery. The water would need to be investigated to see if there were sufficient reserves for the business and also analysed to ensure it didn't contain any harmful additives or too much sodium. He'd also need to get the necessary permissions to use it. But it looked hopeful. Almost too good to be true.

The property seemed ideal; more than ideal with its views stretching away to the horizon over the sea.

'What are your mother's requirements?' asked Mandy.

'Flat as possible, easy access and exit, wet room, with hoist for the bad times. Bedroom and sitting room.'

The whole property had a run-down air to it, but it wouldn't take much to coax the place to life and adapt it to Mrs Frankley's needs.

Graham stopped at one point and grasped Mandy's hands. She noticed Tam pulling an "I told you so face" behind his back.

'Pinch me, Mandy. This is too good to be true, isn't it?'

He turned to Tam. 'Don't tell me this is way over my budget.'

'It's not. Bang on budget actually and no chain. When the mail order business failed, the owner couldn't meet the mortgage payments on this place and so it's been recently repossessed by the bank. They're looking for a quick sale.'

'Wow. Where do I sign?'

Mandy felt her eyes well up at his obvious delight.

'What is the property called again?' asked Graham.

'Bay Ridge Farm,' replied Tam.

'What do you think, Mandy? A range of Bay Ridge Farm themed gins?'

'Sounds good to me. I'm sure Nick can design an appropriate logo.'

Graham sat down on a bench in the ample garden, strategically positioned with a sea view. Mandy thought for one moment he was crying, but when she went to join him, she became aware that his shoulders were shaking with laughter.

'You okay?' she asked.

'More than okay. This feels so right. Just need that water to provide sufficient flow for our needs and to test safe to use then we could be all systems go. Mum will love this garden. I can just see her sitting here with Hazel.'

'Out of ten?' Mandy asked when they'd seen everything.

'Twelve and a half.'

'Wow. So, a serious contender?'

'There's some updating and a few adaptations for Mum, but it's next to perfect. Would you live here?'

She decided not to comment on the ambiguity of the question. 'It's a lovely property and as you say just needs a little decoration and updating. The setting is wonderful with the views over the bay. Your mum and Nick will want to get their paints out straight away. Yes, I'd say it's a good choice.'

'Poor Mum is going to have to take my opinion. It's a bit far for her to manage for just a visit.'

'I can see that might be difficult for her. Take a load of pictures on your phone and perhaps do a video. Would you like me to speak to her? Women always see different things to men.'

'That's a sexist comment.'

'Well whether it is or not, it's true. Men and women see things differently.'

'Anyway, despite the slur on my sex, yes please. I'd really appreciate you talking it through with Mum.'

'Consider it done.'

He stood up and pulled Mandy into a hug. 'Thanks for all your help.'

Tam was winking at her in the background and that was

the only thing that stopped her from sinking into his arms and holding on tight.

'But can it really be this easy?' There was a note of worry in his voice. He went off to have another look at the stream and the pool.

Mandy spoke to a now laughing Tam. 'He loves the property. You might have made a sale.'

'Think he might love you as well, so I hope you like the property too. She winked again, but Mandy felt the echo of Graham's words in her head. *But can it really be this easy?*

It seemed that on the property side it could. Graham rang Mandy at the end of the following week.

'Well, obviously surveys to do, water to fully test and permissions to get but I've said I want to buy Bay Ridge Farm!'

'Wow.'

'Mum says you talked her into being excited too, so thank you.'

'Completion?'

'My solicitor is confident it can be rushed through for a mid-June moving date, providing nothing bad shows up on the surveys and the water is good – initial results are encouraging according to Wendham who is working on the water aspect for me. So fingers crossed we are all systems go.'

They weren't initially going to sell the family home, the childhood home he'd returned to after he and Trisha had parted. They would rent it out. The property they were buying was empty and they had the money from his dad's estate and life insurance to cover the purchase.

Graham had told the staff at Frankley Gins who hadn't left already that the distillery would operate until July. He'd get his mum settled in Borteen and the barn ready first, before moving the gin making equipment. They were still working extra hours so the gin distillery could build up as much stock as possible to tide the suppliers over the transition to the new facility. With Big Al gone to his new warehouse job, Wendham and Graham were having to do most of the heavy work. Hazel was excited about her move of location and job. She'd been spending more time with Mrs Frankley anyway.

For once Graham was positive. The feeling that he was meant to move to Borteen was growing stronger all the time and was reinforced by everything working out.

Chapter Twenty-Three

Eight weeks later, Graham was surrounded by packing boxes when the doorbell sounded. He walked towards the front door. It was half glass, meaning the person visiting could clearly see you were on the way and there was no backing away unless you wanted to be exceedingly and obviously rude.

The unexpected visitor was Trisha. Graham had a rush of revulsion course through his body, which told him he was no way over what she had done. When he opened the door, she barged past him and into the lounge, when Graham would have refused her entry if he'd been quick enough.

'Derek says you're leaving Manchester.'

'How on earth did he get to know that?' Graham hadn't told many people, but then all at Frankley Gins knew and his mother might have spoken to someone who'd told Derek.

'Mutual friend I think.'

'Well, it's none of his, or your, business.' Why did Trisha still have this effect on him, like a knife being twisted in his gut? Remembered trauma. *Put it in a box and close the lid, Graham.* The voice in his head was now that of the expensive therapist his parents had employed to bring him back from the edge of the abyss, the brink of oblivion. It had taken a long time, but it had worked.

'I don't like to think of you going away, Graham.'

'Why on earth would you care?'

'I still love you.' She tossed her long black curls over her shoulder.

'Oh, come on. How can you say that after what you did? How dare you say that.' His gut had tightened painfully.

'I will always love you. I'm beginning to wonder if I made the biggest mistake of my life.'

The collar of his shirt felt too tight. 'Water under the bridge.'

'Not if we don't want it to be.'

Panic was pooling darkly in his stomach. He held up his hands in front of him, as if to ward her off. He didn't need this. 'Look, Trisha. I don't know what game you are playing here, but you made a choice. As far as I'm concerned that was a one-way choice, no going back.'

'No need to get angry.'

There were tears on her lashes. Bloody hell where was his mind heading? What greater revenge on his so-called friend than to nick Trisha back? *No, no, no! Graham put your head back on.*

'That's a bit rich, considering what you did. I'm leaving on Thursday. Bye, Trisha. Have a good life.' How was he going to get her out of the house?

'At least give me a forwarding address so I can send you a Christmas card.'

She wasn't to know he'd ripped up the last few years' Christmas cards in disgust. It was on his lips to tell her to save the postage, but logic told him she'd find him as soon as his new business address went live in any case.

'I'll send you a new address email when I do the business ones, but, Trisha, please no more confusing statements. You and I are over, finished, terminated, right? I would never be able to trust you again.'

'Never?' Her eyelashes were definitely fluttering at him in a flirtatious way.

'Absolutely and utterly never.'

Hazel appeared in the doorway looking like a rabbit caught in headlights. 'Mrs Frankley asks if everything is all right? We heard raised voices.'

'Everything is fine. Trisha is just on her way out,' said Graham.

Hazel turned to leave.

'Hazel would you stay please until Trisha has gone.'

Hazel stood still in the hallway and waited, still looking half scared to death.

Trisha began to snivel and it was all he could do not to

comfort her. After all, he'd never exactly fallen out of love with her. He hated what she'd done to him, but it had been her choice to turn her back on their relationship.

For a second, he was transported back to that moment she'd told him she was pregnant, that moment when his heart had soared in joy at the thought of being a parent and having a real family. That moment just before his heart had been beaten on the rocks and destroyed along with all his dreams for the future. *Close the lid of that box, mate. Hell is that way.*

'Time for you to go,' he said firmly.

Trisha flounced along the hallway and slammed the front door behind her.

'Thank you, Hazel, I'd better come and explain to Mum.'

Graham and his mother were moving to Borteen on 21 June with Hazel. Wendham would follow as soon as the distillery was packed up.

His mother looked pale and wan after the stresses of sorting through her belongings and deciding what to bring with her into her new life. He hoped she would settle in Borteen. In fact he hoped they all would.

The house move went smoothly. When they arrived, Graham was pleased that his mother found the bungalow much easier to move around in than the Manchester house – that was being rented partially furnished with items they didn't want to bring with them.

Mandy had insisted on cooking a meal for their first evening at her house. It was very kind of her, but Graham was so tired he would have preferred to have got the beds made up at Bay Ridge and had a rest. His mother was having difficulty steering her wheelchair, so he supposed she was feeling the same. However, she rallied when she saw Nick. Having a grandson was good for her. And Hazel was good for his mum he reflected as he watched her moving things closer to Ann. Hazel was helpful but not in an overbearing way.

*

When Mandy had heard that Hazel would be moving in with the Frankleys as carer to Ann, she had secretly feared the slim and dark-haired Hazel would have designs on Graham as a partner, but hearing the way she spoke about Wendham in her lilting Irish accent made her attraction to him obvious and Mandy relaxed. From what she could gather, Hazel had worked as a carer for several years after school. She said she'd got fed up of all the travelling between clients and the short amount of time she was allowed to spend with each person on her rota. For the last two years she'd combined a part-time job at Frankley Gins, where she'd become known as an expert at applying the bottle labels and packaging the gin, with a bar job in the evenings.

Mandy looked at Ann and saw how exhausted she looked. 'Mrs Frankley, would you prefer to stay here this evening? I'm sure you must be tired after the journey.'

'I wouldn't want to put you out, dear and I really can't manage stairs these days.'

'That's no problem. The conservatory has a bed settee and I have a small shower room downstairs.'

Ann looked at Graham, longing in her eyes.

'Mum, it might be easier and you can get to bed earlier, rather than waiting for me to sort things out.'

'Thank you so much, Mandy. I think I would like that, as long as you don't mind me going to bed very early.'

'Well, why don't I show you where everything is and then Nick can look after you while I go back to Bay Ridge with Graham and Hazel to help them with some unpacking. I'm sure Hazel can give me some overnight things for you.'

'Sounds wonderful.'

Graham smiled at her gratefully. 'As long as you're sure it's no trouble?'

'No trouble at all. You'll enjoy looking after your grandma, won't you, Nick?'

Nick smiled and nodded his answer.

Chapter Twenty-Four

Mandy and Nick helped with the unpacking as much as they could over the next few weeks. If she didn't know where Nick was, Mandy could almost guarantee that he would be at Bay Ridge Farm, either helping his father or spending time with his grandma.

It became a Sunday afternoon ritual to take Ann to the seafront. Mandy and Graham would stroll companionably along the promenade, while Nick and Hazel looked after Ann. Nick delighted in pushing his grandma's wheelchair fast along the paving, usually causing Ann to squeal in delight and Hazel to run after them with concern on her face.

On these walks with Graham there didn't seem any need for clever conversation. They were at peace with each other in silence, with the occasional observation about birds flying overhead or the weather.

Mandy loved these simple times with no agenda or complication. They would all walk to the beachside café and Nick had his regular berry smoothie as the others sipped hot coffee.

All seemed well with the world for now and even a gull stealing Mandy's cake one time couldn't dampen her contentment.

The moving of the distillery equipment had Graham terrified. A dent in the distillation cylinders or the boiler could be very costly. As the shiny tanks that produced his livelihood were winched into place on the back of the lorry, he held his breath. He hadn't reckoned on this part of the move being quite so stressful.

It was sad to be leaving this site that had links to his father but it felt right, especially now all of the Frankley

Gins employees had other work. He'd paid each of them a leaving bonus from the settlement he'd received from the site development company for giving up his lease early. A couple had turned up today, even Big Al, who had left a while back, to help sort everything for the move. Graham tried to pay them but they wouldn't hear of it – a sign he hoped that he must have done right by them in the end.

In the month Graham had been based in Borteen, he'd worked hard preparing the barn to house the distillery. Walls had been whitewashed with Nick's help, a new floor put in and the necessary plumbing sorted. Graham was exhausted but exhilarated at the same time.

The new distillery was more impressive than the one in Manchester, as it was twice as big. Graham had plans to incorporate visitors' rails and a raised viewing gallery which led off a small room he'd partitioned off for talks or showing videos. The reception area was resplendent with huge canvases painted by Nick of the still and boiler and a fantastic depiction of Graham and Wendham tasting gin. All had been produced from the sketches he'd made on his first visit to meet his grandma. These gave the impression that everything was more finished than it actually was at the moment.

Fitting out the factory was a fiddly business. The old floor space had been square and the new one oblong, so nothing seemed to fit comfortably. It took a good bit of jiggery pokery until the equipment was housed satisfactorily and logically, given the processes needed for gin production.

Graham was weary by the time everything was off the lorry and he could tell by the way Wendham was moving, that he was too.

'Let's make a late start tomorrow and then I reckon we'd better check our connections and flow, maybe run a test batch to make sure everything is working and we have no leaks.'

'Sounds good to me.' Wendham saluted.

They locked the heavy doors to the barn and went to order a takeaway for their evening meal. Wendham was living at the bungalow for the time being, until he could find his own place.

Frankley Gins was back in business.

Mandy went with Nick to visit the new distillery. The first thing anyone saw in the reception area were the paintings Graham had asked Nick to produce. They were very colourful and striking.

'Nick's pictures look amazing.'

'They do, don't they. I'm very proud of him.

Mandy bathed in the look of joy on Nick's face.

'Are you going to change the company name now you've moved?'

'No, Frankley Gins it is, because the brand is known. It doesn't stop us calling some of the new gins by different names relating to Borteen and Bay Ridge though. The possibilities are endless really.'

Nick was sketching the view and preoccupied, so Mandy asked Graham, 'Right decision?'

He turned to her, the light, bright in his eyes. 'So far, very good.'

'Is your mum happy?'

'We still need to get things to rights, but, yes, she thinks it was the right choice too. I do believe she's feeling brighter and she absolutely loves the bench in the garden, especially now we've put a bird feeder close by. We found a gardener and he's been at work so the grounds are looking fantastic. It's a very special place.'

'Is it working out with Hazel?'

'So far perfectly. Mum adores her and Hazel makes sure she remembers to take her medication on time and that she doesn't do anything that might result in her hurting herself. It's freed me up too and I don't just mean timewise. Mum took up a lot of headspace when I was worried about her at home alone when I was out at work, so I'm more relaxed.'

'That's fantastic.'

'We'll go over to the house for tea later and you can ask Mum how she's settling in yourself.' He raised his voice so that Nick took notice. 'How do you fancy a fun trip out this afternoon?'

'Where to?' Nick's eyes were shining.

'Wendham wants to investigate local flavours. We thought you might even show us those native juniper bushes you told me about. Not that we can use them, but it would be nice to see them nevertheless.'

'Cool. Can Mandy come?'

'Of course, and then it's tea and cake with Grandma.'

'Yeah.'

'What sort of thing are you looking for on this trip?' asked Mandy.

'Local herbs, plants, fruits. Anything we can use as a gin flavouring.'

'Surely they are the same everywhere in the country?'

'You'd be surprised at the subtle changes in flavour caused by differences in climate, water and soil.'

Nick looked excited. 'Pink Moor's a good place to start. Is gorse any good, what about rowan berries?'

Graham laughed at his son's enthusiasm and it warmed Mandy's heart to hear the easy banter between the two.

'Anything can be given a try. Wendham is thankfully knowledgeable about dangerous plants to stop us making any fatal mistakes and is a master at mixing flavours.'

Mandy added, 'On the far side of Pink Moor, there are fruit farms.'

'Great, we can visit those another time, maybe?'

She nodded.

'Today then we'll collect some botanicals and then Wendham will brew some test gins and liqueurs for us all to taste in a few days. What do you think?'

'Sounds exciting,' said Mandy.

'More grim gin,' said Nick. 'I'll enjoy searching for herbs and things though.'

'It's a fun experimental time we indulge in every now and then. If we hit on a good formula, we can repeat it on a larger scale to sell.'

'Like a treasure hunt?' asked Nick.

'Sure is, like the blank canvas when you start one of your paintings,' chipped in Wendham, coming into the building and high-fiving Nick.

Mandy was pleased to see Wendham again. He looked as tired as Graham did after the effort of fitting out the distillery. She wondered if he was aware of Graham's past troubles and background. She got the impression he was very protective of Graham any way.

The four of them headed out, walking further up the hill. On the way over the moor, Wendham began to sing in a deep baritone voice you would somehow suspect he had just from looking at him. Mandy joined in with "Donald Where's Your Troosers" and, eventually, self-consciously, Nick hummed along too. Graham was more reserved but she did catch him mouthing the words to a couple of the songs.

Wendham produced hessian bags from his pocket to carry the things they found. Nick was surprisingly good at identifying herbs.

They all spent a happy hour foraging. Mandy noted that Graham stayed close to her and helped her open her hessian bag when she struggled with it trying to put in some comfrey leaves. Graham had gloves, so he added some nettles. Did she imagine his eyes lingering on her a lot? She hoped she wasn't imagining it, because she knew she watched him all the time.

Wendham worked alongside Nick, and Mandy noticed that he subtly guided Nick to things he would have no doubt picked himself, but allowed Nick to think he'd discovered all on his own. Nick exclaimed aloud over pink mallow flowers, meadowsweet that tasted like cucumber and a few blue berries, which Wendham declared were early bilberries.

Wendham stowed the bags of collected items in the distillery and they went for tea with Graham's mother and Hazel at the bungalow. Mandy noted that Nick was no longer shy with his grandma. He'd been up to see her many times since she'd moved to Borteen. This afternoon, he rushed over to give her a hug and to exclaim in delight at the freshly baked lemon drizzle cake on the table, baked by Hazel to Mrs Frankley's instructions.

It somehow felt more formal being here than on their weekly walks at the seafront. There were still boxes piled behind the sofa, but the lounge was beginning to look homely already. Graham sat next to Mandy on the sofa and she luxuriated in the warmth of his leg next to hers. She watched the body language between Wendham and Hazel. The pair obviously fancied each other, but were still skirting around their attraction politely. Mandy wondered if people looking at herself and Graham saw a similar thing.

'How are you settling in?' she asked Ann.

'Surprisingly well. I didn't realise how our other house didn't help my movement. It's so much easier with everything on one level, wide doorways and lots of room in the kitchen. I feel brighter with the lovely view and of course being close to precious Nick.'

'I'm so pleased it's working out for you.'

Chapter Twenty-Five

The Guildhall gates on the High Street in Sowden had been agreed for their meeting place. It had all been arranged through the intermediary, Jonas. The date had been changed several times by Paul and each time she'd got a call to cancel the arrangements, Mandy's spirits had nosedived. She'd begun to think Paul had cold feet about meeting her and doubted it would ever really happen.

With hindsight, Mandy wondered whether this was too public a place for a reunion charged with so much emotion, particularly when there was a chance she might see someone she knew. Also, if things went wrong ... but she wouldn't think negatively ...

She'd added plenty of tissues to her bag, as she felt tearful just thinking about the meeting, goodness knows what she would feel when she actually saw Paul. Paul. It was still weird to actually have a name for her lost son.

She'd looked into one of the many decorative mirrors on the walls of Owl Corner and rearranged the pretty scarf she was wearing a hundred times before she set off for Sowden. Could she actually go through with this?

Her nervous tension threatened to overwhelm her on the drive over Pink Moor. It was as if those long ago events had happened only yesterday.

Amazing how much pain had resulted from a fumble on the beach.

Of course, she'd denied for ages that anything was going on, hiding the changes in her body by wearing baggy clothes. She was petrified that her parents, friends or teachers might suspect something.

She'd known she couldn't buy a pregnancy test in Borteen; everyone, bar the tourists, knew her. So, she'd taken the bus to Sowden. That journey across Pink Moor had seemed interminable with its twisty roads and potholes.

After the embarrassing purchase from a male assistant in the chemist, she'd done the test in a horrible public toilet. She had stayed locked in the smelly cubicle until her shock reached a level she could cope with.

Why had she been shocked, when, really, she'd known what was going on? Had even begun to feel the baby fluttering within her.

The journey home, *the bus of shame*, had felt like she was approaching the gallows. In fact, she'd contemplated not going home at all, but what were her alternatives? They felt limited. No money, no contacts outside of Borteen, in trouble.

Back in Borteen, the next stop had been the lifeguard station above the beach to ask after Cooper. She was told he'd gone back to uni in Australia and her enquiries about a forwarding address were met with gales of laughter by the leering guards. She went away, not wanting to tell them what was going on or to cause any fuss. No father for the baby either. Great. Although in truth she had never imagined that Cooper Green would stand by her. They had never been a serious couple, just a flirtation that got out of hand after an illicit shared bottle of wine on the beach. It had seemed harmless and fun at the time. She'd never imagined that that one night could dictate the course of the rest of her life.

She'd dragged her feet home to face the inevitable recriminations, the level of which even she had underestimated. Her father was incandescent in his rage.

Neither parent spoke to her for hours after her revelation and she wondered if she should just pack a bag and leave. Fond visions of finding Cooper in Australia and being greeted with joy and a marriage proposal drifted fleetingly through her mind, but she knew that she was well and truly alone to face the future, even if she could find the money for a plane ticket, which was unlikely.

Her relationship with her father had gone from bad to worse, as he made arrangements for her baby to be adopted at birth. He would brook no argument. She had no say in the matter. The baby would go as soon as it was born. It was best for the baby and best for her in the long run, so he said.

What about her? Her view? Her needs?

Her mother was just silent and tight-lipped. Mandy had always prayed that she would take her side, but it didn't happen.

She'd dared to ask her father once when she was nearing her term if she could keep the baby and he'd come so close to hitting her, his fist thudding into the door, that she was scared. Her mother was just quiet, had been for weeks, as if her level of disappointment in her daughter was too great to be voiced.

Despite all the fear and confusion, she affectionately called the baby growing within her "Bumpy". She was living daily with the movements of her child and the changes his growing wrought in her body. How could she bear to give her baby away?

Even now, she could feel the sensations from the time he was born – the pressure and bodily pain, followed by a delicious relief and a baby's cry.

She'd only been given time to gaze on his little red pinched face, to her mind already recognizable as a blend of herself and Cooper, as he yawned. Not long enough to decide on a name for him though, so "Bumpy" had morphed into "No Name".

No pictures.

No name.

No future with him.

No name.

No love given, just life.

No name.

No compassion.

No name.

No understanding.

No Name had been whisked away, wrapped in a white towel, screaming his displeasure to the hospital corridor. Then silence. She'd been left to deliver the afterbirth and sob. Even the midwives seemed to have been chosen to be particularly dispassionate and unsympathetic.

Part of her would always be missing, always be gone. She had a baby-sized hole in her heart and her soul cried out to her son.

No Name.

And now, she knew his name, or rather, the name someone else had given him. The person who'd bathed him, washed and dressed him, dried his tears, sent him off to his first day at school, listened to him reading his first words, waited for him in school playgrounds, known his habits, both good and bad, watched his steps towards adulthood. All the things she'd missed, been robbed of, could never get back.

Mandy parked the car in Sowden and hoped she'd driven safely when she'd been so preoccupied with her memories on the journey. She shook herself, wiped her tears away and adjusted her scarf once more, wishing she hadn't worn something that made her fidget. She was nervous, her hands shaking.

Her steps quickened as she walked along the High Street. Where was Paul? Would he be there by the Guildhall gates, or would he have thought again about meeting the mother who had let him be taken away from her. She couldn't really be called a mother, could she?

Then she saw a curly-headed young man by the huge metal gates and her breath caught in her throat. It was like stepping back in time twenty years. He looked so like his father, so like Cooper Green. He saw her, their eyes locked. He must have sensed it was her, or maybe the adoption agent had described her, and a grin lit up his whole face, then she was running. Instincts took over. She just wanted to hold him. Her baby.

Paul's smile was as warm and welcoming as her own, as she flew into his arms. They clung together like survivors from a sinking ship. She drank in the warmth, height and scent of him. He was a head taller than her, again just like his father.

Eventually, she pulled away just far enough to reach up and cup his face in her hands. She had produced this beautiful blond-haired man. Her baby. Although her initial reaction had suggested he was the spitting image of his father, she could now recognize her own mouth, her teeth and something about his eye and brow area that was like looking in the mirror.

'I hardly got to hold you when you were born, didn't get to even give you a name. They wouldn't let me keep you.'

'It's okay, it's all okay. Let's find somewhere to sit down and talk.'

A fleeting thought crossed her mind. Who was Paul and what did he really want? She pushed the doubt away into the recesses of her mind. She was determined to enjoy this precious time.

They walked to the nearby Crimson Sheep Café, arm in arm and sat at a small table with a red gingham tablecloth. Mandy went through the motions of ordering coffee as if this was just a normal outing for a mother and her son. When the waitress had gone to fetch their drinks, she looked across at Paul and drank in his features.

'You look so like your father.'

'I may do to you, but I can see myself in you too. I'd very much like you to tell me about my father and about yourself. Who was he?'

'He came to Borteen on the coast near here for the summer, twenty years ago to work as a lifeguard on the beach – Cooper.' For a moment, she could forget the pain and remember the wonderful feeling when Cooper had noticed her, had wanted to dance with her, touch her. Not one of her friends, not one of the tourists, but her. The glow of the feeling of being special in Cooper's eyes was still there inside.

Paul looked thoughtful. 'Did he know about me?'

'No. Once I'd finally admitted to my fifteen-year-old self that I was pregnant, he was long gone and I'd no way of contacting him. He was Australian, at university over there, had one of those lovely accents, your curls and the same cheeky look you have around your eyes.' She reached out her hand across the table and her heart felt fit to burst with joy when Paul linked his fingers with hers.

He grinned again, accentuating the cheeky look. 'Can I have his full name at least?'

'Cooper. Cooper Green.'

'So, Cooper Green: lifeguard, Australian and university student?' Paul looked thoughtful once more and then seemed to recover himself. He rubbed the back of Mandy's hand gently.

'Yes, he was a lifeguard for the summer in Borteen, but he was studying medicine at university in Australia.'

'I wonder what became of him?'

'I'm afraid I don't know. I never saw him again. The agent said your adoptive parents had died.'

'Yes, very quickly and both of them ... last year from cancer. Incredibly sad. He rubbed at his eyes. But they had launched my sister and I into the world, given us a great loving childhood and good life principles to follow.'

'I always hoped you'd have lots of love in your life.' The words caught in Mandy's throat.

'Hugs galore.' He smiled.

'I'm so glad you had nice parents. And a sister?' The ache of lost opportunity was burning inside her. She'd missed so much.

'My sister is June. She was adopted too.'

'Are you close?'

'Very. She's great – my best friend.'

'You can't imagine how happy knowing these details makes me. I've wondered about you every day, tormented myself with imaginings.'

She looked at the lovely man in front of her and couldn't help but think "I produced this man". My baby all grown up. How could that be? She battled regrets that she'd missed all those years of him growing up and was alarmed to find tears returning to run down her face.

He squeezed her hand and his dear face grew serious. 'It must have been very hard for you.'

'My father insisted that I gave you up. I hated him for it, even though I can see now that he was thinking of both you and me. I was only fifteen, barely out of childhood myself. But his actions made ... still make me ... rebel. I refused to carry on with school and got jobs serving in shops and cafés. He was distraught, but I felt I needed to punish him for making me give up my child. I couldn't forgive him, even on the day he died. Yet, how can I regret any of it when I look at you now? I just hope you don't hate me for what I did.'

'Hate you? Why on earth would I hate you? I've had a great life up to now, great parents, a lovely sister. I'm happy and grounded ... and now I've found my birth mum – bonus!'

She sat silently as she battled her emotions yet again.

'Was your own mother around when you were pregnant?' Paul asked.

'Yes, she never really said anything to me. She let Dad take the lead. She lives on the south coast with my aunt. We exchange Christmas and birthday cards.'

'Will you tell her you've met me?'

Mandy had to think about that one. 'I may well do. I still don't really know what she thought about what happened. Do you want me to give her your contact details – she's your grandma after all?'

'If it's not too painful or difficult, yes please. I'd like to meet her if I can.'

Mandy nodded her agreement. 'What are you doing in your life now? Sorry this must seem like Twenty Questions.'

'I'm at uni in Cardiff – medicine.'

'Wow! You're going to be a doctor like your father? At least he must be if he finished university in the end.'

'Hope to be. It's a long apprenticeship.'

'And your sister?'

'June, she's a year younger than me. She's married with two little ones already – twins. She's been very hard hit by the death of our parents.'

'I'm sure.' It was Mandy's turn to touch Paul's hand. In fact when she touched his skin, she didn't want to stop. He seemed to sense this and held her hand properly with a grin on his face.

'I'm finding myself fascinated in my studies by genetics, inherited traits and illnesses. Another reason I wanted to contact you. I'm sorry I chickened out so many times and changed the date of our meeting. I needn't have worried – you are lovely.'

She smiled because she didn't think she could say any more without the tears flowing again.

'Tell me more about you,' asked Paul.

'I've lived in Borteen all of my life. I run a craft centre, Owl Corner Crafts at the end of the promenade. I'm currently foster mum to an abandoned teenager.'

'Married?'

'Never.'

'But you have someone special, I hope?'

'Hopeful is just how I'd describe it at the moment.' She felt a lurch inside as it dawned on her that's just how she felt about Graham – hopeful.

Mandy didn't want the meeting with Paul to end but knew realistically it had to. She wrote her address, email and phone numbers carefully on the back of one of the craft centre cards to give to him. The fear was, that having had this tantalizing glimpse of her son, that he would never contact her again, would maybe have found her wanting in some way, or was in reality angry, underneath the politeness, at what she had done after all.

She was relieved when he wrote down his contact details too. His handwriting was neat and easy to read.

'You'll have to change that before you become a doctor.'

'Change what?'

'Your handwriting. I've never known a doctor yet whose handwriting was legible.'

They laughed together and it felt good.

Paul hugged her again as they left the café. 'It's been great to meet you. Do you know I don't know what to call you.'

'It's a strange one, isn't it? Twenty years without each other and yet the same blood flows through our veins.'

'Would you mind awfully if I call you Mum?'

She clung to him until her tears of joy dried on his T-shirt.

'Maybe you could come to Cardiff for a visit next time?'

'I would love that.' He must not think she was too bad after all.

Having met her son, Mandy was once more full of emotion. She was grateful for the opportunity of putting a few ghosts to rest. No longer did she have to worry about her son being killed or maimed in childhood, that he hated her for giving him away, that he'd had a dreadful childhood – all of these could be forgotten.

Paul was whole, well and nurtured by his adoptive parents and what's more he wanted to know her, his birth mother. She was overjoyed, but also sad that she had missed out on all of those years of parenthood. Paul had given her copies of some photographs of him at various stages in his life and she had lost count of the times she'd looked at them. She intended to frame them in one of her favourite frames from the craft centre.

She hugged herself in disbelief that she'd met Paul. Life was good.

This feeling was amplified when she found a friend request from Paul on her Facebook account that evening and a long email telling her more about himself. All was well in her world. Maybe she would be brave and tell Graham all about her son. After all, if there was to be a chance of a relationship between them then honesty would be key ...

Earlier the same day, Graham was happy and excited. Everything was working out. His mum was happy at Bay Ridge Farm. Hazel had settled to her new role seamlessly. Wendham had declared himself content and had that sparkle in his eye which Graham took to mean he was hopeful of furthering his relationship with Hazel.

A card in the newsagent's window had resulted in workers to train for the roles in the distillery. They were hours away from bottling the first Borteen distillation. The sun was shining for those sunny days at the beach his mother craved. If he wasn't mistaken, Mandy was beginning to look on him as more than just Nick's dad. Things were coming together at last and he, for once, felt hopeful about the future.

Graham hummed to himself as he drove over Pink Moor to Sowden. The new business premises were ideal. The new living accommodation would be just right, when he'd put in a few ramps for his mother's wheelchair and newly purchased motorised scooter. He felt more settled owning rather than renting the property; no one could evict him at what felt like a moment's notice again. A tenant had been found for the house in Manchester.

He was getting to know his son and maybe, if the plans went well, could even have him living with him at some point soon and, dare he dream it ... Mandy too? He didn't want to count his chickens there, but they were at least good friends and hopefully would remain so. He was intrigued by the feelings he'd begun to experience near to her. Could she be the love of his life? Could he give love a second chance?

Determined to buy some new clothes for his new life and maybe a treat for his mother too, he parked in the car park he'd used when they'd been for pizza here. Whistling quietly to himself, he began to explore the unfamiliar town.

As if he'd performed some sort of magic trick, he caught sight of Mandy up ahead, walking briskly along the High Street. He hastened his steps to catch up with her, a smile on his face already. He toyed with the possibility of asking her out for a proper date. It was time he showed her what he was feeling and thinking.

The smile and his dream for the future died as she began to run and was enveloped in the arms of an unknown man. They clung together in obvious joy.

Graham stopped abruptly, gulping back an emotion he couldn't name and turned away. He walked blindly up an alleyway off the high street, unseeing, uncaring … His good mood had evaporated. Maybe the Mandy part of his future wasn't going to happen after all. He was a fool.

Chapter Twenty-Six

Mandy and Nick were having tea at Bay Ridge Farm for Ann's birthday on 4 August. Mandy had the impression that something was wrong with Graham as soon as she walked into the bungalow. Instead of the long lingering looks he'd been giving her of late, he was avoiding looking at her at all.

Nick gave his grandma an enthusiastic hug and presented her with cards and presents from himself and Mandy. Flushed with the success of the reception paintings for the distillery and the feedback Michael Bryant had given on his portrait, Nick had done a painting of his grandma. He'd based it on a photograph he'd taken of her looking out of the window at Bay Ridge Farm.

Ann was delighted and insisted that Graham hang it above the fireplace straight away, removing the picture of a countryside scene that was there already. Mandy's silk scarf offering was also admired and placed around Ann's neck with care. Mandy was at least never short of present options from the craft centre.

Wendham was also invited to the party and was talking about the things still left to do in the distillery, in between stealing glances at Hazel.

'I know someone who would be able to help you with some high-class woodwork,' said Mandy, in response to Wendham saying what needed to be finished. 'Carver Rogers. I was at school with him. He does commissions for churches, stately homes and such. I sell some of his work in the craft centre at times. I'll look up his number for you. Don't be put off by his manner. He's a bit of the strong, silent type, but he'll deliver and he's really good with wood.' She took out her phone and scrolled through her address book.

'Okay, great. Very appropriate name.' Wendham took down Carver's number.

Graham didn't sound all that interested, which in itself seemed odd.

'Is everything going well with the distillery?' She pointedly addressed Graham this time.

'Yes, all coming together.'

Graham was definitely different with her today. She couldn't quite put her finger on what had changed, but his conversation was more clipped, not as open and friendly. Maybe he was just preoccupied with everything going on in his life. But somehow the little niggle that something was wrong between the two of them wouldn't go away. She began to feel bewildered as she searched her memory banks for something she could possibly have done wrong.

Graham was gutted. He hadn't been able to stop the vision of Mandy in that man's arms leaping into his head as he spoke to her today. He'd seen a look of confusion pass over her face. Yes, he was talking to her in a different, guarded way. How could he help it? He'd been so badly betrayed by Trisha and just when he thought he could risk his heart again – wham!

The shutters had been firmly re-erected. He was doing well. He couldn't risk going downhill again, just couldn't. Yet, was the darkness beckoning to him from just over there? He knew he had to recover his equilibrium; it wasn't fair to put his mother through a load of angst yet again.

And yet …

Wasn't he judging without finding out the truth? And he had to stay on side with Mandy as she was effectively mother to his son at the moment. He tried a different tack, diverting the conversation to safer subjects.

As he'd designed the layout of the new business premises, he'd built in a factor he'd been contemplating for a while, the potential for factory tours. He'd seen other distilleries, particularly in Scotland, make this a part of their marketing strategy. People actually on site seeing the product being made must help sales. All it took was some extra walkways and railings, so that visitors could see what was going on, but not interfere with production in any way. He talked now about his plans and how he hoped to attract the Borteen holiday season tourists. It was a little late for this year, but they could still have a go and see how things went and refine the plans for the following year.

'You'll need tour guides,' said Mandy.

'I will. If you have anyone to recommend, I'd appreciate it.'

He still wasn't meeting her eyes when he spoke, focussing somewhere over her head. Once again, she tried to think if she'd done or said something to make Graham act like this.

'I'll put my thinking cap on.'

'Maybe some kids from school?' commented Nick.

'Hmm. Not sure how the parents would take underage children giving tours of a gin distillery though, mate.'

'Good point.'

'Have you produced any gin since you've been here?' asked Mandy. 'I'm curious if you think there are differences to that made at your other place?'

Wendham smiled. 'I've just brought over a couple of test samples. I thought a birthday party might be a good time to try them.' He went over to the kitchen cupboard and took out some glasses. Graham joined him and they took time to prepare the drinks.

The glass Graham gave to her from the tray of drinks was beautiful, wide bodied, long-stemmed. She'd only ever had a gin and tonic in a straight-sided glass with lemon. Graham had put an edible pansy on top of the liquid that he'd mixed, he also added a nasturtium, a coriander leaf and a slice of orange. The gin smelt different to anything else she'd ever tried. And how it tasted? Wow. The flavour assaulted her senses.

By the time Graham had handed out the other drinks, the only seat left was next to her on the small sofa. He sat down, seemingly at pains to leave a gap between them. This gesture upset her. It felt as if he was stabbing a pin in the tentative dreams she'd had about them possibly being a couple and looking after Nick together.

It wasn't a large piece of furniture and, eventually and inevitably, his leg pushed up against hers. She held her breath to see if he would move away. Sure enough, he did and it physically hurt her to realise he'd inched away deliberately.

'This gin is amazing,' she said, trying to cover up her sadness.

'Glad you like it.'

They all toasted Ann's birthday. Nick had squash in his glass, but swilled it around as if it was gin too.

'Are you settling in here?' she asked, yet again. She'd lost count of the number of times she'd asked him that question over the weeks and it made her feel idiotic, but she had to try to break through his funny mood somehow.

'Yes, I think so. It's nice to be so close to the business and Mum is loving the views and the sea air.

She sipped her drink.

He sipped his drink.

Wendham and Nick were discussing football, Hazel was listening and Ann was laughing at their enthusiasm and antagonism about different teams.

The conversation, which normally flowed easily between Graham and Mandy, had been stilled by their close proximity to each other and Graham's strange mood today.

'Man—'

'Grah—'

They both spoke together and then laughed. It broke the ice a little.

'You first,' said Graham.

'I wanted to tell you about something. Something that has just happened, but I'm worried it might change your opinion of me.' As if something hadn't already driven a wedge between them and she still couldn't fathom what it was.

'Well I suppose you won't know unless you tell me.' He was pointedly staring ahead, looking through the window towards the view.

'I've got a son too,' she whispered. She looked down at her knees in embarrassment but was aware of Graham's head jerking round to face her. The others were too absorbed in the football conversation to notice.

'Now that is a little confusing. Where is he? Why isn't he here? How old is he?'

Mandy had been itching to tell Graham about this, but his attitude today had made her wary. Now she had his full attention, she decided she had nothing to lose by telling him everything. After all, there weren't many people she felt she could talk to about Paul. 'I was forced to give him away when I was fifteen. He's just recently found me through an adoption agency and we met a couple of days ago.'

Graham's hand shot out and grasped her knee, the expression on his face incredulous. 'The guy in Sowden?'

'You saw us?' They were looking directly at each other now.

'Yes. I'd gone clothes shopping. I spotted you up ahead of me, had just decided to catch you up to ask you to come out to dinner with me, when I saw you fling yourself into the arms of another man.'

Things began to make sense. 'Is that why you've been strange with me today?'

'Not strange I hope ... more guarded.'

Mandy couldn't help but laugh. 'Couldn't you tell he was a very young man? I'm not in the habit of dating twenty-year-olds.'

'I couldn't see that much from a distance, just you in another man's arms. I didn't wait around to see any more.'

'Oh, Graham! Here's me thinking you'd begun to believe the rumours about me, that you'd gone off me.'

'No way, Mandy. It made me realise how much I ... like you. I didn't enjoy seeing you in the arms of another man.'

She smiled at him then pushed against his shoulder playfully.

There was no time to continue the conversation as Wendham came into the room at that moment, carrying a birthday cake with the candles blazing. They sang "Happy Birthday" to Ann and the relief Mandy felt lent a joyful tone to her singing. Graham pressed his leg against hers. Deliberately this time.

Chapter Twenty-Seven

It was strange that if you lived on the doorstep of a beach, you didn't seem to use it in the same way as if you had travelled to the seaside for a holiday. These days, Mandy was always rushing around trying to keep up with the various demands of her life and business, so she definitely didn't take enough time to enjoy the sand.

For Graham, who claimed he'd never heard of Borteen before he received Sally Crossten's letter, the town and the beach were a new novelty and ripe for exploration.

Even Nick lifted his eyes heavenward when Graham suggested an afternoon together on the beach.

'Oh come on you two, indulge me. It's a lovely day and I want to sit on warm sand, build a sandcastle, explore some rock pools and jump some waves.'

The light in Graham's dark green eyes made Mandy wonder if he was remembering family holidays when he was young.

Nick shrugged and in unvoiced agreement, the two of them went along with Graham's plans.

Mandy tried to imagine she was on holiday as she packed her rucksack with a selection of rolls, cakes and bottled water.

Graham produced an old blanket from his car and bought each of them a bucket and spade, plus a fishing net for the rock pools.

They walked over to the less commercialised end of the beach, where there were pools for Graham to explore.

When they'd established a camp, probably looking to all the world like a husband, wife and son on holiday, Graham took Nick off to explore the rock pools and Mandy lay back and looked at the sky. It was a rare moment of inactivity.

She spent her life rushing around, thinking ahead, planning themes and marketing campaigns for the craft centre and these days taking more care over meals for Nick and herself. She hadn't bothered too much when she was living on her own.

What happened to the days when she used to bring a towel to the beach and read? Come to think of it, when was the last time she'd read a novel? She vowed to put this simple indulgence back into her routine. Routine? Who was she kidding? Her life seemed chaotic right now.

The clouds scudded overhead in the blue sky. She was vaguely aware of Nick and Graham nearby discussing the colour of crab shells. It was lovely hearing them talking like this and she was pleased for both of them that they seemed to be building a good relationship.

Mandy was enjoying getting to know Paul better through their emails and Facebook posts too. She was hopeful it wouldn't be long until she could invite Paul to spend a weekend in Borteen and then she could introduce her son to Graham and Nick and her family could be complete.

The next thing she knew, she was waking up. There was a huge sandcastle below her feet and a moat all around their camp. She must have been sleeping for a good while. *OMG. I hope I wasn't snoring!*

Graham's face came into view as he leaned over her laughing.

'Hi sleepyhead.'

'Hi yourself. I'm not even going to ask if I was snoring.'

'You must have been exhausted. I'm too much of a gentleman to mention a lady's habits when she's asleep.'

She felt the heat flood her face. 'I don't ever seem to stop these days. What happened to time? Who speeded things up?'

'I know the feeling, but this is our mini holiday.'

He leaned a little closer.

'Where's Nick?'

'I'm timing him running to the far end of the beach and back.' He glanced at his watch.

'Really?'

'Yes, cunning plan to get you to myself for a few moments.'

'Really?' She'd obviously lost the art of normal speech while she'd been asleep. 'So we can talk about Nick?'

'Mandy, please!'

'Graham?' Her heart began to boom. There was something about the look in his eyes.

'I'm a little tongue-tied like a schoolboy.' He blocked out the sun as he leaned in and gently pressed his lips against hers.

The pressure was infinitesimal as if he feared she would shatter if he applied any more weight, but the sparks from the contact radiated throughout her body and desire forked up her spine. She raised a hand to pull him closer. The next kiss was savoured and deeper. Graham glanced across the beach.

'He's coming back.'

'Pity.' Her voice sounded deep and throaty.

They pulled apart.

When Nick arrived red and breathless, he flopped down on the blanket and Graham read the time from his stopwatch.

'I'll have another go later, see if I can go even faster. We could have a race, Dad.'

'Maybe after lunch,' said Graham, mouthing *no way* to Mandy behind his hand.

Mandy laid the picnic on a clean towel to avoid the sand that was accumulating on the blanket. They sat companionably munching sandwiches and cake and Mandy was again struck by the ideal family scenario ... and the fact that Graham had kissed her! She put her fingers to her lips and looked at Graham. His expression and smile told her he knew what she was thinking.

The tide had turned. It took a fair while to get up the beach at Borteen, but their little camp wouldn't survive for too much longer. Pity, because Mandy wanted this time to go on forever.

Graham started to pack up their things. 'Let's make another camp higher up the beach and go and jump some waves.'

'I don't want to get wet,' she moaned.

'Come on, it will be fun.'

They were holding hands and jumping the surf and it was actually fun. It was also great holding Graham's hand, but the laughter was good too.

He kept hold of her hand as they trailed back up the beach and didn't release it until they sat back down on the rug. Mandy hoped that Nick hadn't noticed.

'I'm so glad I've managed to have summer in Borteen Bay.'

'It is pretty special here when the weather behaves.' She stretched her arms overhead and felt Graham move closer.

Nick was enjoying making sand sculptures. Mandy marvelled that he was almost as good at those as he was at painting. Graham caught hold of her hand again and held it in the gap between them.

The beach was thronged with holidaymakers. Mandy commented that it was sad that the locals were usually so busy manning their businesses in the summer that they hardly made it to the beach. In fact, some of the seasonal shop owners spent their winters in sunnier climes like Spain, because they hadn't been able to take advantage of the Borteen summer while earning their living.

Nick announced he was off to get a bucket of seawater for the fantasy castle moat he had designed and headed off down the beach with a bucket.

Graham watched him go. Then he turned to Mandy with a serious look on his face. 'Marry me.'

Mandy froze in shock. 'What?'

'Marry me. We make a fantastic family, you, me and Nick. Marry me and then we can adopt Nick together and be a family. It would be fantastic don't you think?'

'Whoa! Erm … I don't quite know how to say this, Graham, but when I marry, I hope it will be for love … not, not … convenience.'

'Convenience? No – I mean I care for you, Mandy and those feelings are getting deeper every day. I see no reason why we can't grow to love one another, do you?'

Mandy was on her feet now. Her brain couldn't cope with the implications of Graham's proposal. Although it hadn't really been a proposal, not the sort she'd always imagined getting anyway. It wasn't the down on one knee, declaration of love and wanting to spend eternity with you she'd always hoped for.

Yes, she'd started to flirt with Graham, they'd shared that brief kiss earlier. She had no doubt she fancied him and suspected that he was attracted to her too, but there'd been no build up to this, not even a proper kiss or cuddle, just the rapid, tentative kisses of earlier and holding hands. It felt too fast, too soon, too, she kept coming back to the word "convenient". As if Graham thought he had a ready-made family and Mandy would "do" as the mother and wife.

She looked down at his bewildered face and knew that his error had begun to dawn on him. He leapt to his feet and tried to pull her against him, but Mandy was having none of it. She glanced down the beach to see where Nick was. He was paddling and looking out to sea, so she didn't need to worry about him.

'Mandy, I'm sorry that was clumsy. I didn't mean it in the "convenient" way.'

'Really?'

'Really.'

'Well I'm sorry, Graham, but it came out in the "convenient" way. Look. I'm just going to go home now.' She began collecting her things, aware that Graham looked distraught. 'I'll leave you to bring Nick home later.'

'Mandy …'

She shrugged off his hand in his attempt to grasp her arm and stop her leaving. 'Best not say any more, Graham. Please.'

She rushed up the beach, stubbing her toe on the beach steps and swearing under her breath. She needed to get home. It wasn't until she was safely locked in and standing in the shower that the tears began to fall uncontrollably.

Chapter Twenty-Eight

Mandy was so restless after the "incident" on the beach, that she couldn't stay in the house, besides the fact she didn't want to have to speak to Graham when he returned with Nick later. Her heart hammered and her mind couldn't order the confused thoughts teeming through her head.

After a brisk walk the long way around to avoid any route Graham and Nick might take, Mandy went to the craft centre and told Romana she could leave early. She turned the sign to closed and locked the door.

She then swept the wooden floor of Owl Corner Crafts as if her life depended on it, spiders ran for the hills and no speck of dirt escaped her wrath! When she'd finished the floor, she started on the tiles in the toilet. She didn't trust herself to dust the shelves as she knew she was too angry and there were lots of fragile items.

The little demon in her head was speaking to her again. *What are the chances of a decent guy like Graham taking up with you long term anyway?* Had changing her dress, make-up and hair really made that much of a difference? Was this version of herself still one that would attract the wrong men, even though she'd told herself she'd changed? That she no longer wanted to be that Mandy.

She wanted to be a Mandy who attracted and kept a caring guy like Graham. No, she wanted to be the kind of girl who attracted Graham, full stop. But attracted a guy like Graham because of who she was, not for the convenience of being a mum for Nick.

How dare Graham Frankley, gin maker, get under her skin like this? She didn't let men get to her. She took a dance, a meal, a visit to the cinema, a drink and maybe sex and then moved on when they tried to get serious. She did not let them get to her. She stayed aloof, detached, rose above emotional involvement, but not it seemed this time, not now she'd met Graham Frankley.

How dare he? She was so annoyed with herself, so annoyed with him. And worst of all she knew she was so angry because she had begun to care about Graham, had begun to imagine the possibilities of exactly what he had been suggesting on the beach that Mandy, Graham and Nick could be a proper family unit, that they could adopt Nick as their son and become a family, that she could have the happy ever after she'd always dreamed of after all.

Damn Graham and his hasty proposal. Mandy didn't feel she could ever take any advances from him seriously now, even if he was brave enough to ever try again.

Damn, damn, damn! Life was so unfair.

Graham was furious with himself. He'd been stupid and clumsy. He should have known that Mandy would want a proper romance, declarations of love, not a cold marriage proposal. It had all seemed so simple in his head before he blurted it out. So logical. He'd been a complete and utter idiot.

Nick was oblivious to the undercurrent as they walked back to Mandy's. Graham wasn't surprised that she wasn't at home when they got back to the house.

He said his goodbyes to Nick and drove further up the hill to home, his mind whirring with ifs, buts and maybes.

Everything was eclipsed when he got home and found his mother on the floor. She'd fallen and been unable to get up. Hazel was so upset. She said she'd only popped out to get some milk. When Graham tried to move Ann, she yelped. He declared she might have done some serious damage and dialled 999 instead.

They were waiting at the hospital for the A&E consultant and Graham knew he was quieter than normal. He hoped his mum thought it was because he was worried about her. However, even though she was in pain, Ann seemed to know there was something wrong with him.

'What's got to you today, Graham?'

'Nothing, Mum.'

She looked at him in just the way she had when he'd been a young boy. 'Oh yes, nothing?'

'All right.' He sighed. 'I did something silly.'

'And what might that be?'

'I asked Mandy to marry me.'

Her face changed, her smile sunny. 'But that's wonderful.'

'Nope. She wasn't having any of it.'

'Oh dear. Why not? I think you two are perfect together.'

'So do I, but I was a complete idiot. She, understandably, wants the whole romance thing and I blurted out a sterile proposal and mentioned us being great parents for Nick. She thought it was just a proposal of convenience, not love.'

'*Oops!* But speaking as your mother, even though I already adore Mandy and think you'd be perfect together, maybe I'd better be devil's advocate and ask you some obvious questions.'

'Go on then …'

'Why this girl? Is it just because she's been kind to your son?'

'No, it's the light in her eyes, the wideness of her smile, the way she moves, as if she did a lot of ballet when she was young.'

His mother smiled her encouragement for him to continue.

'It's her caring attitude and the way she speaks to everyone, possibly because she knows lots of people in this town, but still she takes the time. There's a lot more to her than I know, hidden depths, hidden pain. Would I have recognised that in the old days, before I had my bad patch? She has depth, in a way that Trisha hasn't. I thought I loved Trisha, thought I wanted to spend the rest of my life with her, but even if

I put aside her betrayal and infidelity, I now recognise that something was missing. We muddled along very well together, had similar interests, but that soulmate thing I used to think was a load of twaddle was missing. I do hope she's found that with Derek. After all I still care about her, despite all the upset.'

His mother was nodding. 'Sounds very much to me like a bad case of being in love with Mandy.'

Well he was convinced that he'd blown his chance ... cocked it up completely. 'So, having found a woman I would like to spend the rest of my life with, how do I go about wooing her now? And can she ever feel that same way about me? This love thing isn't simple, is it?'

'Never is son, never is.'

The consultant chose that moment to come into the hospital bay, brandishing his mum's X-rays.

Chapter Twenty-Nine

Nick came downstairs in his pyjamas having taken an after beach shower. He was happy, Mandy could tell by his whole demeanour. He'd enjoyed being on the beach with Graham. It wasn't fair to burst his bubble by being grumpy about the abrupt end to her enjoyment of the afternoon.

'Can I watch TV?'

'Sure you can. I'm just popping out for a moment to get some things for tea.'

Nick sat down and Merlin immediately leapt up next to him on the sofa.

Dilemma time. Did she go and tell Graham she was sorry and try to smooth things over? No, her emotions were too raw. She'd go and get some pies from the bakery on the high street. At least then she would have the walk there and have the walk back to give her time to calm down. Nick need never know. But then, he'd be sure to be aware of a strained atmosphere between herself and Graham next time they were together.

Wendham was in the bakery. Mandy groaned because he'd spotted her before she could duck out of the shop. He was one of the last people she wanted to meet right now, being as he lived with Graham.

'Hi, Mandy. A right to-do up at the house.'

'What do you mean?'

'Graham found his mum on the floor. We've had blue flashing lights.'

'Is she okay?'

'Been carted off to Sowden General Hospital. They think she's maybe broken her hip.'

'Oh, no, how awful.'

'Hazel feels dreadful – she'd only popped out for milk.'

Mandy bought her pies, said a rushed goodbye, and after a moment of indecision, stopped on the seafront to send a text to Graham: *Heard about your mum. Hoping things not too bad.*

He texted back almost immediately: *Thank you. I do hope you and me are still okay?*

She contemplated what to say and decided to text one of Nick's expressions: *We're sound!* with an added smiley face. She would have to find a way of being easy in Graham's company in the future so she may as well start now.

Poor Mrs Frankley's accident made it easier the first time she saw Graham after their argument. The conversation could focus on his mother and her hip, rather than be intense about them. It was almost as if the poor woman had sacrificed herself to preserve their relationship, fragile as it now felt. Thankfully Ann's hip was badly bruised but not broken, so she hoped to be home soon. They hadn't been happy with her blood pressure readings and wanted to observe her for a couple of days.

Nick had been really upset about his grandmother's accident and made her a lovely card. Which of course she fussed over and got the nurses to admire.

Graham didn't raise his eyes to meet hers. Their conversation on the beach had done serious damage. Nick didn't appear to notice anything, but Mrs Frankley was different.

'Nick, could you get me some chocolate out of the vending machine in reception?' she asked. 'Get yourself a bar too.' She handed him some money and he went off happily on his errand.

Ann didn't waste any time getting to the point. 'What's going on with you two today?'

Graham's head jerked up and he seemed to give his mother a strange look. 'Whatever do you mean?'

'Come on, I've known you for thirty-six years. I can tell when you're unhappy about something. You two haven't exchanged a direct word or looked at each other since you came in.'

'Mum, leave it please.'

Ann glared at him, then turned to Mandy. 'Are you going to tell me what's going on?'

'We had a disagreement and I think we both need a little while to get over it.'

'Well see that you do. That poor child has had enough trauma in his life without the two people he needs most in the world falling out.'

Nick again. Mandy loved the lad, but why did it seem that the world was revolving around him these days? What about *her* needs, *her* dreams, *her* hopes? She wanted to run from the room, pack a bag and escape to the Outer Hebrides. Why there she hadn't a clue, but that was the location that came to mind. She'd still have to take herself along with her though, so would she be any happier?

'Now, Graham, go and find Nick. I want a word with Mandy.'

Oh, dear! Was she about to get a lecture? Graham met her eyes at last and shrugged. He walked off towards the ward entrance before looking back and frowning at his mother.

Mandy sat down on the chair next to Ann's bed.

'He's upset you, hasn't he?'

'Yes, but with hindsight he probably didn't mean to. I just took it the wrong way.'

'You do know he's been hurt rather badly before?'

'Yes, we've had the conversation about past relationships.'

'Did he tell you what happened afterwards?'

Ann's eyes had become haunted, her lips set in a firm line, as if she was trying to hold back tears.

'Yes.'

'Oh good. As a mother, you only want the best for your children, don't you?'

'I understand that.' She'd like to tell Mrs Frankley about Paul, but now didn't seem the right time.

Ann obviously read her expression as meaning something else.

'I didn't mean to upset you too. I know you wouldn't hurt Graham if you could help it and maybe you don't want children. Oh, dear. I think I'd better shut up.'

Mandy took a few moments to recover herself.

'Look, Ann, I can't make any promises about the future, but please believe I care a great deal about both your son and your grandson.'

'I do believe that, dear.' She patted Mandy's hand.

Nick came back into the ward with chocolate bars for everyone, followed by a rather subdued Graham. He was obviously wondering what on earth his mother had been saying to her.

When visiting time was over, he linked his arm with hers in the corridor.

'Am I allowed to ask what that was all about?'

Mandy tapped her nose. 'Woman to woman stuff.'

'Is that the only crumb you're giving me?'

She stopped and faced him. 'Nothing to worry about, honestly. I think, reading between the lines, your mum was warning me not to play around with your feelings.'

'God, sorry.'

'No, no, it's okay. I'd probably do the same in her position. She's seen you go through a lot of crap and is scared it might happen again.'

'Mandy, I'm so sorry about the other day.'

She laughed and twirled away, speeding up to catch up with Nick. 'You never know I might hold you to that proposal after all.'

He stood there open-mouthed in the middle of the corridor

with other hospital visitors having to veer around him to get past.

Nick was the one to be quiet as Mandy drove home. As soon as they were inside the house, he turned to Mandy with a serious expression on his face. 'If Dad asked you to marry him, would you say yes?'

'It isn't as simple as that, Nick.'

'Why do adults make everything so complicated?'

'Probably because it is,' she said, heading into the lounge.

She caught the exasperated look he gave her as he followed, before he then flopped into the chair he'd made his own. Merlin jumped up into his lap.

'Nick, please don't ask your dad the same question.'

'I already have.'

'When?'

'In the hospital, when we went to get the chocolate.'

Great.

She almost didn't dare ask the next question.

'And what did he say?'

'That he didn't think you'd want him and I should forget the idea.'

Great again.

Mandy went off to prepare their evening meal with Graham's botched proposal ringing on repeat in her ears. Would she always wonder if she'd thrown away a chance of happiness, just because she had a set idea about how things should be?

Chapter Thirty

Mandy and Nick visited Ann frequently after she returned home from hospital, often together but sometimes separately. Graham was trying to build up his business again after the move and at least Mandy and Nick's visits allowed Hazel to have a break. The poor girl felt so responsible for what had happened and seemed terrified to leave Mrs Frankley alone after the fall.

On one of her solo visits, Mandy finally told Ann all about Paul. Mrs Frankley listened quietly.

'So have you been in touch with him since he visited?'

'Yes, we message nearly every other day. We're "friends" on social media, so we can see what is happening in each other's lives. It's fantastic, more than I could wish for.'

'And what about your own mother? Have you told her you are in touch?'

'Surprisingly, at last we've talked about what happened. Turns out Mum was rather afraid of my father when he got angry, which he did big time about me getting pregnant. She says she's always regretted what happened and really wants to meet Paul.'

The tensions that had existed in Mandy's body for so many years when she thought about her mother had shifted at last. It was such a relief to have spoken to her openly about Paul and the time of her pregnancy. Her mother had even begged her forgiveness for not having supported her more at that difficult phase of her life. Mandy was hopeful that she could salvage something of their relationship, especially when Paul was added into the mix.

'That's wonderful, dear.' Mrs Frankley clasped her hands together.

'Actually, I know there's loads going on here, what with the gin business and your accident, but I was wondering if you'd have Nick for the weekend when I go south to see Paul and introduce him to Mum?'

'I'm sure we can. Hazel is long overdue a visit home to see her parents, so maybe Nick could look after me for that weekend.'

'That would be wonderful.'

Mandy was just about to get in her car after her visit when Graham came out from the distillery and waved to stop her going.

'Hi Mandy, how did you find Mum today?'

'She seems in good spirits.'

'As am I. Good news … The Ship Inn in Borteen has agreed to trial our new gins.'

'Now that is good news. Congratulations.' She wanted to give him a hug and a kiss but wasn't sure it would be welcome after their recent falling out.

'Also, we need to agree a strategy for dealing with Nick. I'm going to see my solicitor tomorrow and could do with your opinion on what I've decided to say.'

'Are you sure I'm the right person? I mean, I'll brainstorm with you, of course, but I'm kind of involved, maybe in too deep to be objective. If I'm totally honest, although it hasn't been long since he moved in with me, he already feels like my son.'

'And that I'm talking about maybe taking him away from you?'

'That's what it feels like.'

'We really need joint custody.'

Mandy decided not to answer that one. Instead she diverted the subject back to Nick's absent mother. 'Won't any court want an answer about Sally Crossten?'

'There's been no sign of her for over six months.'

'No, but she's still his mother.'

'I would guess she could be facing charges of neglect and abandonment if she ever shows her face here again.'

'Can you ask your solicitor about it please? And I'll make a point of contacting Ethan again to see if the police have heard anything about Sally. Although, I'm sure he would have been in touch if they had.'

'Mandy, can I ask you out on a proper date?'

She stopped rearranging the gravel beneath her feet. She took a moment to give her thoughts time to settle.

'Why would you want to do that?' she finally asked. 'Given all you've heard about me and what I said the other day, I would have thought that was the last thing you would want to do.'

'Hmm, not quite the response I was hoping for.'

'Graham, don't toy with me.'

'Look, I hope I've got to know you by now. I genuinely like you and I know enough to realise you are you because of what you've been through.'

The gravel needed to be level. It felt as if her life depended on it.

Graham had moved closer; she could smell his citrus aftershave. He reached out a hand to hers. She froze, unable to look up.

'Mandy?'

'I'm a disaster.'

'In what way? You look pretty together to me.'

'Relationships.'

'Hmm … If you measure your life like that, then I'm a disaster too. I must be or Nick would never have been born.'

'I think I'd better go.'

'What? Do you really mean that? Do you want to spend your life alone with brief encounters?'

It came out as a whisper. 'It's safer …'

He let go of her arm and she felt like a kite whose string

had broken. Panic invaded her stomach. Had she just turned away again the best thing that had ever happened to her?

'Graham, promise me one thing. Don't let any thoughts about me dictate what you do about Nick. We are separate issues.'

'I know. I guess I just thought in my dreams it might be nice to have the two linked together. A bonus. A family.'

'As I said the other day, too convenient maybe and … not going to happen.'

He shrugged. 'That's told me.'

Then he was gone, back into the distillery.

The void felt complete. What had she done? Staring at the gravel, her vision blurred as tears ran down her cheeks.

The crying continued all afternoon off and on. She didn't seem to be able to stop, or rather she'd stop and then start again. Later that afternoon some tourists came into the craft centre, but when they noticed Mandy crying, they went out again as quickly as they could. For once, Mandy didn't care. They may not have bought anything anyway.

When she closed up early, she made her way back up the hill towards home but diverted off and walked to Graham's. She went into the distillery, guessing he would still be at work. If he noticed her dishevelled state, he didn't say anything about it. Of course, he was being tactful. Wendham darted past them and announced he was finished for the evening.

'Graham, I'm sorry.'

'There's nothing for you to be sorry for. It's me who should apologise. I've made assumptions, taken your good nature and friendliness as a sign of something more, made huge leaps in my imagination.'

'No you haven't.'

He looked confused. 'What do you mean I haven't?'

'I do care for you … fancy you … I guess I don't feel I deserve something so good.'

'Mandy …'

'Look can we rewind a little, take things slower, maybe go back to that kiss?'

He was smiling now and she swore he sighed. With relief?

Instead of answering her direct question, he went over to a table in the corner and beckoned her over. His face looked more animated than she'd ever seen it. He had an array of bottles with different coloured liquid in them on the table and rows of small glasses.

'Will you join me for one of my favourite things, tasting day?'

She laughed too. 'Let me text Nick to tell him I'll be late. He can get fish and chips for his tea.' She turned away to type into her phone and sighed with relief herself. She had another chance. *Don't blow it, Mandy.*

They drank rather a lot of gin and tonics. Mandy began to feel very mellow and could tell Graham did too.

Strange the thoughts that went through your head when you'd had a drink. Mandy knew that if she and Graham were to make a go of a relationship, it was important they were completely truthful with each other.

'If we're going to be a couple, you're going to have to realise that everyone around here thinks they know me. Has an opinion about me it seems, but none of them really know why. Why I act like I do, what brought me to the place I'm at now. How much I despise and hate myself at times.'

'I imagine a lot of it has to do with giving away Paul when you were so young. Am I right?

'Do you ever feel that your life has been defined by one event?'

She watched him stiffen opposite to her.

'Yup, frequently.'

'After I gave away my baby, I found it difficult to settle back into normal life. I went off the rails, did stupid things, didn't care if I lived or died. Took drugs, walked on the train tracks, waded too far out in the sea, hurt myself with razor blades.'

She showed Graham the faint scars on the insides of her wrists. 'I hated my dad so much after the adoption of Bumpy.'

'Bumpy?'

'It's what I called my baby when he was a pregnancy bump – Paul.'

Graham looked thoughtful. 'It's lovely you've now got the opportunity to get to know Paul at last. You know it strikes me that we have similar life patterns.'

'What with our sons?'

'Yes. At least I was spared the angst of knowing my son was out there somewhere though. It must have been purgatory not to know where he was, or how he was doing for all of these years.'

'It never leaves you. Some days you forget, only for it to hit you full force on the next one. Silly things, like a coach crash or earthquake and I'd wonder if my son was involved. If he lived, or if he'd died as a child and I would never have known. You give up all rights when your child is adopted.'

'Do you wish you'd been able to keep him?'

'I don't know. I wanted to at the time. Maybe it would have been better for my sanity, or maybe not – the life of a single parent can be extremely tough. I mean would he be studying to be a doctor if I'd kept him? We would have been living pretty much on the breadline, I'd have thought. He might not have got such a good education, but I would have loved him, oh how I would have loved him. Seeing that little scrap of humanity that you've grown inside you is so special, a miracle. The wrench when they took him away ...'

Graham rubbed her arm.

'I can see why you went off the rails. Did you have any help for this? Counselling?'

'Yes and lots of it. Most of the time I'm fine these days, just the occasional bad thoughts.'

'You know I had a breakdown, but you don't know that I also felt my dad's death was all my fault.'

'I'm sure it wasn't.'

'I ended up with lots of counselling too.'

'We make a right pair!'

'Yes, but I think our past experiences will allow us to understand each other more deeply.'

'You're probably right.' She smiled and tried to stifle a hiccup.

'I think I'd better get us some supper to soak up the gin,' he said and she could tell it was a real effort for him not to slur his words.

'Aww, I was enjoying this feeling that we can talk on this level and the fact we are friends again.'

He linked arms with her, grabbed the one bottle they hadn't sampled and locked up the distillery. His mother and Hazel were nowhere to be seen and Mandy suspected they had been tipped off by Wendham that Mandy and Graham were drinking together and had made themselves scarce.

Graham put some tortilla chips and salsa on the coffee table in the lounge and mixed two more gins. 'Wendham has taken Hazel and Mum out to dinner in Sowden apparently. There was a note in the kitchen.'

So Wendham had picked up the vibes. 'Mmm this gin is the nicest. You saved the best till last.'

'Liquorice and ginger. We've called it Borteen Secret.'

Graham looked suddenly so adorable with his hair flopping over his eyes. She took his drink from him and placed their two glasses on the coffee table. She turned back to him and he put his arms around her. Their lips met.

She deepened the kiss, her tongue playing with his. He tasted different, but somehow so familiar. She pulled away from his lips and teased her mouth up his neck, her breath on his ear. She nibbled his earlobe and ran her fingers up his back. Pausing, wondering if she'd gone too far, too fast; she was relieved to hear Graham sigh. He moved his body closer, his hands in her hair, as he, in turn, nibbled her neck.

Relaxing into the sensations, Mandy was shocked as he broke off and stood up. Bereft of his warmth, she wondered what she'd done wrong? Then he was pulling her to her feet and back into his arms. Their bodies were full length against each other, so she could tell how aroused he was and it was so flattering.

'Are you sure about this, Mandy? We did say we were going to take things slowly?'

'Mmm ... mmm.' Mandy's gin-fuelled desire ignored the plea in his voice.

'Off to my bed then,' he ordered – but he raised his eyebrows in silent question. She nodded.

She'd never been to his room before. It was at the far end of the bungalow. He threw some clothes off the bed and onto the chair, then closed the blinds, shut the door and pulled her down on top of the duvet. There was a noisy creak from the bed that set them both giggling.

'You sure no one is in?' Mandy asked urgently.

'Don't worry, we'll hear the car on the gravel when they come back.

Graham pulled her on top of him as he fumbled with the fastening of her jeans. Pushing her back on the bed, he pulled off her trousers, before starting on his own. They were both laughing together now, in-between kissing each other.

'Why do you have to have a creaky bed? It keeps making me laugh.'

'I know. If Mum was in, there would be no way she wouldn't know what we're up to – her bedroom is just next door.

Graham and Mandy giggled in unison again.

Mandy felt as if she'd had a large gin. Actually she'd had several. 'I'm drunk on you.'

He looked at her puzzled.

'Euphoric, high on feelings.' She began to unbutton his shirt.

'Two can play at that game.' He reached to lift her top over her head. The bed groaned and they both started laughing again.

'Had we better go back to mine?'

'No, Nick will be there. We'll be fine.'

'Less talk, more action, Mr Frankley.'

'Yes, madam.' He lay gently full length against her. Senses on overdrive they moulded to each other.

Chapter Thirty-One

Mandy woke the next morning mortified. Not because she and Graham had made love exactly, but because she'd repeated old patterns, getting drunk and sleeping with a man. Only this time, it was a man who meant something to her. A man who she'd only just asked to take their relationship slowly! What would Graham think of her? The terms not being able to teach an old dog new tricks and leopards not changing their spots came to mind.

From what she remembered about Graham walking her home last night, thankfully before Wendham, Ann and Hazel had returned from Sowden, Graham had been thrilled to bits that they'd made love and had held her hand tightly all the way down the hill to her house. She somehow remembered him insisting that he walked on the road side of the pavement, changing sides if they crossed the road, as that's what a gentleman did, he said. It was mildly irritating and sweet all at the same time.

She'd told him he couldn't come in or kiss her on her doorstep as it wasn't fair to raise Nick's hopes if he saw them. He'd complied and kissed her thoroughly before they reached her door.

Having sex changed things. Having sex complicated things. Her head was throbbing with overthinking. She would have to get the first meeting with Graham post-sex over before she could relax. She needed to know how he would react when he hadn't drunk a lot of gin.

She scrubbed herself vigorously in the shower and went to work. Distracted and a tiny bit hung over, for once, she sat and did nothing.

Mid-morning she glanced out of the one window of Owl Corner from which she could see the promenade. There was a woman sitting on the bench near the sea wall. Her stance seemed odd and, as Mandy watched, she doubled over. Was she ill? Upset?

Mandy was working alone today, as Romana had a bad cold and had rung to apologise for not being in. Still, there was no one in the sales rooms, so Mandy grabbed the key and her bag, locked up and walked briskly across the paving towards the bench.

The woman's shoulders were shaking and Mandy could now hear loud sobs.

She had a moment of indecision, but then went over to the distressed woman.

'Excuse me, are you all right?' Silly question when she blatantly wasn't, but what did you say?

The woman jerked upright; her expression shocked. Her face was streaked with tears and puffed up with redness caused by her overflowing emotions. She was probably normally quite pretty. Her hair was pulled back tightly to her head, secured with a clip and straggly long locks hung down her back. She wore a summer dress that hugged her figure. A fringed bag on her lap overflowed with used tissues. She mopped at her face with one of the tissues.

'I'm sorry.'

Mandy dropped to her knees in front of the distraught woman. 'There's no need to apologize to me. Just tell me what I can do to help you.'

The woman flailed her hands and began to sob again. 'I chose the wrong man. Had a child with the wrong man. Should have kept my mouth shut. I've made such a mess of everything. What a life.'

'We all feel like that now and then, been there myself many times I can tell you.'

The woman tried to sit up straighter but was off balance and fell to one side. Mandy helped her to sit up and sat down next to her on the bench. She sat quietly while the woman appeared to calm with her presence, sorting out her tissues and closing her bag.

'Can I get you a coffee?'

'That would be lovely. I find I'm feeling rather shaky all of a sudden.'

'Let's go to the café, just along here.'

'But I must look a terrible wreck.'

'Do you know anyone in Borteen?'

'Not really. No one that would want to see me anyway.' She sobbed again.

'Well then, it hardly matters. You can sneak off to the loo and wash your face, while I get the coffees.' Why did she feel the need to comfort this stranger? *Because you relate only too well to how she is feeling. You've been there so many times.*

When they were settled at a table, coffees in front of them, Mandy was able to examine the woman more closely. The redness was receding from her face and she'd brushed her hair in the toilet so that it hung in long curls either side of her face. She had dark rings under her eyes as if sleep had eluded her for a while.

'I'm Mandy Vanes. I run the craft centre, Owl Corner Crafts at the end of the beach. I saw you from the window … could feel your pain even from a distance.'

'I'm Trisha Vardy.' The woman offered her hand and Mandy squeezed it briefly.

Why did that name send a chill through her? She waited, senses on full alert. Alarm bells were sounding, but she didn't yet know why.

'I've messed up my life big time. It's one great big pile of pooh.' The woman stirred sugar into her coffee.

'I've been there, got several T-shirts. Probably still there in some ways, even now.'

Trisha smiled in sympathy. 'Thank you for coming over to me.'

'I couldn't just watch you in distress. I know if I was like that, I'd hope someone would at least ask if I was ill or needed help.'

'You didn't think I was going to do anything silly, did you?'

'I didn't really think that far ahead, but I wouldn't have wanted to take the risk that you might.'

'Okay. Thanks.'

'Is there somewhere you need to be today? Can I give you a lift? Call someone?'

'You've been kind enough, thank you. I'll be okay from here. I know what I need to do. I must go and see someone and it's time for humble pie.'

The icy dread had begun to multiply. She'd remembered that Graham's ex was called Trisha. Could this woman be *that* Trisha? Had she come to see Graham – to claim him back?

Mandy rationalised that she was worried for Graham and that Trisha reappearing would upset his mental state again. But was that true?

She decided that in any case she'd better go up to the distillery and warn Graham that Trisha might very well be in Borteen to see him.

Chapter Thirty-Two

Graham couldn't believe Trisha had found him here in Borteen. Someone had obviously given her his new address. His mother? Wendham? Then he realised. The company website had been updated and now the business was located next to his home, it can't have been difficult to find him.

Sweat gathered on his upper lip, as the feeling of being cornered grew in intensity. Trisha had come upon him when he was stoking the boiler. As she was standing in the doorway of the small, hot room, Graham had no choice, unless he pushed past her, but to listen to what his ex-wife had come to Borteen to say.

'What are you doing here, Trisha? Where's your baby?'

Trisha looked momentarily shocked. 'Monika, my daughter's called Monika. She's not a baby any more, she's five.'

'Where is she?'

'Monika is with her nanny, of course.'

'You're a long way from home. How can you bear to be this far away from your child?'

'I don't want to go back.' Her face had become ghostly white. 'I don't want to live with Derek. Don't want to be a mum.'

He felt a shiver of fear. *Red alert. Red alert.*

'What are you saying?'

'I made a mistake. I never should have left you.'

'Trisha, you did much more than simply leave me. You scythed my life into pieces. You left me broken and penniless in your wake.'

'And all because I was honest. I should never have told you the baby wasn't yours.'

'Honest! Honest?! You had an affair with my best friend,

my business partner to boot.' Graham was too incredulous to be angry.

'I should have kept quiet about everything and stayed with you. You loved me. You'd have loved Monika too if you hadn't known.'

'And you don't think the enormity of the lies would have eaten away at you?'

'I'd have loved you just that little bit more. Made it up to you.'

'Until it happened again, you mean? Or I recognised that Monika was the spitting image of Derek?'

'It wouldn't have happened again, should never have happened in the first place. I was wrong and I'm sorry. So, so, sorry. Forgive me, Graham.'

'Yeah, right. It's that easy, isn't it?'

He couldn't believe she would have contemplated lying like this about the father of her baby. How would he have felt if he'd thought the baby was his, enjoyed the joy of being a father, only to discover years later that the child wasn't his? How awful would that have been? He'd thought what had actually happened was bad enough.

The feeling of claustrophobia was growing, getting overwhelming. He had to get away from this woman who had once meant everything to him and whom he now despised. He bent down to check the boiler was safe, the door closed against the flames. He straightened and could stand being cornered no longer. He pushed past Trisha, taking care to present his back to her body as he passed by.

He turned to face her as soon as he was through the gap, fighting a resurgence of the feelings that had submerged him in the past, the black waves threatening to close over his head and drown him once more.

His breathing sounded laboured even to his own ears. Was he going to have a panic attack? Iron chains of tension closed around him as she walked toward him, her arms outstretched, reaching for him. *No!* He couldn't go there again, but the overwhelming emotions surging through his body seemed to have robbed him of both speech and movement.

'Hold me, Graham. Forgive me. Take me back. Please.' Her voice held a tremulous pleading note, her eyes were red from crying. It tore at the part of his heart that had once loved her. But his head was screaming back. *No! No way!*

'Are you joking?' He finally managed to utter some words. She leapt backwards as if he'd punched her.

'Please, Graham. You must still have some feelings for me.'

'None I'd care to voice in polite society.'

She started to cry.

He watched her, strangely detached. Did he still have feelings for her? He watched the tears flowing down the face he'd once thought he would stare at every day for the rest of his life. The woman he'd promised to have and hold until his death. The woman who had as good as stabbed him with a spear of pain. Did he still care for her?

After a search of his inner feelings, he was certain he felt only revulsion when he looked at her, not even any compassion for her distressed state. What on earth was she thinking coming here like this? Did she think he was an idiot, a fool to be played once again? He'd always thought she was out of his league, but now he knew she wasn't for him. Mandy, with her genuine feelings, was worth ten of Trisha, but was Mandy out of his league too?

While he'd been thinking, he hadn't noticed that Trisha had moved closer to him and before he had time to even protest, she draped her arms around his neck and planted her lips firmly over his.

He recoiled, feeling sick, but was unable to immediately free himself from her vice-like grip. Now she was betraying his former best friend too, showing her true colours yet again. She tried to kiss him once more, but he moved his head ... just in time to catch sight of Mandy's shocked face in the doorway and her flight from the scene.

'No, no! *Damn*!'

He finally shrugged Trisha off. She staggered and fell against the wall.

'It's over, Trisha, completely over. It has been for over five years, ever since you told me about the father of your child. Go back to Derek and Monika. They're your family now. I don't understand how you can leave your daughter for so long. It's time to be responsible, grown-up and think of someone other than yourself!'

Trisha's face crumpled. 'Graham we were perfect together. I don't know what came over me going off with Derek. Please give us another chance.'

'Trisha, it's not going to happen! If you think I'd *ever* trust you again you are off your trolley. Go away from here. I never, ever want to see you again.'

But now it looked as if the damned woman might have messed up his future as well as his past.

Wendham came into the distillery. The look of horror on his face when he saw the two of them together spoke volumes.

'Wendham, can you please see Trisha to her car and make sure she leaves the premises? I have something urgent to attend to.'

Graham launched himself towards the door and ran after Mandy as if his life depended on it. He tore across the yard and left the gate swinging on its hinges. While he ran full pelt, he tried to decide which way Mandy would go.

The timing of Trisha's visit sucked. Why had she arrived just the day after the night he'd made love to Mandy. He had to find Mandy and quickly.

Mandy had finally started to allow herself to believe in possibilities, which is why Trisha draped over Graham gave

209

her such a jolt and shock. She shot out of the distillery as if she had truly been shot out of a gun.

Having just walked up the hill, she began to run back down towards the sea. She needed to stand on the beach to ground herself. She was sick with relationships and the pain they caused. For years she'd stood alone because it was safer and never dreamed that the love word would enter her vocabulary, but the way Graham wrapped around Trisha had hurt her made her realise the depth of her true feelings.

How did you unlove someone?

She supposed she'd have to heap hate on top of her love, but it didn't seem to be working.

She didn't stop running until she reached the edge of the surf.

Graham paused at the sea wall, heart pumping and breathless from running. He really must take up some form of fitness training.

He knew as he stood there trying to recover, that he must never have truly loved Trisha. He'd never felt this heart-rending, senses on fire, emotional mind-bending before. It seemed to him that Mandy could do anything to him and he would still love her. But how to convince her that he was the man she wanted in her life. Her past experiences had made her so cautious. He wasn't sure he'd ever make it completely through her armour.

What he couldn't understand was that she wasn't like any woman he'd ever fancied before. The attraction seemed to be beyond his control, beyond his conscious thought, even beyond his better judgement. He failed to understand it, but then knew it was pointless to try and deny it or resist it. He was in love with Mandy Vanes. Full stop.

Where that left him if Mandy turned him away, he wasn't sure. Broken-hearted he supposed.

He scanned the expanse of sand. It was low tide and the

beach seemed massive and full of holidaymakers. A woman stood with her back to him right at the water's edge. Was it Mandy? He wasn't totally sure, but the possibility had him sprinting down the steps to the beach. As he ran over the sand, dodging other people, he became more sure it was indeed Mandy.

She turned, just as Graham tripped in a dip in the beach and went flying full length on the sand. The fall winded him and he rolled over on his back, just as a concerned looking Mandy reached him. He found he couldn't speak.

Her face changed from looking concerned, to angry and then seemingly despite herself, she began to laugh. Graham laughed too, even though he could feel the wetness from the sand seeping into his jeans.

'I love you, Mandy Vanes,' he spluttered.

She looked surprised and then her smile was brighter than the sun. 'I love you too, Graham Frankley, even when I think I hate you. I may change my mind if I find you in a clinch with your ex again. I'm not sharing you.'

She extended a hand and helped him to his feet.

'You have to believe me, Trisha jumped me.'

'I kind of suspected she might have, but even so I didn't like it. I didn't like it at all.'

'I can assure you neither did I.' He pulled her in for a kiss.

They stood for a long time at the water's edge holding each other close.

Chapter Thirty-Three

Up until now, by seemingly unspoken agreement, Mandy and Graham hadn't been overtly lovey-dovey when Nick was around. Over the past few weeks they'd met as often as possible and managed to snatch a few precious times to make love.

From Mandy's point of view, it was nothing to do with not wanting Nick to know they were getting closer, but more the terrible disappointment Nick would undoubtedly feel if their relationship didn't come to anything, fizzled out and died.

Mandy was also scared of that happening. Despite her new image, she still struggled to believe that Graham could truly be interested in her.

Graham had come down to the craft centre to see Nick after school. The rooms were quiet, he moved closer. She could hear his breath, feel its warmth at the side of her neck. He put his arms around her and rested his chin on her shoulder. He stood there just leaning into her. It felt peaceful, calm, as if they fitted together, belonged together.

Butterfly kisses traced up her neck and along her jaw. It was difficult to keep still. She wanted to grab hold of him. He found her mouth and began to explore, her lips, the edge of her teeth with his tongue and then that warm tongue was inside her mouth. His kisses aroused her and she was in danger of getting carried away, until her mind tried to interfere and inject her old insecurities.

He knows you are an easy lay. He's just trying his luck. He doesn't care about you at all. Just wants sex.

She jerked away. Graham almost fell over he was so surprised. Why was she feeling like this again? Was it because they were getting on so well? Because it seemed almost too good to be true?

'What?' asked Graham, a look of bewilderment on his face.

'Nick will be here any second.'

'Okay.'

She began to rearrange the decorative paper bags she used to wrap sold items. As she tried to calm her rebellious unbelieving thoughts, it felt as if her life depended on the edges of the bags being level. 'Besides, I've great news for Nick.'

Just as she said it, Nick came through the door, making Mandy grateful that she'd not given in to Graham's advances.

'Hey.' Nick looked so much healthier and tidier these days, but even so his shirt was hanging out of his trousers and his rucksack was slung at a precarious angle on his shoulder.

'Hey, yourself,' said Mandy.

Graham went over to him and they performed their still clumsy high-five, man hug routine. 'Good day?' he asked.

'If you count double physics and double maths as a good day.'

'Well it is a *great* day,' announced Mandy.

Nick and Graham turned to her and she knew she had their full attention.

'I had an unexpected visitor today – Tanner Bryant, Michael Bryant's son. The family and Michael are delighted with the portrait you did, Nick. So delighted that Tanner bought another three of your canvasses and has commissioned a picture of himself to hang next to his dad.'

Nick whooped and did a victory lap around the craft centre rooms, making Mandy fear for her pottery shelves.

'So, Nick, you have a nice amount of money coming to you. You'll need to think if you want to save it or spend it.'

'*Mmm*.' He did another victory lap with Graham watching him with obvious pride shining in his eyes.

Nick had been bemoaning the fact he hadn't got a PlayStation like some of the other kids. She knew if she mentioned it to Graham, he would probably buy one for him, but so far hadn't wanted to. She didn't like the thought of Graham buying his son's affections. She wasn't even sure it was a good thing for Nick to get into electronic devices, as at the moment he defaulted to his sketchbook if he wanted something to do. However, now he could have a choice about whether he spent it on electronics.

'Also, Tanner has invited us to afternoon tea at Lucerne Lodge, so that we can see where they've hung your pictures and where he wants the one of him to go.'

Mandy had sold three large canvases that Nick had painted of individuals looking out to sea to the rather dishy Tanner Bryant. They'd been bought as a gift for his father, who had apparently not stopped talking about Nick's portrait of himself.

She was particularly thrilled that Mr Bryant had suggested Nick go and see his pictures hanging in the places for which they'd been chosen. When she'd been speaking to Tanner, she'd told him a little of Nick's backstory and that he'd never really seen his work on display apart from at the craft centre. Now Nick could combine sketching Tanner and seeing his pictures on Lucerne Lodge's grand walls. She had no doubt that her foster son was excited.

'Do you think I could sneak in too?' asked Graham.

'I don't see why not. You are Nick's dad after all. I've been in the grounds before. The family hold charity auctions and dances there once a year. I hoped I could sneak into the big house to go to the ladies' but they'd hired Portaloos so I didn't get the chance. It's a huge stately home type house. I'm excited about going inside already.'

Nick asked if they could go for a pizza in Sowden to celebrate, and Mandy and Graham readily agreed after both chorusing *not pizza again*.

Mandy wondered if she and Graham should say anything to Nick about their own news, but she kept coming back to the fact that it was early days for their relationship. She was still having doubts that she deserved or could achieve the future of her dreams that Graham seemed to be offering.

At the pizza restaurant in Sowden, where they were no doubt becoming known as regulars, they chatted away easily in each other's company about all sorts of subjects, ranging from the moon, to Nick's art. Mandy sent out a silent prayer that the happy-ever-after could really be possible for all of them.

Graham could tell that Mandy didn't want to declare them a couple or even an item. He was happy to go along with this for now, because in truth he too was scared that things between them could go wrong at this fragile early stage. So, instead he talked about safe subjects.

He declared that his gin tours were taking off. He'd set up a simple online booking system and restricted the tours to Tuesday and Thursday afternoons and the spaces were booking up fast, mainly at the moment with curious local people. The beauty of having visitors on site and keeping the tour fee low was that people were more likely to buy from his makeshift shop on a trestle table at the end of the tour and tasting route.

'I'll need to look into a more permanent shop area and also maybe gift boxes. I've heard some other spirit makers make extra money by selling fancy glasses, especially when they're in gift boxes with gin.'

'That sounds a great idea. Well, would you believe that Michael Bryant's business is glass-making? Maybe you could ask him about glasses when we go to see Nick's pictures?'

'What a happy coincidence – or is it a sign?' Graham laughed.

Nick started fanning himself with his napkin.

'You okay, Nick? Was that piece of pizza too hot?'

'Nah. Just can't believe I've actually sold those pictures and have another commission. Just having a moment – as Grandma Ann would say!'

Mandy and Graham exchanged looks and smiled at each other. It was lovely that Nick's talent had been recognised – and that he was picking up expressions from his grandma.

Graham laid his hand on Nick's arm. 'I for one couldn't be more proud of you.'

Mandy felt a tear leap to her eye at the pride and affection flowing between father and son.

They munched pizza in silence for a little while, then Mandy asked how Graham's mother was doing. She couldn't help a little frisson of guilt that they hadn't invited Ann along to share the pizza celebration. They must bring her along next time.

'She's doing well. In fact, it's quite ironic that following the exercise regime dictated by her physio – watched over by Hazel, of course – if anything she's more mobile than she was *before* her fall.'

'How wonderful,' said Mandy.

'I was discussing the possibility of having a stall at the October Sowden arts festival and I nearly fell over when she asked if she could sit behind the stall and look after the cash from sales. That's the first time since Dad died that she's shown any interest in the business.'

'Can I help too?' asked Nick.

'Sure thing.' Graham high-fived him again.

'And, Nick she says if you're agreeable, she'd like a painting afternoon with you soon.'

'I'd love that.'

Mandy felt an alien emotion creeping over her and decided after a little thought, it was contentment.

Chapter Thirty-Four

Nick had been finishing his cornflakes when she left the house that morning and then he'd been under strict instructions to clean his teeth, lock up and get to school. But, now, as Mandy looked across the promenade, she couldn't believe her eyes and the hairs on the back of her neck stood to attention.

In a strange deja-vu parody of the day when Nick told her his mum had gone away, Nick was hurrying down the road towards the craft centre, clutching a drink and pursued this time by a woman.

Mandy leapt to her feet and went to the craft centre door, just as Nick arrived outside.

'Mand, help!' yelled Nick. He vaulted up the steps and stood next to her.

'Excuse me, but why are you following Nick?' Even as she said it, she thought the woman looked familiar.

'I'm his mum for goodness' sake.'

'You're Sally Crossten? I'm Mandy Vanes.'

She was pretty sure she'd never spoken to Sally Crossten before but she must have seen her around town.

'Couldn't believe she's back,' piped up Nick.

'Don't be cheeky.' Sally Crossten had an exasperated tone in her voice.

Mandy held the craft centre door wide open. 'Let's sit down and talk about this. You'd better come in.'

She watched as Nick and his mother eyed each other suspiciously as they sat down. Mandy made three cups of tea, handed one to Nick and left one on the table for Sally. She sipped her own and then decided that leading the conversation was the best option. 'We really thought you'd gone for good.'

'Saw the chance for a better life, didn't I?' Sally looked a little embarrassed.

'Couldn't you have taken Nick with you?'

'Richie didn't want that. He said just me, or not at all. Don't think he really wanted to take me either, but I didn't listen to the vibes, did I? Stupid where men are concerned see.'

Mandy felt a burn of remorse. Wasn't she just like Sally, stupid with men? Having said that, she'd never banked on one to provide her every need, trusted one enough to change her whole life for … until now maybe.

'I still don't understand how you could leave your son.'

'He's gone all teenaged. Asks awkward questions. Makes comments about how I live my life.' Sally jutted her chin out defiantly.

It struck Mandy that this woman appeared to be stuck in her teenage years too. 'Isn't that just normal? I've been living with him for six months now and he's fine apart from the odd grumpy phase.'

'Oi!' said Nick.

'But you're not his mum. They act differently with others. I just wanted to run free for a bit. No ties. No burdens.'

Mandy couldn't believe Sally had described Nick as a burden. Nick was watching the two women and appeared to Mandy to be trying to decide whether to listen or to run off. 'You do realise that the police will want to talk to you.'

'What've you been saying to them?'

'I haven't, but I had to get the proper permissions for Nick to stay with me. I'm now his temporary foster mum by the way. Social services told the police you'd abandoned him.'

'What the devil?'

'There are rules, Sally.'

'Bloody rules, he's my son for goodness' sake. I can do what I like.'

Above all else, Mandy was finding it hard to visualise Graham being with this woman. She must have been very different as a young girl.

Sally Crossten's mood was deteriorating and Mandy knew

she'd have to call a halt to this encounter soon. Sally seemed outraged that Nick wasn't living in the house she'd left him in. Had she expected him to live there alone with no money for food, bills or rent? Mandy felt her hackles rise. The woman was unbelievable.

Sally was reciting a list of her valuables out loud, things she was annoyed Nick hadn't rescued from the rental house. If she hadn't come home, Mandy wondered if she would ever have thought anything about these items again.

'Mum, I thought you'd gone off with that man for good.'

'Might have done if he hadn't proved to be a wanker.'

'Did you miss me?'

His tone tore at Mandy's heart.

'Of course I did, my little man.' Sally made as if to cuddle Nick, but he ducked under her arm and backed away.

Mandy thought she was going to be sick.

'So, where are we going to stay now?'

'I live with Mandy and I see my dad all the time.'

'Graham got my letter then?'

'Why didn't you tell me about him before? He's cool.'

'I thought he was pretty cool when I first met him. Maybe it would be worth renewing our acquaintance.'

That just finished Mandy off. Despicable woman. How low could she sink? But, it was more than that – Mandy had to bite back the retort that Graham was hers, so hands off.

'Well I haven't got the money for a hotel,' growled Sally.

Mandy could see the way this was going and she didn't want to invite Sally to stay at hers after all the pain she'd caused to Nick and the trouble she'd given Mandy and Graham.

'Look, as a one off, I'll ring the bed and breakfast and pay for a room for two nights for you, after that you're on your own. Maeve is still looking for a cleaner, I do know that.'

Sally huffed but seemed to realise she'd been given a good deal and picked up her things to leave. She didn't say goodbye to Nick or Mandy.

When she'd gone, Nick's eyes were full of unshed tears.

'Nick, it will be okay, it will all work out.'

'I don't want to go back to living with Mum. I've been so much happier since I've lived with you. Even living with Dad would be better.'

Mandy was pleased at his comment, however upset she was about the encounter with Sally.

'You going to be okay?'

'I'm embarrassed that mum would act like that. She was awful. So rude to you.'

'It's you I'm worried about,' said Mandy.

'I'm just disgusted with the way she spoke and worried I'll be sent back to live with her.'

Mandy stopped herself saying "over my dead body", because she knew she might not have the final say about where Nick would live. 'Nothing is going to happen immediately, Nick. The police will want to speak to your mum about leaving you on your own anyway. And I guess social services will get involved too. Now come on. I'll walk with you to school and have a word with the headmistress about what's happened and then I'll phone Graham and Harriet Drew.'

As soon as she'd ensured Nick was safely at Borteen High and had gatecrashed the headmistress' morning teacher meeting to give an alert about Sally, Mandy walked back down the hill. She dialled Graham's number as she walked and blurted out, 'Sally's back.'

'What! Really? How is she? Is her man in tow?'

'No, she's on her own. She says the man she went off with is a "wanker". She was horrid to Nick, blamed him for the loss of stuff she'd left in her rental house as if it were treasure and yet I doubt she'd have thought about it if her man had worked out.'

'Where's she staying?'

'I paid for a B&B for her, or rather I thought it was less painful to pay for the B&B.'

'Why's it your responsibility to make sure she has somewhere to stay?'

'It seemed the easier option. You'd have loved some of the conversation. Sally must be completely mercenary where men are concerned. Nick said you were cool and she asked him if she should make a play for you next. I think she's after a meal ticket.'

'She's the last person I'd be with after what you've said and what I know.'

Mandy felt better hearing this – although it would have been reassuring if he'd mentioned his feelings for her too as reasons not to be interested in Sally! She wished now that she'd made her way to the distillery after Borteen High because she felt in need of a reassuring hug.

'Is Nick okay?'

'Rather unsettled, as you'd guess. Embarrassed by his mum and worried he will be expected to go back to how things were before Sally went away. She was mad that Nick wasn't still living at her rented house. I don't know what she imagined he was going to live on as she left him no money, let alone how she expected him to pay the rent. She accused me of taking her son too.'

'That's awful. You've been golden to him. How would he have managed if you hadn't taken him in?'

'I'll tip off Ethan. The police are keen to speak to her anyway. I don't know if they'll prosecute. Nick's devastated. Says he won't live with her again.'

'I'm not surprised. Would you?'

'Yet, she seems to expect to slot back into her old life as if she's not been away. I can't see how that's going to happen. A lot has changed in six months.'

'Just a bit. I suppose I'll have to speak to her at some point, but I'm not looking forward to it at all. I'll speak to my solicitor.'

'I'll ring Harriet Drew to get advice. I don't want to get into hot water for keeping Nick away from his mother.'

'Poor lad. This must be so confusing. And we've only been sorting out the mess she left behind her. I'm afraid I've got to go. Sorry. Bye.'

'Okay. Bye.'

He seemed to cut the call off rather abruptly. She knew he was as unsettled and worried about Sally Crossten reappearing as she was, but it was disappointing he didn't finish the conversation with "love you" or "see you later". She really wished she wasn't still so insecure about Graham's true feelings, but given her past experiences she couldn't help it.

Nick had an art class after school and Mandy was determined to be home well before him. She sat at the kitchen table, nursing a mug of tea and thinking over the encounter with Sally Crossten.

She stopped her musings as she heard Nick come through the door, shouting a cheery hello.

The contrast to the boy she'd taken in was marked. Nick no longer skulked into the house as if he was trying to be invisible, but strode in with his head high and a smile on his face.

His new correctly-sized clothes and neat haircut made him appear taller and more mature.

Mandy felt a momentary glow of pride that she'd had some influence in this, immediately followed by the dread of how Sally returning would affect them.

'Got an "A" in history today.'

'Wow. An *"A"*?' They high-fived.

'Yep, an "A". Can you believe it?' He put his hand behind the strap of his rucksack and did a little strutting dance.

Even his progress with schoolwork had improved with Mandy showing an interest in his homework. She remembered how dismayed he'd been when he came home with a Dickens text to read for English. His face when he showed her the book had said it all. Mandy had suggested they read it aloud to each other for an hour each evening. Last night, they'd spent two hours on it, because Nick was enjoying using different voices for the characters.

A clutch of fear grabbed at Mandy. How would Sally's return change Nick? She didn't want things to alter – she was enjoying being his mum. She'd never got the chance for any of this with her own son, until now, of course, but he was past this stage of needing so much input and guidance.

'Can we read some more *Great Expectations* tonight?'

'Sure we can. Graham knows your mum is back in Borteen by the way.'

Nick's face changed in an instant. 'Wish she wasn't.'

'I know, Nick, but she's your mum and I'm not, I'm afraid.'

'She can't come back and mess everything up again.'

'Graham and I are here for you. You do know that?'

'She only came back because her man didn't work out. They never do. I wish she'd learn that.'

'She's not gone off before, has she?'

'Not like this time, but she's let men come live with us. They weren't always nice.'

Mandy could see the panic running through Nick's body and mind.

'I won't go back to live with her. I want to stay with you.' Nick leapt to his feet. 'I have homework. I'd better go and do it.'

'Okay, tea will be about an hour.'

'Anything nice?' His smile was back.

'Sausage and mash.'

'*Yes!*'

Chapter Thirty-Five

After a very disturbed night of anguished thoughts, Mandy decided to visit Graham at the distillery early that morning for a reassuring hug and chat.

She'd tried to be calm and confident with Nick and had even cooked them both bacon sandwiches for breakfast as a treat. Nick brought tears to her eyes by flinging his arms around her when he left for school and thanking her for being there for him when he'd needed her.

It was quite a trek to walk to the distillery and although she would ordinarily have enjoyed it, she decided to drive so she could get to Owl Corner Crafts at a reasonable time. As she parked her car, she could see that the big double doors to the distillery were open, so she wandered over, hoping Graham was already at work.

When she did catch sight of him, Mandy was almost sick. The bacon sandwich she'd just enjoyed was in danger of making a reappearance. Clinging together in front of the beautiful copper gin distilling vessels were Graham and Sally Crossten.

Mandy stood frozen. She'd thought Graham had begun to commit to her, had promised to make a new life with her and Nick. How could she have been such a fool to trust a man?

Sally Crossten had her hands either side of Graham's head, but it was the fact he had his hands on her hips that unnerved her.

'You utter bastard!' Mandy yelled, before stumbling to her car and driving off. The shock reverberated around her head. Her eyes were dry; she knew she had to get away before allowing her emotions to get the better of her.

She didn't own Graham, they hadn't got any formal sort of understanding, but she'd hoped, oh how she'd hoped. She drove like a mad woman down the high street and screeched her car into the car park at Owl Corner Crafts.

Mandy's anger made her clumsy. By the time she'd broken a glass, stubbed her toe and tipped sugar all over the floor she'd only just cleared of glass shards, she was fit to burst. She left the sugar on the floorboards, locked the door and went down to the beach. She was useless in this mood anyway.

Seeing Graham with Sally Crossten in an almost carbon copy of the other day with Trisha was too much. The fact that only this morning she'd been fantasising yet again about being married to Graham with Nick being happily their child, didn't help. Her hopes sank to the bottom of her stomach.

She'd thought Graham was a different sort of guy to those she normally dated, but was he? She'd thought him steady, safe, caring and responsible, but was he?

Damn Sally Crossten and damn Graham Frankley!

Thankfully, there was a strong breeze on Borteen beach. Mandy walked fast, the wind drying the tears on her cheeks.

No! Graham had seen Mandy come into the distillery from the corner of his eye. He couldn't believe she'd caught him in a clinch with another woman yet again. Her timing was impeccable. The fact it was Sally Crossten of all people that had her arms around him must have made the hurt of his perceived betrayal even harder. And now he was aware of what it must look like to Mandy, as he'd just put his hands on Sally's hips to try to push her away.

There was no way he wanted Sally Crossten's advances but she'd taken him by surprise. He shoved Sally hard and even though she was clinging to him like a limpet, he managed to shake her off. He ran outside but Mandy was already driving full speed for the gate.

'*Mandy!*' he yelled ineffectually as he watched her car disappear down the lane. Sally Crossten caught up with him. She was angry and shouting.

'You hurt me. I fell against that table. I'm going to have a right bruise. I should sue you.'

Graham saw red. 'Right, you do that and I'll bring a sexual harassment claim against you. Your advances will be taped on our security cameras, so I have the proof. For your information, I have no desire to kiss you, or even to be in the same room as you. *Stay* away from me! Your behaviour towards Nick disgusts me and I've filed for full custody of him. How I ever could have seen you as attractive in the long gone past, I don't know. How you could not tell me that Nick existed, I don't know. And now it seems you've probably ruined the best thing that's happened to me for a long time. Well done. Now get off my property and stay away or I will call the police!'

Sally looked for a moment as if she was going to say something else. Obviously thinking better of it, she went back inside to retrieve her bag from the floor where it had fallen and then flounced past him and out of the gate.

Wendham peered around the door of the distillery. 'Is it safe now?'

'I've got to go out. Relationship crisis again.'

'You're making a habit of this.'

'Please don't tease me, it really isn't funny. Hazel is with Mum. Please don't mention any of this yet. I may be some time if I'm to have any hope of salvaging my future with Mandy.' He turned to leave.

'Graham. You can't go like that.'

'Like what?'

'I think you'd better have a look in the mirror.' Wendham was having difficulty controlling his face, his moustache twitching.

Graham went to look at his reflection in the mirror on the reception wall and could see that pursuing the love of his life with his face smeared with the lipstick of Sally Crossten was probably not the best idea he'd ever had.

A little while later, he caught up with Mandy on the beach. He'd guessed where she would be, but he'd parked at Owl Corner next to her car and tried the door to the craft centre first. With his face still red from scrubbing at the seemingly immovable lipstick, he ran over the sand towards her. She was striding across the beach in the opposite direction, oblivious to his even being on the beach.

'Mandy, wait.'

'I'm not waiting for you ever again. I'm done.'

'She grabbed me!'

'I'm sure.' Her tone was heavy with sarcasm.

He caught up with her and pulled her around to face him. 'She's desperate, Mandy. You must see that.'

'From where I was standing, it didn't look as if you were exactly resisting her advances.' She pulled her arm out of his grasp and carried on walking.

He followed her, matching her pace. 'She took me by surprise, launching herself at me like that.'

'Two times, Graham Frankley! *Two times* I've caught you being kissed by another woman!'

'I know.' He hung his head. 'But neither of them was the woman I want, because that's you. It must be the sea air or something. I've never had women throwing themselves at me before. When I'm kissing you, I get sparks and fireworks and the feeling everything is right in the world. Please believe me.'

Despite herself, Mandy wanted to believe him. 'No sparks and fireworks with Trisha?'

'None. Not even in the early days.'

'No sparks and fireworks with Sally Crossten?'

'Absolutely and utterly not. All I felt was revulsion. No bodily reaction, apart from thinking her breath didn't smell very nice. Please don't tell me a misunderstanding, something not my fault, means I'm going to lose you. I couldn't bear it. Not now I know for certain.'

'Know what for certain?'

'That I love you. That I want to spend the rest of my life with you. Mandy, think logically about this. I hope you know me pretty well by now. Why would I hook up with Sally, when she is the epitome of all things I try not to be: unreliable, selfish, disinterested in her own child?'

Mandy stopped walking.

'She launched herself at me just as you came in. I soon shrugged her off and told her not to do it again, but she was like a limpet. I think she's so desperate to be looked after that she'll try anything. She's more of a child than Nick. If he's not careful, he'll end up providing for his mother when he's older.'

'Maybe we can find someone for her. I can think of a few candidates.'

'Are you being sarcastic?'

'Maybe ... but going back to what you were saying about wanting to be with me.'

'With Nick too, as a family.'

'But would you really want me if there was no Nick? I don't think so somehow.'

'That's not true. You've grown on me.' He grinned at her with such a look on his face that her heart was melting. 'You've got under my skin, all those things people say when they've fallen in love. They may be clichés but they are so true. Give me another chance, Mandy? *Please*. If you don't believe me about Sally launching herself at me, it will all be on the security camera recording at the distillery. You can watch it. Please watch it. I need you to believe me. I love you, Mandy. I love you like I've never loved anyone else in my life.'

He put out his hands and she took them, but kept him at arms' length as she looked into his eyes, searching for the truth, for sincerity, for love. The look on his face was so heart-wrenching. Could she trust him? Was it just her past insecurity rearing its ugly head? After all, Sally Crossten was a vile woman. They'd had their youthful fling so many years before. Why would Graham want her now? Before she'd even consciously registered her decision, she was smiling.

'I might forgive you – again, but don't think I'm kissing you to seal the deal till you've washed your mouth.'

'Where's the nearest sink?'

She grinned. 'There's always the sea.' She pointed to the ever-present ocean.

'Okay, whatever it takes.' He began to jog toward the water.

Mandy followed him. 'Graham, I wasn't serious.'

He turned his head but didn't stop moving. 'Well, I am.'

She raced across the sand behind him.

When he reached the surf, he fell to his knees, heedless of his jeans getting wet. He grabbed a handful of sea water and began to scrub at his mouth. When he'd scrubbed his lips thoroughly, he took another handful and swilled his mouth out with it and then another and put his head back to gargle. He spat out the mouthful and his face showed his disgust.

He stood and joined her just out of reach of the waves, the legs of his jeans completely sodden. 'Satisfied? I think I'm cleansed ... heck that's salty water and colder than I expected for September.'

'So, let's get this clear, Graham Frankley. You want to spend the rest of your life with me?'

'Sure do.'

'And you'll be true to me, forsaking all others?'

'Yep.'

'In sickness and in health?'

In answer, he dropped to his knees on the sand. Reaching for her hand, he looked up at her, the green of his eyes like emeralds in the sunlight. 'Mandy Vanes, will you do me the honour of becoming my wife?'

The doubts had gone and as if to confirm she was doing the right thing, the sun came out from behind a cloud and bathed them in sunlight.

Mandy's phone began to trill in her pocket. Even though it seemed the wrong time to answer it, or even to look at the screen when Graham had just proposed, the ringtone was the one she'd set for Borteen High School and she had a strange premonition. An icy feeling was spreading rapidly down her body. Her reply to Graham's question died on her lips.

'It's the school. I have to take it ...' She whipped out her phone. 'Hello?'

The headmistress told Mandy that Nick hadn't come into school that morning. 'I wouldn't normally be as concerned, but with what you told me about his mother being back in Borteen, I thought I should be cautious.'

Mandy glanced at her watch. It was now ten o'clock. 'But he left just before me. He was wearing his uniform and had his school bag.'

She was having difficulty understanding what Karen Brookes was saying. 'Given the reappearance of his mother, the uncertainty over where he might be going to live, is it possible he's taken the day off to think, gone to see his mother or maybe even his father?'

'His father's here with me. We'll go and look for Nick and report back as soon as we can.'

Mandy finished the call and the icy feeling took over completely. She began to shake. Graham held her tight against his body and she could feel he was shaking too.

'We'll find him.' He squeezed her arm and took her hand. 'Come on. Let's check Owl Corner Crafts as it's nearby, then your house. I'll ring Wendham to check at mine while we walk. Let's go.'

Chapter Thirty-Six

Fear, anger and bewilderment threatened to overwhelm Mandy. She kept thinking back to how strangely Nick had acted that morning before heading off to school. She told Graham how Nick had hugged her and thanked her for being there for him. Tears began to stream down her face.

'Do you think he was saying goodbye?'

Graham pulled her against him for a moment. 'We need to stay as clear-headed as we can. I'm parked next to your car at the craft centre. Let's start searching there.'

Nick wasn't at Owl Corner; she'd not really expected him to be there, but Graham was right, they had to rule it out. They left her car parked outside and Graham began a slow drive back up to Mandy's house. They looked out for Nick as they went, but saw nothing.

When he parked at Mandy's, Graham called Wendham again, but an initial search of the distillery and garden had come up with nothing. Graham stressed that Wendham wasn't to worry his mother.

Mandy had clung to the possibility that Nick would be at her house watching television, having decided to skive off school for the day and lie low being as his mother was in Borteen. She walked into the hallway with Graham close behind her, talking as if Nick was there.

'Nick, come on, you're late for school.'

He wasn't in the lounge or the kitchen-diner. Merlin mewed from the windowsill. Mandy fought down the thought that if Nick was at home, the cat would be with him. He rarely left Nick's side these days.

Mandy checked the bathroom – he wasn't there. She knocked on his bedroom door: there was no answer. She pushed it open. It was tidy and neat as always.

Graham touched her arm, but she shrugged him off and rushed over to the wardrobe. She flung open the double doors. She couldn't be sure whether anything was missing, but one thing she saw clearly was gone was the big winter coat he'd brought with him from his mother's house. Why would he need a big coat at the beginning of September? She gulped. She seemed to remember his school bag looking rather full this morning.

Telling herself not to panic, she pushed past Graham and systematically searched the rooms of her home, firstly to establish to her complete satisfaction that Nick wasn't there and secondly, to see if she could find his coat. The search proved fruitless.

Now she was really scared.

'Graham, I think he planned to leave. Now I think about it, his school bag looked rammed this morning. I didn't question it, but I think he may have had his big winter coat in there.' She clutched her chest as panic threatened to overwhelm her.

'You think he intends to sleep rough?'

She could feel her lip trembling. 'Yes.'

Graham gave her a quick hug and then searched the rooms again himself, his face set in a mask of worry.

Mandy picked up her phone, trying to think who to ring for help and then threw it into her bag. She turned to Graham. 'I think he's really gone.'

'I suppose Sally being back in Borteen has spooked him and he's taken off. But where would he go?'

'Absolutely no idea, but that young man knows this area so well. He's told me before how he used to wander around for ages in preference to being home with Sally and her man friends. He could be anywhere. My hope is that he's still in Borteen ... Oh, Graham.' She staggered and almost fell over.

'Come on. We are no use to Nick if we make ourselves ill with imaginings. Let's sit down for a moment and have a hot drink while we decide how to approach this. You look very pale.'

'I'm fine really, just shocked and worried. I'm supposed to be keeping him safe and I've let him down.'

'Do not blame yourself for this.'

'What else can I do? If I'd reassured him enough, he wouldn't have gone.'

'Ifs and maybes. It's happened and we need to deal with it.'

'Police?'

'Not just yet. That will definitely traumatise him if the police track him down, maybe with dogs.'

'But what if he's got himself in a dangerous situation?'

'Ifs and maybes again. Right, I propose we search for an hour. If we find nothing in that time, we alert his case worker and the police. Any ideas at all as to where he might go?'

Graham made two mugs of tea, all the time prompting Mandy to talk about places in Borteen that Nick had mentioned.

'He's always talking about the plants on Pink Moor, but that's a huge area and if he's intending to sleep rough, there isn't much cover up there. He may want to get away, but I believe he's sensible enough to realise he needs a safe place to stay. He knows the buildings in the alleys off the high street like the back of his hand. I wonder if he could be squatting in an empty building? Or even in the church – it has lots of empty nooks and crannies.'

'Drink up. Let's try the church and then even though I hate the thought of it, I think we need to speak to Sally.'

'Why Sally? Oh Graham, you don't think she'd try to abduct him?'

'I doubt he'd go with her willingly, but I meant she might have spoken to him again, seen him ...'

'This is all my fault.'

'Don't be silly, of course it's not. Nick has just got worried about what might happen to him.'

'He was scared about being sent to a children's home when I first took him in.' Mandy began to feel a little faint and spooned sugar into her tea in the hope it might help.

'He's had a glimpse of what life could be like while he's been living with you and I know he hopes you and I will get together to make his family complete.'

Mandy wailed in despair. 'I told him that wouldn't happen.'

'You did?'

'I didn't want to raise his hopes.'

'Didn't want to raise his hopes, or didn't want it to happen? And you haven't answered my question from earlier yet.'

'Graham, we need to find Nick first.'

'But wouldn't it be better if we were clear about what we could say to him when we find him?'

'Stop please ...'

'I'm just impatient. I mean I got as far as proposing – again. Remember, men in general, and this man in particular, don't do subtle signs. We need certainties to work on.'

She leaned over and gave him a kiss on the cheek. 'Let's find Nick and then propose again so that I can give you a proper answer.'

This was one of those life-defining moments. One of those times you couldn't unsay what you said, one that might determine your life path. She gulped. She didn't want losing Nick to be one of those moments too.

Graham stood up. 'Wow, I feel so much better after that tea. That saltwater gargle didn't agree with my mouth.'

He put the empty mugs by the sink, grasped her hand and made for the door.

'Now, let's go and find Nick. Only positive, remember – we *will* find him.'

They scoured the high street again on the drive down the hill and parked at Owl Corner. The church was empty. There was nowhere in the churchyard to shelter. Mandy scanned the beach from the sea wall. No sign.

'Graham, where is he?'

'Let's try Sally next.'

Mandy led the way to the cheap B&B she'd paid for when Sally arrived. The owner said that Sally had left with her bags just half an hour before, declaring she was leaving Borteen and never ever coming back. She'd heard her ask the taxi to take her to Sowden railway station.

'So it sounds as if Sally has gone, probably just after she visited you and before the police catch up with her,' said Mandy as they walked away.

'Sounds like it and good riddance. Let's hope she meant what she said about not coming back.'

They walked in silence for a while, both absorbed in their thoughts.

Graham pulled Mandy to a standstill as they reached the sea wall again. 'Nick might have got the bus out of Borteen. Do you know if he had any money?'

'I didn't look to see if his cash was still there, but I gave him his pay from the sale of his paintings only yesterday.'

'Where would you go if you were in his position?'

Mandy felt the stirrings of an idea and hope. She was remembering a conversation with Nick when they were talking about the hidden parts of Borteen. 'Quarry Point! I'm almost sure he'll be there.'

'Quarry Point?'

'The caves at the far end of the beach.'

'Why there?'

'Just far enough away to avoid detection, reasonably dry and protected from the weather, high on the cliff so no danger from tides. Nick was once telling me about the places in Borteen he'd explored. He talked about the caves on the headland at Quarry Point and how he was convinced he could live there. That's where I'd go. I think that's where we'll find him! Please let that be where we find him ...'

Graham grabbed both her hands and squeezed. 'Let's try

Quarry Point and if not, we'll contact the police. Is it best to walk or drive?'

'Drive. Have you got a torch?'

'There's one in the side pocket of my car.'

On the short journey along the beach road, they continued to look left and right, desperately trying to catch sight of Nick.

'Graham, I'm scared. What if he's not there?'

'So am I. I've only just found my son and don't want to lose him again.'

They parked in the lay-by at the far end of Borteen beach.

'The tide's coming in.'

'Are the caves safe when the water's up?'

'Yes, you'll see. The caves are high on the cliff wall. The problem will be deciding which one to search first.'

'If he's here at all.'

They scrambled down the dunes from the road, Graham clutching his torch in one hand and Mandy's hand in the other. They jogged along the sand. Mandy scanned the cliff face. The gaping mouths of the caves were clearly visible. Some were inaccessible unless you had a ladder, but several had rough-hewn steps leading up to them. As the water rose a way up the cliff side at high tide, the bottom steps were covered with seaweed.

'Which one?' asked Graham.

'Well, if I was running away, I wouldn't choose the first one, or the second.'

'Let's try the third then.'

The water had almost reached them as they began their climb and the steps were slippy with seaweed, sandy and worn away completely in places. Graham helped Mandy up the difficult bits.

The cave was dark and surprisingly cold away from the entrance. Rivulets of water ran down the walls. Graham shone the torch around, but there was no sign of recent habitation apart from a couple of beer cans piled up near the entrance.

'I've spent nights sitting here with friends drinking in the past,' said Mandy. 'There are quite a few passageways leading into the cliff face. I've never been brave enough to go very far in.'

Tears began to fall down her cheeks yet again.

Graham caught sight of her face in the torch beam. 'Hey.' He put his arm round her shoulders.

'I'd convinced myself he'd be just here, sitting waiting for us. He's talked about this cave before.'

'And he could still be here – we've not looked properly yet. Come on, deep breath, and let's be systematic about this.'

Graham led the way down the passage on the far left, but it quickly came to a dead end. The next passageway was narrow and smelt musty. It too petered out. They retraced their steps. The next stone corridor led to a larger cavern with stalactites hanging from the ceiling.

'Oh, I remember coming in here once,' declared Mandy. She stood in the darkness and began to shiver a little, waiting while Graham shone the torch into all of the nooks and crannies around the space.

'What if we never find him?'

'We *will*.'

Graham pulled her close and she tried to drink in his warmth, to shield herself from her fear with his body.

'You know, I've come to love him as if he's my son.'

'Me too and that's not just because he "is" my son.'

'I can only hope he's not gone off somewhere like London. We'd never find him. How could we ever be a proper family without Nick?'

'My instincts are telling me he's still in Borteen. Don't give up yet. Come on there's still more to explore here.

A disembodied voice came from somewhere at the back of the cave. 'Can I come home?'

Mandy and Graham lurched apart and Graham shone the torch beam in the direction the voice had come from. A rather grubby-looking Nick, wearing the oversized winter coat, emerged from behind a kink in the rock.

Mandy was over to him in seconds, yanking him into a bear hug and Nick made no protest.

'I'm hungry and it's cold in here, but I don't want to live with Mum again.'

'Your mum has gone, Nick. She's left Borteen again.'

Nick's face brightened in the torch light.

'There's a lot of things we need to sort out, but running away won't solve any of them,' said Graham.

He grabbed Nick close for a hug as Mandy released him.

She ruffled Nick's damp hair, still not quite believing they had found him. Relief gushed through her. 'Nick, it will all work out.' Now they'd found him anything was possible.

'Let's get you both home.' Graham put his arms around their shoulders.

As the three of them got to the cave entrance it became clear they were going to have to stay in the cave a while longer. The tide had come in during their search, cutting them off from the beach.

Mandy was grateful she had a mobile signal so that she could call Borteen High School and tell Karen Brookes that Nick was safe and well. As soon as that call was made, she felt the tension beginning to leave her body. Graham rang Wendham – he and Hazel sounded relieved Nick had been found too.

'Have you anything to eat or drink in that backpack, Nick?' asked Graham. 'I'm starving after all this drama and tension.'

Nick produced two bags of crisps and a large bottle of water with a grin and the three of them sat with their legs dangling over the edge of the cave, munching the potato snacks and passing around the bottle of water. Nick sat in the middle of the two adults. There was a spectacular view out to sea from where their little *family* was sitting.

'Is there anything you want to say to Mandy and me while we're here? No rules as this is no man's land.'

Nick looked surprised. 'Adults are strange,' he said. 'Not sure I'm looking forward to being one.'

Mandy and Graham laughed in unison.

'Mandy's cool though,' continued Nick.

'And I'm not?' asked Graham, putting on a hurt face.

'You're my dad, of course you're cool, but Mandy is when she doesn't have to be.'

She felt tears pricking her eyes.

When they eventually left the cave, as the tide turned and ebbed away from the steps, Mandy held Nick's hand on one side, despite his initial protest, and Graham's on the other. She felt exhausted but so happy.

'You haven't answered my question from earlier, Ms Vanes,' said Graham.

She dropped both of their hands and twirled away. 'I think you'd better ask me again, Mr Frankley, especially now we have a witness.'

Graham grinned. While Nick looked on with a confused face, Graham dropped to his knee on the sand in front of Mandy.

'What's going on?' asked Nick.

'I'm about to ask Mandy a question for the second time today. Note that the first time I didn't get an answer, because someone decided not to go to school and the headmistress rang at just the wrong moment.'

'What question?'

Graham ignored Nick and reached for Mandy's hand. 'Mandy Vanes will you do me the honour of becoming my wife?'

She glanced at Nick – he looked as if he was holding his breath. 'Yes,' she said simply. 'I would most definitely like to be your wife, love to be your wife, love you, love Nick. I really believe we are truly a family already.'

She was enveloped in a huge hug by Nick before Graham could rise up from his knees and then the teenager who had changed her life so completely in so many ways was running in delighted circles on the beach, shouting *yes* to the sky and punching the air in triumph.

Mandy and Graham sealed their summer beach promise with a lingering kiss.

Thank You

Dear Reader,

Thank you for reading the fourth book based in my fictional seaside town of Borteen and published by Choc Lit (I still have to pinch myself when I say this).

I do hope you enjoyed Mandy's story. She's had a role in all of my books so far and I thought it was time she got to be the leading lady.

It is always nerve-wracking to launch a new novel into the world, as each time you feel as if you reveal a little more of the inner workings of your mind.

If you did enjoy this story then please leave me a review on the retail site where you purchased it. Just a few words in a review really make a difference to the sales of a book as they raise the profile of an author's work.

You can find details of how to keep in touch with me, or to contact me at the end of my author profile.

Best wishes and happy reading,

Morton x

About the Author

Morton lives with her husband, two sons and Lily, the little white dog, in Worcestershire, UK. She has been reading and writing fiction for as long as she can remember, penning her first attempt at a novel aged fourteen. She is a member of the *Romantic Novelists' Association* and *The Society of Authors*. Her debut novel *The Girl on the Beach* won the Choc Lit's Search for a Star competition.

Morton previously worked in the electricity industry in committee services, staff development and training. She has a Business Studies degree and is a fully qualified Clinical Hypnotherapist and Reiki Master. She also has diplomas in Tuina acupressure massage and energy field therapy. She enjoys crafts, history and loves tracing family trees. Having a hunger for learning new things is a bonus for the research behind her books.

For more information on Morton visit:
www.twitter.com/MortonSGray
www.facebook.com/mortonsgray/
www.mortonsgray.com
www.instagram.com/morton_s_gray/

More Choc Lit

From Morton S. Gray

The Girl on the Beach

Borteen Secrets series

Who is Harry Dixon?

When Ellie Golden meets Harry Dixon, she can't help but feel she recognises him from somewhere. But when she finally realises who he is, she can't believe it – because the man she met on the beach all those years before wasn't called Harry Dixon. And, what's more, that man is dead.

For a woman trying to outrun her troubled past and protect her son, Harry's presence is deeply unsettling – and even more disconcerting than coming face to face with a dead man, is the fact that Harry seems to have no recollection of ever having met Ellie before. At least that's what he says …

But perhaps Harry isn't the person Ellie should be worried about. Because there's a far more dangerous figure from the past lurking just outside of the new life she has built for herself, biding his time, just waiting to strike.

Winner of Choc Lit's 2016 Search for a Star competition!

Visit www.choc-lit.com for details.

The Truth Lies Buried

Borteen Secrets series

Two children in a police waiting room, two distressed mothers, a memory only half remembered …

When Jenny Simpson returns to the seaside town of Borteen, her childhood home, it's for a less than happy reason. But it's also a chance for her to start again.

A new job leads to her working for Carver Rodgers, a man who lives alone in a house that looks like it comes from the pages of a fairy tale – until you see the disaster zone inside …

As Jenny gets to know Carver she begins to unravel the sadness that has led to his chaotic existence. Gradually they realise they have something in common that is impossible to ignore – and it all links back to a meeting in at a police station many years before.

Could the truth lie just beneath their feet?

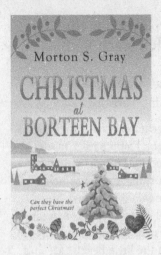

Christmas at Borteen Bay

Borteen Secrets series

Christmas has a way of bringing family secrets to the surface …

Christmas is a bittersweet time for Pippa Freeman. There are good memories, of course – but some painful ones too.

Then her mother is implicated in a mysterious occurrence in their home town of Borteen, and Pippa wonders if she'll ever experience a happy Christmas again – especially when a family secret is revealed. But when police officer and old school friend Ethan Gibson offers his support, Pippa begins to realise that even though her life has been turned upside down, a happy and hopeful Christmas isn't impossible …

Visit www.choc-lit.com for details.

Christmas at the Little Beach Café

Run away to the little beach café this Christmas …

Five years ago at Christmas, solicitor Justin Sadler made the decision to leave his comfortable existence behind and move to the coast. Since then, he's tried his best to ignore the festive season and, as he sits in the little beach café and reflects on that fateful night when his life was turned upside down, he expects his fifth Christmas alone to be no different to any of the others since he made his escape.

But when he encounters a mystery woman on the beach, he soon realises he may have found a fellow runaway and kindred spirit. Could Justin finally be ready to move on and let Christmas into his life again?

Visit www.choc-lit.com for details.

Summer at Lucerne Lodge

Could a beautiful old house and a handsome stranger hold the key to a life-changing secret?

Rosie Phillips could be forgiven for not being immediately won over by Tanner Bryant. After all, their first meeting involves him knocking a tray of prawn cocktail over her very expensive dress at a charity event in the grounds of Lucerne Lodge.

But little does Rosie know how pivotal that awkward first meeting will be, or how the Lodge will become the unexpected backdrop for a summer spent finding out who she really is, and who she could be ...

Visit www.choc-lit.com for details.

Introducing Choc Lit

We're an independent publisher creating
a delicious selection of fiction.
Where heroes are like chocolate – irresistible!
Quality stories with a romance at the heart.

See our selection here:
www.choc-lit.com

We'd love to hear how you enjoyed *Sunny Days at the Beach*. Please visit **www.choc-lit.com** and give your feedback or leave a review where you purchased this novel.

Choc Lit novels are selected by genuine readers like yourself. We only publish stories our Choc Lit Tasting Panel want to see in print. Our reviews and awards speak for themselves.

Could you be a Star Selector and join our Tasting Panel?
Would you like to play a role in choosing which novels
we decide to publish? Do you enjoy reading women's
fiction? Then you could be perfect for our Tasting Panel.

Visit here for more details...
www.choc-lit.com/join-the-choc-lit-tasting-panel

Keep in touch:
Sign up for our monthly newsletter Spread for all the latest
news and offers: www.spread.choc-lit.com. Follow us
on Twitter: @ChocLituk and Facebook: Choc Lit.

Where heroes are like chocolate – irresistible!